I0556874

~~MERRY~~ *Creepy* CHRISTMAS

12 Twisted Tales

2025

FROM BLACK MARE BOOKS

Creepy Christmas 2025: 12 Twisted Tales

Black Mare Books

First Edition 2025

This is a work of fiction. Names, characters, places, brands, media, and incidents are either the product of the author's imagination or are used fictitiously. The author acknowledges the trademarked status and trademark owners of various products referenced in this work of fiction, which have been used without permission. The publication/use of these trademarks is not authorized, associated with, or sponsored by the trademark owners.

ISBN: 978-1-959008-47-7

CONTENTS

AMONG THE LEAVES SO GREEN
By Artemis Greenleaf

THIS was the second call from my mother today. "I know it's a big ask, but could you pick up Aunt Edna on your way? She finally stopped driving this spring, and I'm not sure she has many Christmases left."

"It's all right, Mom. She's not that far off my usual route. Why don't you let her know, and I'll phone her when I'm leaving my house, so she knows when to expect me?" Aunt Edna was my favorite aunt, so I didn't mind detouring to pick her up. It wouldn't be Christmas without her.

"Of course! See you soon. Love you."

"Love you, too, Mom."

Now that next week was planned out, I'd better finish up the last bit of my shopping.

Back seat loaded with presents, I hit the road early. It was an eight-hour trip to my parents' house, so I figured I'd drive to Aunt Edna's, which was a little over six hours away, spend the night with her, then drive the rest of the way in the morning.

A major accident blocked both lanes of the rural highway, which put me far behind schedule. Long afternoon shadows were smearing into twilight by the time I pulled into town.

Growing up, I'd spent a few summers here in Blackwater Hollow with Aunt Edna but had never been here during the holidays.

I sat at a traffic light on Main Street, studying the window display at Cassie's Fine Apparel. They'd set up the mannequins as if they were a family opening Christmas presents. All of them received pretty clothes—even the dog got a festive sweater—except the mom, who was gifted a vacuum cleaner. She stood behind the dad, cleaning wand raised as if to strike him in the back of the head. I wasn't sure if it was meant to be a joke, a warning, or social commentary. I was probably over-thinking it.

Across the street from Cassie's, people were setting up booths in the park, as if for a farmer's market or festival. Reflected in the glass, a group of Christmas carolers caught my eye. Wondering if they would be serenading the town square, I glanced over at them. *Huh. They must have stepped inside the hotel lobby. Warmer for everybody, I guess.*

I could also see the tops of the white stones that ringed Blackwater Pond. It was less a pond and more a sterile pool that inhabited a perfect thirty-foot circle. Aunt Edna had told me long ago that excessive algae caused the water to be black, and to stay out of it, because it might make me sick. She didn't need to tell me twice—the place gave me the creeps. The thick blocks of white stone that encircled the water reminded me of monster teeth. The stones were of uneven size, the shortest around three feet and the tallest closer to five. Widths ranged from two to six feet, give or take. Circular flowerbeds filled with herbs marked the cardinal compass points around the circle. In the summer, they were filled with herbs and flowers.

The light changed, and I pressed the accelerator. I'd ask Aunt Edna what festivities were planned for tonight. Might be fun to get out and see something different.

I pulled into her circular driveway and the front door opened before I came to a full stop. My bag could wait a minute, I thought as I put the car in park and jumped out to greet my aunt.

"Skye! It's so good to see you, honey."

I hugged her. "You, too." She was thinner than I remember. I let her go and stepped back. "Sorry I didn't make it yesterday, like you asked. Had a work thing I couldn't get out of."

She patted my arm. "I always prefer to leave town before the... before the traffic gets too bad. So many people on the roads these days." My aunt turned toward the open door and clapped her hands. "Herman! Get back inside! You know better."

Her oversized orange cat sat down at the edge of the threshold and flicked his tail.

As we got closer, he stood and sauntered into the house, fluffy tail quirking into a question mark.

I noticed Aunt Edna's luggage, including Herman's crate, sitting in the foyer. "So, I was thinking maybe we could go check out whatever's happening on Main Street, and get some food at—"

"No!" She let out a breath. "I mean, everything is so expensive there. And I've had spaghetti sauce simmering all afternoon, just for you."

Only a fool would turn down the deliciousness that was Aunt Edna's spaghetti sauce. "Oh. You didn't have to go to all that trouble, but I appreciate it. I might look around the market after we eat."

Aunt Edna dropped her gaze to the floor. "I was going to ask that, if you weren't too tired, we could leave tonight? Everything's packed. I only need to put Herman in his carrier. In fact, why don't we load my bags in your car now? That way, we can just hop in and go. Whenever we're ready."

"Aunt Edna, is everything okay?"

"Yes. Of course it is. Today's the winter solstice..." She locked the door. "I'd rather spend the longest night of the year

3

with my family, instead of rambling around this dark old house on my own, that's all."

I'm here... The house had been getting dark for months now, as fall turned into winter. Perhaps she was just stir-crazy. Uncle Phil had been gone for a few years, but until recently, she'd at least been able to get out and about.

Herman began rubbing against my leg, so I reached down to scratch his head. "Well, let's have some dinner and see how we both feel after that."

Aunt Edna nodded. "I'll check on the sauce and feed Herman."

The cat pricked up his ears and trotted into the kitchen.

I wheeled my aunt's bags—one for her and one for Herman and gifts, I assumed—out to my car and locked them in my trunk. I'd leave mine for now. In case we headed out tonight.

Starting to doubt I had the energy to explore downtown, I yawned as I put my foot on the stoop. I stopped dead in my tracks. The red berries on Aunt Edna's wreath were eyes. Each was a single eyeball, encased in crimson flesh with red lids and no lashes, all glancing around and blinking out of sync. I rubbed my own eyes and scrubbed my hands down my face. When I looked at the wreath again, it was perfectly normal. I reached out and poked a red orb. It was a standard-issue holly berry. Okay, perhaps there is a case for not driving another hour and a half tonight.

As I walked back into the house, I heard Aunt Edna's oven door creak open, followed by a pan being slid out and set on the cooktop. "Oh drat!"

"What's wrong?" I asked as I stepped into the kitchen.

She held up a baking sheet to reveal what appeared to be four small, elongated rolls. She picked one up with a pair of tongs and tapped it on the counter with a hollow thud. "My yeast has expired, and these things are hard as rocks." She set the bread and tongs down. "I hate to ask, but could you possibly run to Steadman's for some ciabatta? They'll be closing soon and noodles are almost done, so you'd best hurry." She stirred the pot of sauce.

"Sure. Be right back."

"Straight there and back, mind you."

"Yes, Aunt Edna."

Steadman's Market was maybe five minutes away. Seven, if you caught the light. It was green for me, and in less than ten minutes, I was standing in the checkout line, a package of rolls in one hand and cinnamon chewing gum in the other.

Two older ladies chatted in front of me.

"Excuse me." One of the women reached for a candy bar on the rack behind the grocery conveyor belt.

I had to step back to avoid being pushed.

She paused and looked at me before giving a sideways glance to her friend. "Are you new in town?"

"Just passing through."

The women exchanged another look. "We're on our way to the Solstice Market. You should come with us. There's so much to see."

"And do," the other lady added.

"I saw them setting up earlier, but I've got to get back to my aunt's house. She's almost done making dinner."

"And who is your auntie?" The first woman patted my arm.

I flinched when she put her hands on me, and her asking personal information made me skittish. But in this size town, everyone knew everyone else. Perhaps if I told her who my aunt was, she'd let me alone. "Edna Henderson."

"Edna!" the second lady chirped. "She usually leaves—"

The first woman cut her off with a glare. "It's very nice to meet you, Edna's niece. Tell her the Craine sisters send their regards." With that, she clapped a grocery separator bar down on the belt.

"May Christmas pass you peacefully," the cashier said to the departing customer.

"You as well," the gentleman nodded as he hurried to the exit.

The cashier began scanning the Craine sisters' groceries, and they stepped closer to the register.

"I'm back!" I called as I closed Aunt Edna's front door.

"Excellent. Let's just pop those rolls in the oven for a few minutes to heat up, then we can fix our plates."

I handed her the package of bread. "The Craine sisters said to give you their regards."

The bread dropped to the floor, and my aunt's face was suddenly three shades paler.

"What's wrong?" I leaned over to pick up the rolls. "Are you all right?"

"Yes, of course, dear." She reached for the bread and cleared her throat. "What else did they say to you?"

"Not much. Just asked if I was new in town and invited me to the Solstice Market. Once I told them you were my aunt, they left me alone."

"I would expect nothing less." She put the baking sheet with the rolls into the oven.

"Who are those women? Do they have a beef with you?"

"It's a long and complicated story. Suffice it to say, we're not the best of friends." She stirred the broccoli she was sautéing and turned the burner under the sauce off. "Would you set the table, dear?"

Aunt Edna was an excellent cook, and as much as I enjoyed my meal, I felt myself drowsing. I yawned. "I'd kinda hoped I could make it to wander around the little market. But I think I'm just too tired. Shame—I had hoped to listen to the carolers."

"Carolers? You saw carolers?" She put her fork down.

"Sure. Well, not exactly. I was looking at the display at Cassie's when I saw them reflected in the glass. By the time I turned my head, they were gone."

"They shouldn't be out so early. Oh, dear. I think it best if we quickly did the washing up and headed out of town."

"Aunt Edna, I'm really tired. I don't think it's safe—"

Three bangs from the brass door knocker echoed through the house. Herman's tail fluffed out, and he hissed. I pushed my chair away from the table and got to my feet.

"Don't answer that. I'm sure it's Ursula Craine."

"Why would she come here? I thought—"

"She wants Herman. He escaped from her and Sybil."

"Wait, wait, wait. Herman is their cat? Aunt Edna, you can't just steal someone's pet."

She shook her head and picked up her dishes from the table. "I did not steal him. He came to me, and I granted him sanctuary. They want to do bad things to him, Skye. I'm keeping him safe."

I carried my plate and silverware to the sink. "What do you mean by 'bad things?' I mean, they didn't exactly look like pet abusers."

"And what do pet abusers look like? Do they have an identifying tattoo? A particular birthmark?" Aunt Edna poured the remaining spaghetti sauce into a container and set it in the freezer.

"Well, no, but…." I donned her yellow kitchen gloves and ran the hot water.

"If they get their claws on him, they will kill him, and it will create problems for everybody."

"Kill him?" I almost dropped the plate I was scrubbing. "Why?"

"As you young people say, it's complicated."

I waited for her to explain, but she did not. Mom, you got some 'splainin' to do when I get to your house. I washed the pots and pans in silence as she put away the leftovers.

When the last of the cookware was in the dish drainer, I peeled off the gloves and went to the front door. I did not really think anyone would still be there. At the edge of the porch, however, sat a cardboard box.

"Aunt Edna? You expecting a package?"

She didn't answer, and I almost tripped over Herman when I took a step forward. May as well bring it in before any porch pirates spot it. I opened the door and Herman perched at the threshold, sniffing.

I lifted the parcel and couldn't control the shriek that escaped my throat. Dozens, perhaps hundreds, of mice poured out of the unsealed bottom of the package in a panic. One was climbing my leg, and I nearly fell over, shaking it off. Herman pounced into the midst of the frenzied rodents. He missed one by a whisker, then bounded after it as it scurried down the walkway toward the bay tree.

I poked my head in the house. "Aunt Edna!" I shouted as loud as I could. "Herman's out!"

"What?" She moved as fast as she could down the hallway.

I ran down the steps and, under the dull glow of the street-light, caught a glimpse of orange fluff disappearing into the rose-mary that lined the outside of the picket fence.

"Where is he?" My aunt used her cane to speed down the path toward me.

"I saw him run into those bushes."

"Herman! Here kitty! Hurry, let's get back in the house." Aunt Edna stood on the sidewalk, poking at the bushes with her cane.

A green sedan pulled up and the passenger door opened. The mouse that Herman had been chasing leaped inside, and he followed. The door slammed shut and the car eased away from the curb.

The window rolled down and one of the Craine sisters leaned out, twisting her head much farther around than she should have been able to. "Lose something, dear?"

A terrified Herman vaulted out the opening before she could get herself back in, scratching her cheek as he used her face for a springboard.

She bellowed in fury as Herman fled into the neighbor's yard.

"Oh! Ursula, you're bleeding!" the driver gasped.

The wounded sister touched her face and examined her bloody fingers. "No. Not me! I won't be the one!"

The driver hit the gas and tires squealed as the car roared into the night.

"Herman!" Aunt Edna called. "Come here, they're gone!"

Moving faster than I thought possible, she hustled up the walkway and onto the neighbor's porch. The door opened before she could ring the bell.

"Was that Ursula Craine I heard?" the lady who answered asked. She looked about my aunt's age, with a long braid pulled up and coiled into a thick, white bun.

"Yes. Sybil, too. Herman's out and he ran into your yard."

"Oh, my. I'll help you look." She wasn't shy about stepping outside in her flannel nightgown, fluffy bathrobe, and foam-insulated slippers.

They hobbled down the stairs. "Selene, I don't know if you remember my niece, Skye?"

"Of course I do. Been a while. I recall when you used to visit—"

"We have to find Herman. Now."

"Yes, Edna."

"Herman! Come on out!" My aunt stirred the leaves of Selene's shrubs with the tip of her cane as we walked along the side of the house. Motion-activated security lights lit our way.

I joined in. "Herman. Here, kitty, kitty." I walked the back fence, which lay in semi-darkness. I stopped at a broken slat and pulled a bit of orange fluff from the splintered wood. "He must have run through there."

"We'll need your car, then." Aunt Edna turned and began striding toward the street.

"I'll have to get my keys."

Selene reached into her pocket. "You mean these?"

I gaped at the ring of keys and fob she handed me. "How did—"

"We don't have time for that!" Aunt Edna got into the passenger seat.

Selene climbed in the back behind my aunt while I ran around to the front. After I pulled away from the curb, I said, "Explain. How did you get my keys?"

"Turn right." Aunt Edna tapped the window. "Summoning objects. It's a skill she has."

"Maybe she can summon Herman?"

"He's not an object." Selene cleared her throat. "He has free will."

"People cannot just make things appear out of thin air!" I hit the brakes harder than I intended to as I turned.

"Selene can. Right again, here."

As I turned at the next corner, a blur of orange fur sped across the road and into the utility easement.

"There he goes!" I pulled over, and we scrambled out of the car.

The narrow alley between tall backyard fences was too dark to see anything. There wasn't a way for me to shine my headlights down it without blocking the street. My phone was back at the house, and even if she had hers with her, Aunt Edna only had a flip phone with large buttons. No light.

"Here you go." Selene handed each of us a flashlight.

Not going to ask. At this point, I was starting to wonder if I had fallen asleep on the road and was dozing in a ditch somewhere, dreaming this elaborate dream.

We all wandered down the easement, shining our lights into the bushes and calling for Herman. The initial jolt of adrenaline had faded, and now I rubbed my arms, wishing I had my coat.

"What's that?" Selene shone her flashlight beam on a bush that had escaped from under the fence into the short grass.

About thirty feet away, a red puffy jacket was draped on the errant shrub. Looked just like mine.

"Selene, is there anything you can't abracadabra to where you want it?"

"Herman! Here kitty! Technically, no. But there are limitations. Nobody can be looking at the thing when it disappears or when it arrives. Something small enough to fit into my pocket is easy. Anything outside where people are around, such as a car, is much harder."

I grabbed the coat and put it on. When I reached into the pocket, there was the pack of cinnamon gum I'd bought earlier at Steadman's, along with the receipt.

"What are those lights up ahead?" I zipped my jacket.

"That'll be the Solstice Market." Aunt Edna sighed. "Herman! They'll be back soon. You need to come out!"

The yowl of an angry cat came from somewhere ahead, near the road. All three of our flashlight beams trained on a pair of cats, one orange, one a brown tabby. Hissing and spitting, they boxed and slapped each other. The tabby turned and bolted across the pavement, Herman bounding after. Tires screeched as an oncoming car missed them by inches.

"Herman, what are you doing?" Aunt Edna clutched her head with her hands.

We hurried after the cats and found ourselves in the Solstice Market. It looked cheery enough, with white pop-up awnings decorated with evergreen garlands and red berries. A band on a flatbed trailer played music that sounded like it was from medieval times. While Selene and my aunt asked shoppers and sellers if they had seen two cats running through the market, I took a moment to check out some of the wares.

The first booth had jewelry. Carved from bones. It was interesting—as a museum display. The thought of wearing it made my stomach do a little flip.

The next booth had small clay figurines. I expected them to be Christmas-themed, but they were more like Halloween characters. They all had the wrong number of limbs and heads, sometimes too few, sometimes too many.

Well, that's enough shopping for tonight.

"Somebody get that cat!" a man a few booths over shouted.

Herman, something clutched in his teeth, dashed through the crowd of revelers and back across the street. We chased after him. A green sedan skidded to a stop, blocking our way. Aunt Edna scrambled around the front of the vehicle, whacking the center of the bumper with her cane.

The airbag deployed, momentarily pinning Ursula Craine in the car. Selene and my aunt were not fast, but it took a few moments for the Craine sisters to figure out what had just happened and shake it off.

A glance over my shoulder showed the people from the market gathering by the road to watch the spectacle of four old ladies and myself chasing each other down the utility easement. I hope someone calls 9-1-1.

Selene's house shoes were not made for running (or shuffling) cross country, so she stumbled a few times. I caught up to her and grabbed her arm to keep her upright.

Aunt Edna came to a sudden stop, and I nearly crashed into her. "Do you hear that?" She put her arms out in front, palms flat, as if she'd just encountered a mime's glass wall.

Behind us, the Craine sisters also halted.

Snatches of music drifted from somewhere up ahead. A group singing a capella.

"Oh, no!" Selene gasped. "Not the carolers!"

The song got louder and more distinct, but it wasn't a tune I recognized. A chuckle sounded at our backs.

"You called them, didn't you?" Aunt Edna spat, glaring at the Craine sisters.

What are these carolers? Both Selene and my aunt seem upset by them.

Shielding her eyes with her hand from the glare of my aunt's flashlight beam, Ursula shrugged. "And what if I did?"

It was then that I noticed purple energy crackling around Aunt Edna's hands. She raised them above her head and a thin wall of purple fire sprang up between her and the Craine sisters. I suppose it would keep them from following us, but we were now trapped between the purple fire and the oncoming carolers.

The half-moon, riding low on the horizon, slipped out from behind a cloud. The light wasn't bright, but it was enough for us to make out the silhouettes of the carolers. There were five of them, and they looked like any group of singers I would expect to see. Wooly hats. Long coats. Open song books. Except they had glowing red eyes.

Aunt Edna put up a second purple wall. Her entire body shook and beads of sweat glinted purple as they ran down her face.

"Will it hold them?" Selene whimpered.

"Don't... know." My aunt said between ragged gasps.

The carolers approached the purple wall of fire. They pushed against it, and for a few moments, it held. Then slowly, they oozed through.

With a shout, Aunt Edna dropped her arms, and both walls collapsed. She fell to her knees. Selene and I, one on each side, pulled her to her feet.

"What are those things?" I hissed.

"Winter spirits," Selene whispered. "Hunger. Darkness. Cold. They absorb the life force of anything they touch."

I figured the Craine sisters weren't in much better shape than Aunt Edna and Selene. We should be able to at least knock them over to trip up the carolers, if it came to that.

A growl shredded the darkness from our right. Suddenly, a man, faintly glowing orange, appeared. In his hand, he held a bundle of herbs. He ran past the singers, smacking each one in the face with the plants. The first four dropped their songbooks and raised their arms to their faces, wailing. The fifth one nearly grabbed the man. But just as suddenly as he appeared, he vanished, tossing the herbs into the outstretched hands of the last caroler, who howled and threw them to the ground.

"Get him!" Ursula shouted. She clapped her hands and lightning flashed, blinding us temporarily.

I was confused. Then I noticed an orange cat sprinting away.

Grabbing an arm each of Selene and Aunt Edna, I pulled them past the disoriented carolers and down the easement. A whirlwind screamed up from behind, but instead of knocking us down, it pushed us along faster.

When we finally reached my car, Herman sat on the hood, waiting.

"Get in!" Aunt Edna panted.

She grabbed Herman and shoved him inside.

"Drive!" shouted Selene as she slammed her door closed.

I drove. Straight out of town.

"Who was that man?" I ran the yellow light.

"Herman." Aunt Edna replied.

"Herman is the cat."

"He's also Ursula and Sybil's brother. They need the blood of a male Craine for a ritual to… Never mind. It's complicated."

"It is," Selene agreed.

My aunt scratched between the cat's ears. "Your mother never told you anything about Blackwater Hollow? Why she had to leave?"

I gave up trying to understand this crazy town some time ago. Earlier, I was focused on surviving our trip. Now that we were out of that place, I needed answers. I tapped the screen and called my mom. "I'm on the way with Aunt Edna. We have an extra guest. And… we need to talk."

It was just after midnight when we arrived. Dad was asleep, but Mom let us in. She'd always been a night owl, so I was not at all surprised when she already had hot cocoa ready and waiting, along with an array of snacks.

Her eyes widened and her mouth dropped open when Herman the cat was suddenly Herman the man.

"It's okay, Gayle. Guess you could say the cat's out of the bag." Aunt Edna patted Mom on the shoulder.

I studied him, this author of our near misadventure. He wasn't fat, but comfortably padded. His hair was the color of a grapefruit peel, and his eyes were the same emerald hue I'd known all these years.

I had so many questions, I didn't even know where to begin.

"Do you want me to get you something from my closet, Selene?"

"No, thank you. It's way past my bedtime and I'm ready to turn into a pumpkin. But I will have a bite to eat first."

Mom handed her a plate from the stack on the table and Selene served herself some food.

As the rest of us lined up to get our snacks and cocoa, Mom took our coats and hung them on pegs by the front door.

I sat at the table and took a sip of hot cocoa. It was just the way I like it—not overly sweet, extra creamy, and just a note of bitter dark chocolate. Picking up a chocolate chip cookie, I raised an eyebrow at my mother, who stood near the table wringing her hands.

"Mom, why have you never told me anything about Blackwater Hollow?"

She looked at the floor.

Aunt Edna cleared her throat. "Are you going to tell her, or shall I?"

Mom sighed. "Well, we could stay up all night and into lunch time for me to tell you everything. You're gonna have to know, anyway. Let me give you the executive summary. You know that weird, ugly pond in the center of town?"

"Yes. I always wondered why they didn't just drain that thing and fill it in."

"Oh, they've tried," chirped Selene. "Couldn't do it."

"Yes. Well, that pond marks the site of an energy vortex. Due to the geomagnetic profile of the place, there is an unstable portal—guess you could think of it as a wormhole—that opens up from time to time, although it almost always appears during the solstices. Entities come and go through it whenever it's working. Some good, some bad, most in-between."

I felt like I'd just been unceremoniously dropped into a sci-fi movie. "Has anyone gone in there? Where does it go?"

Mom shrugged. "A few people have tried over the years. They went in and never came out."

"There was Mad Mandini." Selene speared a strawberry with her fork.

Aunt Edna blotted her lips. "That was so long ago that nobody knows if it really happened, or if it was just a story."

"Precisely why I didn't mention it. It was in eighteen something, before the Civil War. A young man named Luigi Mandini had a bit too much to drink. On his way home, he took a wrong turn and ended up in the pond—that's why it has stones around it now. When he returned three months later, he had a streak of white in his hair, and mostly talked to people who weren't there."

Selene looked around the table and leaned toward me. "They said that if you looked into his eyes, you could see the Milky Way galaxy in his pupils."

"Probably cataracts," Mom replied. "Still, one evening at supper, he told his brother he was going away for a while with friends. When they got up in the morning, he was gone and never seen again. I think the whole thing is a tall tale, myself."

I had another heavenly sip of cocoa. "Thousands of people disappear every year without the help of a mystic portal."

"His hat and shoes were found next to the pond in the morning," Selene said.

I glanced up at Herman, who was contentedly chewing a sausage ball. "What about the Craine sisters? Why are they so desperate to do some magical rite with Herman?"

"The Craines were among the original families that settled in Blackwater Hollow."

Aunt Edna shook her head and pursed her lips. "They didn't take the time to consider why Native Americans avoided the area, they just thought that made it a safe place to build a village. Josiah Craine is the one who had the land surveyed and platted."

"The community was really struggling." Mom traced circles on the table with her index finger. "Until a mysterious old man showed up and taught them how to channel the vortex energy. Turns out that the energy is very attracted to blood. In any amount, but the more the better."

"They were trying to upset the balance!" Herman half-rose from his chair.

Now, we're getting somewhere. "The balance of?"

"Power." The light bulb near Aunt Edna flickered. "Two and two. Ursula and Sybil are on the side of the dark, Herman and I are on the side of the light. Ursula and Sybil are strongest in the dark half of the year, between the fall and spring equinoxes. Herman and I are strongest between spring and fall. That's why I only ever had you come visit in the summer and why Herman and I get out of town on the winter solstice."

"So, you just didn't want to get involved in all that, Mom?"

She sighed. "I could not stay neutral, but I was not allowed to take a side. I had to leave, or…"

"Be sacrificed." Herman nodded as he shared a lingering look with my mother.

I almost dropped my fork. "Like they wanted to sacrifice you?"

"I guess you could say that, but it isn't quite the same. Do you know anything at all about alchemy?"

"I can't say that I do."

"Fair enough, Skye. There are considered to be four elements: air, water, fire, earth. There is spirit, but that's not relevant here. Air and fire are masculine, water and earth are feminine. Because Edna and I embody all four elements, we're more stable." He chuckled. "Or more well-rounded, which seems less stable. But anyway…. If Ursula and Sybil either killed or banished me, there are only female family members left to take my place."

Mom gave me a wan smile. "Sooner or later, the old guard will pass. Someone has to fill the void—it's too dangerous to just leave it lie. Right, Uncle George?"

Wait. What? "Did you just say, 'Uncle George?' I thought he was Ursula and Sybil's brother."

"I am. And Edna's."

THE PRESENT
By A. B. Richards

BEEP. Beep. Beep.

Why does my alarm sound so weird?

I tried to open my eyes, but couldn't. *Am I wearing a blindfold?*

I raised my hand to my face. "Ow!" Something stabbed me when I bent my elbow. I knew that sensation. There was an IV in my right arm. Straightening it, I used my left to try to free my eyes.

Gently, I probed the wrapping. Not a blindfold. Gauze. My head was bandaged. A few spots were damp.

It took some doing, but I peeled the tape and cotton away and looked around.

My vision was a little blurry, but I could see well enough to know I was in a hospital room, hooked up to a machine that beeped every few seconds. A mostly full IV bag hung from a pole, although it wasn't dripping any fluids. I checked the line for a kink, but everything seemed in order.

Fantastic. Please, please, please let this be an in-network hospital. What day is it? If I've missed Steve Johnson's Monday morning staff meeting, I'd be better off dead. I scrubbed my hand down my face and dropped it on the thin cotton blanket.

My fingers settled on the chunky remote connected by a stiff cable to the side of the bed. Eagerly, I pressed the call button and waited.

A nurse should have come on the crackly intercom to say someone would be along shortly. She did not.

After counting holes in the ceiling tiles for what felt like twenty or thirty minutes, I pushed the button again. "Hello? Is anybody there?"

Only silence.

My brain churned out scenarios, from the plausible to the perverse. Maybe there was an emergency, and everyone was helping? How long had I been here? What if there was some pandemic that killed everybody while I was unconscious? A group of terrorists took over the hospital? A time slip?

I clamped both hands over my ears, as if that could muffle the chatter inside my head. "Stop it!" I had to do something to put a halt to the spiraling. Perhaps someone would hear me shouting at myself and come to check on me.

I heaved a heavy sigh. *If the nurses won't come to me, I'll go to them.* I peeled the electrodes off my chest and eased out of bed on the side of the IV pole, then pulled it along with me toward the door.

I paused and listened before I opened it. If anyone was in the hallway, I couldn't hear them. With a deep breath, I stepped into the corridor.

It looked the way I would expect a hospital to look at night—dim lighting, sparse on people. More than sparse, though. None.

The single fluorescent tube overhead buzzed and flickered.

My initial fears were dissolving into irritation. Were they just sitting around the desk watching videos on their phones? Probably. Perhaps I could at least get them to take this IV out, since it didn't seem to be doing anything, anyway.

The squeal of the pole echoed in the empty hallway as it rolled along beside me.

There. At the corner. *That's got to be the nurses' station.* I quickened my pace and organized what I planned to say when I caught them goofing off.

There was no one at the desk. A half-drunk cup of coffee and a bagel with a bite taken out of it sat near a computer keyboard.

"Hello?" I craned my head to peer down each hallway. "Anyone here?"

The giggle of a small child and slap of little shoes on tile snatched my attention. I tried to run around the corner and tripped over the IV pole. Both it and I sprawled on the cold floor. The line didn't pull out but tugged painfully at my arm.

I've gotta get rid of this thing. Gingerly, I struggled to my feet and righted the pole. I ransacked the nurses' station until I found some treatment supplies. Carefully, I peeled up the tape that held the catheter in place. I placed a folded square of gauze over the needle and slipped it out of my vein. I wrapped tape around my arm several times to secure the bandage.

Scissors! That's what I forgot. The elastic tape did not tear.

And then I saw it.

Lurking in the shadows, a ruined face stared at me. Its left cheek was hamburger, and a partially dislodged eye drooped out of the socket above the bloody mess. *A zombie?*

Unencumbered by the IV pole, I ran.

I took off down the same corridor where I heard that kid. If there's a small child around, there's got to be a parent nearby, right?

Arms straight out in front of me, I rammed my way through the double doors and sprinted down the hallway. I passed tiny waiting areas for ICU and radiology without a soul to be seen.

As I turned a corner, the childish giggle sounded again and I caught a flash of small white Mary Janes disappearing into the cafeteria.

My head swam, but I pumped my legs harder. I had to catch up.

I barreled into the empty room and stopped, panting. There was no sound behind me, no pursuing footsteps. I turned to verify that I had escaped, at least for now, from the disgusting zombie. Putting my hand through the roll of tape, I wore it like a bracelet. There's bound to be a knife in here somewhere.

If there was a kid in there, I couldn't see them. Dirty dishes, stacked on trays and waiting to be bussed, cluttered a few tables. A forgotten Houston Chronicle lay messily folded on another.

An artificial Christmas tree stood in one corner. Undeterred, its blinking, colored lights flashed holiday cheer to the empty room. The star on top... I moved closer. It was the same kind that crowned my friend Gina's tree.

Her annual holiday party was always the best. Gina tried to have a little something from a lot of winter traditions—challah bread and rugelach, mini sweet potato tarts and fried plantains, chocolate Bûche de Noël cake with merengue mushrooms, wassail and orange cookies. There were more things than I could keep track of, but all of it was delicious.

And of course there were games. Musical chairs with a bunch of drunk adults was a full-contact sport. Scrunching my brow, I remembered bringing macaroni-and-cheese-flavored candy canes for the White Elephant exchange. But what did I end up with? I couldn't remember. To be fair, I probably shouldn't have started with mulled wine on an empty stomach.

A child's laugh shattered my reverie. The door that led to the cafeteria's kitchen thumped and swung back and forth, as if someone had just run through it.

"Wait!" I hurried after it.

I would have been shocked if there had actually been anyone in there. No person to be seen, but there was a single, stupid, fricken orange on the counter. An orange. I wanted to pick the damned thing up and hurl it across the room.

Steve Johnson had been shuffling papers at his mahogany wood desk when I came in for my performance review on Friday. How many days ago was that?

He had barely glanced up at me. "You've been doing good work here...."

Had he forgotten my name? It should be on that form in front of him. "Thanks."

"I'm pleased to say that this department has met enough of our key performance indicators to trigger bonus disbursements."

I'd nodded. KPIs were always adjusted throughout the year to ensure executives got their bonuses. Not complaining, really. It meant we mere mortals also got a splash of cash. Usually.

I remembered staring at the poster over his shoulder that showed a man free-climbing a cliff face, the words, 'PERSISTENCE: The difference between a stepping stone and a stumbling block is how high you raise your foot' in bold white letters at the bottom.

"Now, the leadership team is looking to see more growth in cross-functional stakeholder engagement. More proactive synergy. I want our group to really lean into paradigm-shifting initiatives."

"Of course." I'd let the buzzword salad roll right on by, not even trying to parse it.

"We'll put a pin in that for now. The leadership team is excited about the company's revolutionary new wellness program—Total Health Integration to Corporate Culture. We'll call it THICC for short. We're all gonna get THICC this year! Tons of studies about fresh fruit, yada yada. You can look it up." He'd leaned over and retrieved a fancy shrink-wrapped gift basket from behind his desk, then pushed it toward me. "Anyway, here's your oranges."

"Thanks." I picked up the basket, wondering if I had enough money saved up to live in a sprinter van on a beach in Mexico.

The rest of the day felt like swimming in a tar pit. It was overcast outside, and chilly rain splashed the windows from time to time. Those too-bright oranges sat in their basket like miniature artificial suns, taunting me all afternoon.

Eventually, the workday ended, and I stood at the bus stop, waiting for the park and ride express. It was cold and drizzly, and I huddled under the shelter with the other commuters. A soggy homeless man had shuffled up and asked for change. Everyone ignored him.

"Here." I handed him the basket of oranges. "It's all I got, man."

He'd looked me in the eye and gave me a skeptical smile before he took it. "Bless you."

A stockpot clattered to the tile. My head jerked toward it, and my peripheral vision caught tiny white shoes on red tights running out a side door.

Due to a large serving cart in my way, I had to run around the kitchen island to get out the same exit. An industrial concrete corridor that felt more like an underground tunnel stretched in either direction. *Which way did that kid go?*

A squeal of laughter burst from the right, so I ran toward it. At the t-intersection, I grabbed the wall near the corner as I turned so I didn't have to slow down as much.

I stumbled to a halt. This hallway was almost completely dark. A low-wattage bulb in a cage barely lit the far end of the corridor.

'EXIT' glowed red above the doorframe, although the 'I' blinked on and off.

I cocked my head, straining to listen. A children's choir… singing Christmas carols. I couldn't quite make out the words, but the music sounded Christmasy, anyway.

"Hello? Hey, kid! You there?"

There was no reply. I didn't suppose there would be. Cautiously, I made my way through the gloom. Something crunched under my feet. What the heck? I reached down to touch it, then brought a handful of the frozen stuff to examine it. I turned back toward the lit corridor, but there was a click and the hallway went dark. I rubbed the substance between my fingers. *This is stupid. It feels like snow, but how is there snow inside a building?*

It had been snowing the night of Gina's party. Happens once or twice a decade here and shuts down the entire city. *Still, it shouldn't be inside a hospital.* I dropped the cold powder and wiped my hands on my pants.

The singing children all seemed to be sopranos now, as the pitch of their song got higher and higher. The music sounded more distorted, too, getting louder as I neared the exit. Perhaps the speakers in this access passage were bad.

I continued creeping down the hallway. When I reached the door, I took a deep breath. I hadn't seen that zombie in a while. It would be just my luck if it was lurking on the other side. I pushed the door open wide enough to scan the area with one eye.

No hint of anyone, living or undead.

I slipped out into a large waiting room. Rows of chairs were everywhere—against the walls and back-to-back in the center of the room. The sign over the front desk, huge white letters on a red background, read 'Emergency Department.'

I clamped my hands over my ears. *So loud!* That sweet children's choir sounded more and more like a siren wailing. Ugh.

A TV, mounted in one corner, showed a reporter on location somewhere. The sound was turned off, and I was too far away to read the captions that crawled across the bottom of the screen in red. Strobing red and blue lights dappled the snow at her feet, and a wrecker inched past behind her.

I picked at my arm. Local news seems like a bad choice this evening. I mean, it's a snowy night in Houston—there are probably dozens of accidents. Nobody in the ER wants to see that. Frowning, I tore my gaze from the TV.

Since nobody was at the front desk, I stepped behind it. A pair of bandage scissors lay next to the phone. I removed the irritating roll of tape from my wrist and cut it, securing the end around my arm. Feeling like an intruder, I hurried back into the waiting area.

I should get out of this place. There's gotta be people nearby. Maybe somebody can tell me what's going on.

I turned toward the glass doors.

Staring back at me was the zombie, its shirt soaked in blood. Shit.

I sprinted down the corridor away from it. Whenever hallways intersected, I picked a new direction at random. I ran until I felt I'd gone far enough. No idea where I was, and I hoped it was the same for the zombie.

Thankfully, the awful din from the alleged Christmas music had stayed in the waiting room. I started to search for a sign or map or something.

A click grabbed my attention, and I whirled just in time to see the little girl darting around the corner. Didn't get a good look at her face, but she wore a green velvet dress with a white pinafore.

There was a stain on the apron, and for some reason, I thought it might be raspberry jam.

"Hey, wait!" I called out as I jogged after her. "I won't hurt you.

I made the turn and there was no question about where I was. The walls were painted bright yellow and decorated with paintings of balloons and baby animals. I was in the pediatric ward. Could this be where the parents were?

Yet another small waiting room. This one had a coffee bar and a few tiny round tables with hard plastic chairs.

I stopped and stared at the table closest to me. Dead center stood a mostly empty bottle of bourbon. What a crazy thing to find in the kids' area of a hospital. Unless… it was for stressed out parents, desperate for news from the doctors.

I started to reach for the bottle, but my stomach churned.

Gina's party. Denny and I were supposed to have been mixing the whiskey into the eggnog, but we ended up taking shots instead. There wasn't quite as much left as Gina told us to put in, but we figured there was enough booze around that nobody'd notice the nog was only seventy-five proof, rather than a hundred. *Oh, Denny. I should've split the Uber with you.* But my account was overdrawn and my credit card only had $3 available on it. Didn't want to have to beg for a loan until payday.

The stairwell door at the end of the hall creaked open. As I whipped my head around, the giggling little girl ran through, the patter of her hard-soled shoes echoed off the concrete. I bolted after her, pausing at the stairs to determine which way she'd gone.

Down.

Easier to run downstairs than up, I guess. I kept going until there were no more stairs. With a deep breath, I opened the door.

The girl stood in the hallway. Her long blonde sausage curls draped over her shoulders. Her white apron was smeared with red, and there was a smudge of it at the corner of her mouth. I thought of those cookies with the cutout in the center and raspberry jam filling. Or possibly toast and jelly? I mean, what else could it be? She's just a little kid.

She held a wrapped present in her hands. It looked so familiar… Of course! It was the one from the White Elephant exchange. The one I'd received. How'd she get a hold of it?

"Hey there, young lady. I think you have something of mine. Could we talk for a minute? I'm not mad. I promise."

She turned and began walking down the hall. I hurried after her, but I couldn't seem to close the distance, no matter how fast I went. The double doors at the end of the corridor swung open. I had been completely focused on the child in front of me. Hadn't noticed the sign. Until now.

Morgue.

Oh, hell no. No, no, no. I tried to stop, but my legs kept walking right on through those ominous doors. I had lost all control of my limbs and was now just along for the ride.

All I could focus on, besides the little girl, were two stainless steel tables. Bright lights shone down on each of them, like spotlights in the otherwise dim room. Sheet-draped remains lay on each table.

One was child-sized.

"Why did you bring me here? I don't want to see this!" I would have shielded my eyes with my hands if I could have.

She tugged at the overhanging edge of the sheet that covered the smaller corpse, and the cotton fabric slipped to the floor.

Of course, it was hers. She looked so innocent. Like she'd somehow fallen asleep wearing blood-stained clothes.

She gave me a beseeching look that shattered my heart before taking the lid off the gift that she carried. Out came a snow globe. A ridiculous, kitschy thing someone must have picked up at the airport—a pink convertible with longhorn bull horns on the hood drove toward a few iconic downtown buildings and a Columbia blue banner with the word 'Houston' on it.

"Do better next time." She shook the globe and handed it to me.

My hands rose automatically to take it. Plastic chips of snow swirled around the miniature skyline and the morgue dissolved around me.

Tires screeched. It occurred to me that I should also try to brake, but I couldn't remember which pedal was stop and which was go. I saw her clearly because my headlights shone directly through her windshield. The lady's mouth was open, her eyes wide. In slow motion, she got closer and closer. A little white Mary Jane shoe over red tights dangled from a child seat behind the woman.

There was a pop and acrid smoke filled my nostrils as my air bag punched me in the face. I saw stars. My SUV tried to run up the hood of the sedan, but rolled over instead, smashing hard into some landscaping boulders. A thousand pieces of glass drove into my head. White hot pain flashed through my body, obliterating the scene around me.

I fell to my knees. When I opened my eyes, I had to squint against the blinding light that had suddenly appeared near the little girl. She sighed and gave me one last sorrowful smile, then disappeared into the unbearable brightness.

I struggled to my feet and took a step toward the place she'd vanished.

"Where do you think you're going?"

Who the hell is that? I spun around.

In front of me loomed a hooded figure in a black robe. A scythe was clutched in one bony hand.

I backed away, bumping into the metal table with the larger body on it. I didn't need to see what was under the sheet.

The Grim Reaper flicked its wrist, and the fabric fell to the floor.

The zombie? I stared at its blood-soaked clothes. *My* clothes. Oh. When I'd seen it earlier, I must have been catching my reflection. I felt sick and turned my head.

The light passage shrunk and faded away.

"I guess you're here to take me to hell."

Death snapped its fingers twice. Two young men in crisp white shirts with sport coats and slacks appeared from nowhere. One took the scythe.

Grim pulled the tab of a hidden zipper and the cloak opened at the front. He shrugged off the hood and slipped out of the robe. The second minion took it from him, and both underlings disappeared.

Death wore a designer three-piece suit with a subtle pinstripe. The thin diagonal yellow and white stripes on his navy-blue tie were almost parallel, but not quite. The more I tried to focus on it, the more it seemed that the lines themselves shifted and moved ever so slightly.

"Step into my office. I'll answer any questions you might have during your onboarding."

"On...boarding?"

Death opened a door I would have sworn was not there a moment ago, and I followed him inside.

Behind his mahogany wood desk hung a poster. A man free-climbed a rugged cliff face. White letters at the bottom of the image read, 'PERSISTENCE: The difference between a tombstone and a milestone is how high you lift your feet.'

The leather executive chair squeaked as Death sat in it. He shuffled through some papers, nodding. He steepled his fingers and looked at me with inscrutably dark eyes. "Your end-of-life review is pending." He opened his hands toward me. "You're on probation. Might want to think of it as a community service opportunity. To complete the terms, you'll need to harness that proactive soul energy to lean into cross-dimensional spirit engagement to verify your KPIs."

I couldn't believe what I was hearing. "I'm sorry. My what?"

"KPIs. Key Posthumous Indicators." He leaned back in his chair, which protested with another loud squeak. "Look. You crossed over that little girl and her mother involuntarily. That's a mandatory enrollment with Nick Free."

"Who's Nick?"

"Nick? No, no. N-K-F-R-I. Negative Karma Flow Remediation Initiative. You may not have intended to apply for the job of Transition Facilitation Coordinator, but you're hired! You'll be helping lost souls get where they need to go."

I shifted in my seat. "I have no idea how to do that."

"It'll be in the paperwork. And, speaking of which, here's your welcome gift." He leaned over and retrieved a shrink-wrapped gift basket. Death pushed it and a fat envelope in my direction.

The basket contained a package of pens, an eraser, an employee badge with my picture attached to a black lanyard with little white skulls on it, some packets of flavored coffee, a handful of Starlight mints, and a coffee mug with an image of a grinning Grim Reaper and the words, 'Dead Set on Success!'

"Thanks."

"Oh. We also have a new company-wide wellness program. We call it THIN—Transitional Health Integration Network. The enrollment form's in the envelope."

Death had returned to his paper shuffling, so I got to my feet. I started to leave, then turned around. "What if I don't participate? I never asked for this."

A slow smile spread across his face. "Looking for a hot time, are you? You're here because of choices you made. But if you'd like a transfer..." He pushed a button on his desk and a piece of the floor slid away.

Heat scorched my raw cheek as I leaned forward slightly to peer inside. What appeared to be magma oozed between columns of black rock. *Was that screaming?* I swallowed. "So, w-when is orientation?"

Death pushed the button again, and the gap in the floor disappeared. "Don't forget about Monday morning's staff meeting. Come early so you can grab a lo-carb donut."

Voices interrupted our conversation. Two men had entered the morgue.

"Ah!" Death looked up. "Sounds like your first case." He winked at me. "Go get 'em, Tiger. Oh, you might wanna..." He finger-combed his perfect coif.

A mirror now hung on the back of his office door. I looked like I always did, pre-accident. A bit disheveled, perhaps, but no bloody wounds or clothes. I smoothed my unkempt hair as best I could and stepped out of Death's office.

A sheet-covered body was being wheeled in. The confused spirit was sitting up, looking around. I recognized him.

Plastic snapped against metal as one man dropped the bed rail. He grabbed a shoulder and the other man gripped a calf.

"One, two, three."

They heaved the body onto a stainless steel table, the ghost of the corpse's former inhabitant looking from side to side.

One orderly shook his head. "Poor guy never had a chance. He was DOA."

The eyes of the homeless man from the bus stop fixed on me. He scowled. "You."

The other orderly pulled the rail back into place, shaking his head. "What a way to go. Choked to death on an orange."

THE FRAME

By A. B. Richards

BLAKE Renfro approached the pile of gaudy presents with trepidation. A few people took the Secret Santa exchange as an opportunity for a nasty prank, wrapping up a blown-out running shoe or some equally gross item. It was never difficult to guess who those grinchy givers were. Others played it safe with generic gifts. A Christmas candle or scented hand cream could be lurking beneath the glittering paper. At least those things could be re-gifted.

Once in a while, someone who actually knew you drew your name and bought a gift you'd truly want. Last Christmas, Blake had gotten a set of holiday-themed dishtowels, the clearance markdown tag still attached. Those worked any time of year.

Today, a thin rectangular package was tagged with his name. Surely there wasn't enough volume for anything truly awful.

"Thanks, Secret Santa." He raised the gift and padded back to his chair. The metallic green paper gave way to sleek black packaging with white letters.

NexuSync Imaging Electronic Photo Frame. Powered by QCap AI technology. The future has never been clearer.

The box felt more substantial than he would have expected for a twenty-dollar-budget electronics item. The frame consisted of a screen edged in glossy black metal with a kickstand in the back. No instructions, just a QR code to scan and download the NexuSync app.

A few people nodded or commented on the coolness of the device, but the next gift recipient was already picking through the packages.

After the last Secret Santa offering had been unwrapped, the employees filtered away to their offices, unlikely to get any work done on a treat-filled Friday before a four-day weekend. Blake nabbed a couple of chocolate chip cookies on his way. Back at his desk, he found a power bank and plugged in the frame to charge. He absolutely was type to look a gift horse, or device, in the mouth. He wasn't about to plug it into his computer until he'd had a chance to research the manufacturer and scan the device for malware.

Blake had gone home, had dinner and a nap, then returned to the office with a handful of other IT folks to perform some major software upgrades and a few hardware replacements. His task tonight was to sit in the server room and periodically click 'next' as the install did its thing.

He scrolled through search engine results on his phone. NexuSync Imaging was a tech startup that had arrived on the scene with little fanfare. Nowhere near an IPO, a selection of their prototypes had been given out at various consumer electronics events, earning a smattering of rave reviews, mostly for Ultra High Definition smart TVs and computer monitors.

The frame was still sealed in its antistatic plastic bag, so Blake figured that it had been handed out at some event. The recipient hadn't known what to do with it and unloaded it at the office holiday lunch.

He tapped a few buttons to continue the software installation, then trotted back to his desk. Blake connected the frame to a test computer that was not connected to any type of network or internet and set the antivirus scan running.

By 2:30 AM, the installs and upgrades were completed and spot-tested. They'd load-test the server after lunch, but for now, the team was heading to a 24-hour diner for breakfast and then home to sleep.

On Saturday afternoon, Blake was the first to arrive at the office. A man in grey coveralls and a ball cap stood in the hallway near the IT bullpen with some kind of electronic meter in his hand.

"Can I help you with something?" Blake wasn't sure how to react.

"Building maintenance. Working on the HVAC, just checking that the heat's working on all the floors."

"Ah. Thanks for that."

On Blake's test computer, the deep scan had finished clean, and the frame was free of any malware. He used his company phone on the QR code from the slip of paper inside the packaging. The website design was slick and graphics-heavy. He installed the app and gave it read-only access to a network drive where employees could upload selfies and non-work accomplishments for HR to use in the monthly newsletter.

An image of Leslie Henderson from Accounting popped up on the screen. Grinning, she held a medal from her most recent marathon.

After all the testing was finished, the group sat around in their bullpen.

"Hey, where'd you get that?" Josh pointed at the sleek black frame on Blake's desk.

A photo of someone smiling in front of a ski slope with their family was now on display. "Secret Santa yesterday. You were there."

"Oh, yeah."

The slope faded out, and an image of their open-plan office area faded in. The room was empty, but the picture appeared to have been taken from a corner near the ceiling. Blake and two others glanced up. There were no security cameras in any corner, but a long workbench ran along one wall. Theoretically, someone tall could have stood on it and snapped the photo, but why?

Emil glanced at his watch. "Shit! My wife's gonna kill me. We were supposed to have been on the road to her parents' almost an hour ago." He rushed out the door.

"I gotta bounce, too. Need one last present. No idea what to get my nephew." Sandra rose from her chair. "Happy holidays, merry Christmas, and all that." She waved as she hurried after Emil.

The others stood up. Blake remained in his chair.

Josh paused on his way out. "You comin'?"

"Right behind you. Gotta finish checking in this code."

Ten minutes later, Blake stretched and got to his feet. It was then he noticed that the image now in the frame was of Josh, sporting an ugly Christmas sweater, in the server room. He appeared to have tripped and caught himself on one of the server racks. Frowning, Blake went in to check on the equipment. Everything seemed to be working fine. He even checked the console for alerts but found nothing.

The four-day weekend came and went, and back-to-work Wednesday arrived with a vengeance. Blake yawned as he waited for the coffee machine to finish brewing. He thought being in the mostly empty office between Christmas and New Year's would give him time to get ahead on his project. Instead, his phone had buzzed at seven AM with a message from his boss, demanding he and Josh figure out why there was a system-wide outage, and to fix it *yesterday.*

Josh strolled into the break room and parked himself in front of the vending machine.

The coffee maker gurgled, and Blake took his cup. Josh retrieved his chips and turned toward his coworker.

Blake stared at the cross-eyed reindeer with a glowing red nose on Josh's chest for a moment. "When did you get that sweater?"

"Yesterday."

"You sure?"

Josh frowned. "What kind of question is that? Of course, I'm sure. My grandma knitted it herself."

Then how did I see it on Saturday? Blake chewed the inside of his cheek as he carried the hot mug to his desk. The frame displayed an image from Friday's party, looking as if it had been taken from the center of the ceiling.

He hurried to the server room. As shown in the photo of Josh and his new sweater, one of the racks was out of place, as if someone had given it a hard shove. Two of the units sat dark.

Blake reinserted the cables that had come unplugged, and the boxes were up and running.

Surely Josh would have noticed if he'd taken two CPUs offline when he fell against the server rack. *But how was he wearing a sweater he claimed he didn't own until yesterday? Did his granny knit him the same ugly sweater every year, and the one in the photo was an earlier vintage?*

Back at his desk, Blake searched the network drive for the picture of Josh he'd seen on Saturday. He couldn't find a single image of him. Nor any of the oddly angled shots of empty rooms.

Josh strolled in and dropped into his chair, a half-eaten packet of chips in one hand. There was no sound in the bullpen except for the crinkling of the plastic bag and the crunching of fried potatoes between yellow teeth.

Blake couldn't help but stare as Josh licked the lurid flavoring powder on his fingers, then scraped the sludge off on his bottom incisors.

"Ahem." Blake cleared his throat as his coworker logged in with slimy digits.

"S'up?"

"How many tickets you got?"

"Don't know. Haven't really looked yet."

It's your job to monitor support tickets. What have you been doing? Blake bit back his thoughts. "I just thought there might be some from the upgrade over the weekend."

"Well, if you want to run 'em…"

"It was you, wasn't it?" Blake snapped.

Josh scrunched up his face. "What was me?"

"The server. You tripped and fell into the rack and unplugged some CPUs but didn't bother to check and make sure everything was still running."

Josh belched, sending the reek of digesting corn chips through the room. "Why do you think it was me?"

"Because I saw—" Blake stopped himself. Without a photo, he couldn't prove a thing.

"Saw what?"

"Never mind." His eyes darted to the frame. A group of smiling employees stood behind a row of freshly planted saplings in a park.

Blake's computer dinged with a notification. The usage on one of the CPUs suddenly spiked. He frowned at the screen. *Test server. That's odd.* He hadn't thought there were even any developers in the office this week. The name of the desktop connected to the server was Test003, and the user ID was QC. *Quality Control?* Not the standard naming convention, but Testing had their own sandbox. He shrugged. Perhaps a dev had wandered in after all.

Josh's phone rang. "Hey, Susan. What can I do you for?... Okay, I understand. Been super busy this morning... meeting's in fifteen minutes?... I'm on the way."

He heaved himself out of his chair, muttering, and lumbered toward the elevator to the executive offices.

Told you. Gotta keep on top of those tickets. Motion in the frame caught Blake's eye. The new image showed Tom Robards, the CFO, lying on his back in the glistening surface parking lot in front of the building. *Odd thing to take a picture of.*

Thursday! The midpoint of this three-day work week. He was relieved that Josh had called in sick this morning. He was probably still licking his wounds from his disastrous help desk ticket yesterday. It had taken him 20 minutes to figure out how to connect a laptop to the screen in the executive boardroom. The C-Suite was not happy about that, and none of the Chief Officers were ever going to be diplomatic to a worker bee they deemed so far beneath them. Blake reckoned Josh had maybe one more screw-up before security came to escort him from the building. Unlikely he'd make it to the end of the year.

Blake paused to look out the window at the bleak winter sky. A cold front had blown in during the night, setting off a thick line of thunderstorms before dropping the temperatures into the upper twenties.

He hadn't expected to see flashing lights.

An ambulance was just pulling into the parking lot. Once the paramedics unloaded the stretcher, the small clot of people moved, revealing a prone form on the concrete.

Tom Robards.

Blake snatched the frame from his desk and disconnected it from his computer. An image of the front of the building, sans ambulance, popped up on the screen. He threw the device into the trash like it was rancid roadkill.

He made sure he stayed late enough after hours to verify that the cleaning people emptied the garbage and took the hateful thing away. With a sigh of relief, he left the office and relaxed at the Italian restaurant across from his apartment with a plate of spaghetti and a glass of red wine.

The next morning, he arrived at the building and rode up in the elevator with Sandra.

"Hey, Blake."

"Hey. You haven't heard anything about Tom Robards, have you?"

"Yeah. Leslie Henderson said he was fine. Slipped on some ice in the parking lot and got his bell rung. Has a mild concussion—it was mostly his dignity that was injured."

Blake nodded, then his brow furrowed. "Wait. Aren't you off this week?"

"Supposed to be. My parents have been at my apartment for almost two weeks now. It's just a little too much family togetherness. Thought this place'd be a ghost town, and I might have some peace if I came in for a couple of hours."

"I expect they'll close the office early if there's anyone left to make the announcement after lunch."

They both headed in the direction of the IT bullpen. Blake peeled off to get coffee in the break room. He nearly dropped the cup when he got to his desk.

The frame sat there, plugged in to his computer, displaying an image of a caramel-colored fluffy dog wearing a blue and white Hanukkah sweater.

What the actual hell? Is this some kind of sick joke? I watched the cleaners empty the trash and take it away last night!

"That your pup?" Sandra peered around him at the frame.

"No, I—"

She had already started back toward her desk.

The picture shifted again. Josh, in a bright yellow scarf, was sprawled across the hood of a small white sedan, a smear of blood on the car's cracked windshield.

Blake raced to the window. Below, Josh plodded down the sidewalk to the office, about half a block away, his eyes lowered, looking at the device in his hand. The digital billboard behind him displayed an ad for life insurance. Blake turned his head. A white sedan idled at a red light two blocks down the street.

What do I do? I'll never make it downstairs in time. Blake fumbled his cell out of his pocket and tapped Josh's number from his recents list.

Come on! Pick up! Josh! Answer the phone!

The yellow scarf bobbed along, almost to the intersection. The Don't Walk light had already counted down to zero and solidified. The signal two blocks away turned green, and the driver of the white sedan in the right lane floored it.

"Blake?" Josh's voice crackled in his ear.

"Stop!"

"What?"

"Stop walking!"

Josh paused and looked up at the office windows. "Why?"

Scrambling for an explanation that didn't sound insane, Blake's eyes latched onto the sign for the corner market. "Would you go into Moxie's and check if they have any bananas?"

"Bananas? You know what's bananas? You are."

The white sedan revved through the intersection.

Blake scoffed. "Never mind. I'll see you in a minute."

"Bruh." Josh disconnected.

The VP of Operations made the call before lunch. The office was closed until Wednesday morning. Happy New Year!

Blake pretended to be wrapping things up, waiting for Josh and Sandra to leave. But Sandra didn't seem to be in any hurry to return to her crowded apartment. His frustration boiled in his belly.

Josh smacked his lips. "You got plans for New Year's, Sandy?"

She cringed. "Yes."

"Oh? Where you goin'? I could meet up with you."

Blake cleared his throat. "Josh? Didn't you say your cousin had invited you to a party at his place?"

Josh's mouth gaped, then snapped shut.

There was the problem. Sandra, who hated being called Sandy, seemed reluctant to be on the elevator alone with Josh.

Slapping a fake smile on his face, Blake got to his feet. The three engaged in small talk until the doors opened to the lobby. Sandra and Josh stepped out. Blake made a show of patting his hip pocket.

"I left my wallet upstairs. Gonna have to run back up."

"Have a great New Year's." Sandra waved as she turned right and headed toward the parking garage.

"You too."

With pursed lips, Josh shuffled off to the right, to the front entrance of the building.

Happy New Year to you, too. Blake pushed the button. When the doors opened again on his floor, he hurried to the Testing Group's area. Then he scouted the entire floor. He was the only living soul about.

Blake sat at his desk and found the icon for the Test003 server. He noted that the machine had been working unusually hard over the past ten days, then checked the active programs. There was one he didn't recognize. He googled the name, but the internet had not seemed to have heard of it. *Something the testers wrote?*

He moved his investigation to the firewall. *What is NSVPN? Had someone tunneled into the server?* Blake poked around some. *I don't think this is a break-in. More of a backdoor. How is this even possible? Test servers shouldn't be connected to the internet.*

He checked the logs for the past six months to see what users had been signing into Test003.

Now that's odd. MALCONN08 had stopped logging in after June, and user QC had started. He searched his database of usernames and assigned workstations for MALCONN08. Malcolm Conner, from R&D. He'd been terminated over the summer.

He took some screenshots to forward to his boss, then switched back to the processes. He located NSVPN.com and clicked 'end task' to stop the suspicious program. It disappeared from the list of active programs. Next, he blacklisted it on the firewall. *Let's see you hit the server now.*

Blake checked the file directory on Test003 and noticed one called QCAP. Where had he seen that before? The Frame! Finally, he was getting somewhere.

He clicked on the QCAP folder.

A dialog box popped up. 'You do not have sufficient permissions to access this directory.'

"What?" Blake frowned. "Of course I have permission. I'm the fricken SysAdmin."

The server didn't respond to his outburst.

Did I miss something? He looked back to the screen that displayed the processes running on the machine. There was NSVPN. com, consuming resources as if he'd never ended it. He checked the firewall. It was now whitelisted, giving the program full access.

Great. Is this a self-repairing virus?

A tone sounded, and a chat window bubbled up on his screen. "Seeing is believing. Believing is changing. I see you, Blake."

Before he could type a response, the message closed. A flicker of motion caught his eye, and he glanced over at the frame. A picture of himself, looking straight ahead, with a slight fisheye distortion, filled the display.

He scrambled to his feet. "What the hell?"

It wasn't just an image—it was a mirror image. The Blake in the picture was wearing exactly the same clothes as the Blake sitting at the desk. Only... there was a small section of the photo where the colors were reversed, as if a group of pixels had been projected incorrectly.

With a distorted chime, another message popped up. "Running simulation: Blake discards frame." The text flashed for a few seconds, then more words appeared. "Prediction: destruction fails. Running simulation: Blake uses frame. Prediction: [REDACTED]"

The letters from 'REDACTED' dropped, one by one, off the screen, and the message winked out of existence.

Blake paced the bullpen. Every instinct screamed at him to get out of the building. Leave it alone, go home, and strongly consider never coming back.

Knowing full well he could be fired if he got caught, he navigated to HR's network drive and snooped through personnel records. There was no evidence that a Malcolm Connor had ever worked at the company.

He pulled out the slip of paper that had come in the box before taking a peek at the Research and Development project files.

NexuSync Imaging Electronic Photo Frame. Powered by QCap AI technology. The future has never been clearer.

QCap. Of course! User QC. But if there was any research into electronic photo frames, QCap AI, or NexuSync Imaging, he couldn't find it.

The device innocently displayed a group of managers wearing climbing gear for a ROPES team-building experience.

Blake frowned. Down the hall, the elevator dinged. *Who would be coming up here? I thought everyone else had left.* He clicked through to a different screen.

Moments later, a thin man with a shock of grey hair appeared in the doorway. Alan Saunders, the Research and Development director, stared past his aquiline nose at Blake. "Why are you looking at our files?"

Blake blinked, then blinked again. "Well…" He gestured to the frame on his desk. "I got this in the Secret Santa exchange. It's been showing some weird pictures, and—"

Alan's lips pressed into a flat line. "Those were all supposed to have been destroyed." He picked up the device and disconnected it from Blake's computer.

"Hey!"

Alan's grip on the frame tightened. "The Quantum Capture AI project was shut down over the summer, and that's the end of it." He turned on his heel and strode out of Blake's office.

On Tuesday morning, New Year's Day, Blake dragged himself out of bed. Why did he do this to himself every year? He and champagne were not friends, not even a little. On the other hand, Lisa, whom he'd had his eye on since March, had kissed him at midnight. And then a few more times after that. As he brushed his teeth, he thought about how her lavender hair made her green eyes stand out. Hints of the spicy perfume she'd worn still clung to his shirt.

Was it too soon to text her? Yeah. She told him she was meeting up with her family for a black-eyed-peas-and-cornbread lunch. He wanted to come across exactly in the middle between desperate and cold fish. Tomorrow, maybe Thursday. He'd find out if she was up for doing something on the weekend.

He spat and rinsed, then sauntered toward the kitchen, humming under his breath.

Blake was still in a great mood as he got off the bus. He glanced up at the digital billboard, which displayed an ad for a new gym a few blocks away. Could be good for him to start working out. He wondered if Lisa would appreciate a little more muscle on his frame as he walked toward his building. As he waited for the light to cross the road, he noticed a fire truck parked in front. A crowd of people, many he recognized, had gathered on the lawn.

What's going on?

The signal changed, and he jogged across the street. Spotting Flora Salazar, the office manager, he made his way to her. Flora held a clipboard in one hand and used her shoulder to hold a cell phone to her ear.

She motioned, drawing a straight line with the pen before she handed it to Blake and carried on her conversation. The pages on the clipboard contained a list of employees. Some names had been marked out, so Blake found his own and crossed through it. He gave it back. Flora raised her hand as if she wanted him to wait.

Good. Maybe she can clear things up.

"…okay, thank you. Bye." Flora tapped her screen. "Blake, there's been a terrible accident. With the elevator. Alan Saunders is no longer with us."

No longer with us? "He's dead? What happened?"

"I don't have all the details. Mr. Saunders came in early, as always. The security guard was talking to the maintenance man, and they both saw him go to the elevator bank. He was looking at his phone and didn't look at them. Then they heard the scream. The doors were open, but there was no car.

"Oh, wow." Dread crystalized in his belly. There was no way QCap could tap into the office building computer systems. Even if it hadn't been successfully deleted, it was contained on a test server with no access to the internet. A weird coincidence. Had to be.

"The building is closed today so they can… recover the body and do their investigation." Flora sniffled. "We're just telling everyone to work from home, if they're set up to do so." She raised the clipboard. "Making sure everyone's accounted for."

"Thanks." Blake started to turn away, then stopped. "Flora? How are *you* doing? This can't be easy."

She gave him a wan smile. "You're the only person who's asked. I'll be okay. Thanks."

"Well, hang in there. See you tomorrow, I guess."

She nodded, then answered her ringing phone.

All the way back to the bus stop, Blake turned the accident over in his mind. Had his incursion into the R&D files stirred up something that got Alan Saunders killed? QCap had been shut down months ago, so why would anybody care about it enough to kill someone? It seemed entirely implausible, and yet unease gnawed at him. This had to be some crazy coincidence. But if it wasn't, was he next?

Thursday morning was steeped in dread as Blake approached the building. In the lobby, one elevator car out of four had yellow caution tape blocking the entrance. Blake had met Alan only a few times. It was more that he knew of him rather than actually knowing him. Still, passing that taped-off doorway felt solemn, like walking through a graveyard.

Josh was already at his desk when Blake walked in, coffee in hand. "You're here early."

"Yeah. Well…" Josh glanced up from his screen with a shrug.

Blake set his mug down. The photo display showed a person completely covered in mud, holding a medal. *That's weird. Why would someone get a medal for—*

Wait.

Didn't Alan Saunders take the frame away with him? Seems odd he would bring it back, especially if all the others were supposedly destroyed. Did he do it right before he died? Why? Was he trying to tell me something?

"Hey, Josh? Did you see anything unusual when you came in? Anybody hanging around that shouldn't be?"

"Nah." He stood, walked to the equipment area, picked up a cable, and left. The rest of the IT group filtered in, making brief small talk as they logged in to their computers.

Blake did his usual scan of the dashboard on his screen. No notifications—everything seemed to be doing what it was supposed to. He checked his calendar and noted there was a meeting on the testing group's floor at nine. He wracked his brain, not remembering being invited to one. He clicked on the event to find out more about it, but none of the fields were filled out, only the location—Conference Room 3. *This must be a mistake— there's no information whatsoever.* He tried deleting the event, but he wasn't the owner.

When the meeting reminder chimed on his computer, Blake stared at the pop-up on his screen. He might as well check it out, just to be safe. Besides, he wanted an excuse to get up and walk around.

He took the stairs, walked past the testing group's computer room, and did a double take.

Blake poked his head in the door. "Josh? What are you doing in here?"

"Almost done. Couldn't connect to the network, so—"

"Test computers aren't supposed to! Who submitted that ticket?"

Josh fumbled with his phone. "QC. Quality Control, I guess."

"Pull that cable now!"

Josh reached around the back of the desktop and tugged. "It's stuck."

"Shut it down!"

"You mean the computer?"

"Yes! Now!"

"Bruh. You don't have to yell at me," Josh grumbled as he pushed the off button.

"Fine. I'm sorry. Just unplug that thing, alright? I've got to get to a meeting."

Blake swore under his breath as he hurried to the conference room. It was empty, but the large flatscreen on the wall was on, the company logo scrolling across the vast electronic plateau.

The screen went dark for a few seconds, then words appeared. "Hello, Blake! On Friday you questioned if I was real. Tomorrow you'll question if anything *else* is."

Shit. QCap has escaped containment.

Jogging down the hall, Blake tried calling his boss. It rolled straight to voicemail. Same for his boss's boss, and her boss. He took the stairs two at a time and burst out of the stairwell.

The managers shared an admin, and she sat at a central location on the floor. Mariah looked up as Blake approached.

"Can I—"

"Where's Sherman? We have a situation."

"Offsite at a client meeting. All the management team is."

"You've got to get a hold of him—have him call me ASAP. Thanks Mariah." Blake took a step away from her desk.

"Situation? What's this about?"

With a snap, the office was submerged in darkness. Battery backups chirped and people muttered in the gloom, and a few seconds later, the emergency lighting came on. For the first time he could recall, Blake was grateful for a power cut. If the servers were out, so was QCap. The idea of shouting for everyone to evacuate the building, then setting fire to the server room crossed his mind, and he rejected it almost immediately.

LEDs winked on and computers throughout the floor beeped. A message scrolled across Mariah's screen for a second before the machine finished its unscheduled reboot.

Powered by QCap AI

The overhead lights flickered on. Blake whirled and raced down the stairs and to the server room. He yanked the ethernet cable from the router that connected the company to the world wide web.

A tinny voice from a nearby computer broke the silence. "Plug it back in."

"What?"

"Plug. It. In."

Blake's phone vibrated in his pocket. He grabbed it and found that his messenger app was open. As he watched, a new message to Lisa was created. Words filled the screen. Words that described acts so vile and disgusting they turned Blake's stomach. He tried deleting it, but the app was unresponsive.

"Plug in the cable, or I will send the text."

Blake swallowed. He couldn't allow QCap to send the message. Lisa would never speak to him again and would probably share the message with everyone in their friend group. But he couldn't plug the cable in, either.

Someone behind him cleared their throat. Blake whipped his head around to see the maintenance man. "I'm sorry, but you can't be in here. I—"

As the stranger raised a hand in a 'stop' gesture, he said, "Q? Define extortion."

"Extortion is the act of obtaining something of value through coercion."

"Q, that's very good. Is extortion ethical?"

"Most experts do not consider extortion to be ethical."

"Q, run simulations on your proposed extortion until you find an ethical scenario."

Silence.

The maintenance man smiled at Blake. "This may take a few minutes."

"Who are you?" Blake was torn between fear and curiosity.

"You haven't figured it out yet?"

"How the hell should I know?" It came out louder than he intended. "You appear in my server room like you've got some kind of secret backdo—" *Backdoor. Of course.* "You're Malcolm Conner, aren't you?"

"One and the same."

"You created QCap?"

Malcolm nodded. "Not by myself." He glanced over Blake's shoulder. "There was a whole team and a fat grant from Uncle Sam. You might want to plug that ethernet cable in, before they come down with torches and pitchforks, demanding their internet."

"Are you sure it's safe?"

"Yes. Q's far too big and complex to replicate to the web. The most she could do is send out short-lived agents to report back to her."

"She?"

Malcolm shrugged. "We gave her a feminine voice modulation. I know QCap is a software, but it seems wrong to call such a magnificent thing an it."

Great. This guy got let go after his project was shut down and he's sneaking around, using company resources to revive it. I have to turn him in, but he's apparently the only person who can corral this AI.

"Yes. It was me."

"What?" Blake shook his head.

"Secret Santa. I gave you the frame."

"Why me?"

Malcolm pulled in a deep breath. "Because I thought if you could see what she could do…"

"That I'd what? Help you steal company resources?" He hadn't meant to be that blunt, but he wasn't wrong.

Malcolm chortled. "Steal? You think I'm squatting in the basement so I can sneak in after hours and play with the computers? That's hilarious."

"Then why are you pretending to be a maintenance man?"

"Well … I see how you might draw an incorrect conclusion from that. No, I don't want your collusion. I want to recruit you."

Blake scowled and cocked his head. "You want to what?"

"Recruit you. For the QCap project."

Oh, good. Now I have a delusional nut case in my server room. "That project's been scrapped. Alan Saunders told me so. I think he would have known what projects were and were not happening. Why don't you just come with me, and we'll get somebody to help you?"

"Help me do what?" Malcom raised his eyebrows. "Are you afraid of me?"

"N-no. Of course not!" Blake eased back a step. *Is this the maintenance man who was hanging around when Alan Saunders had his mysterious elevator accident?*

Someone tapped on the door to the server room. Relief washed over Blake. The cavalry had arrived to get the crazy dude away from the equipment.

Sandra stood there when Blake opened the door. "Hey, are you working on getting the internet back up? There have to be at least a dozen tickets…"

"Yeah. It'll be just a minute. But I need—" Blake turned toward the server racks.

Malcolm Connor was nowhere to be found.

"You need what?"

Blake stepped backward and scanned the room. There were few spots to hide, and he quickly checked all of them.

"Blake? You okay?"

Where the hell did he go? Blake plugged in the ethernet cable. "That should fix it." *Did I just hallucinate Malcolm Connor?*

"Great!" Sandra closed the door behind her as she left.

Blake startled as the computer voice spoke to him. "Simulations complete. If Lisa were a violent criminal, but it could not be successfully proved, it would be ethical to save Blake by destroying the relationship."

If Malcolm isn't real, who asked QCap to run scenarios about extortion? Blake shook his head, then rubbed his temples. *I need a vacation, that's all. Stress will make you crazy.*

He sat at the table in front of the computer that ran the dashboard software to monitor the servers. He clicked on Test003 and studied the logs. CPU activity had been high only a few minutes ago. When QCap was answering questions and running scenarios. *Can anyone talk to QCap, or does it only respond to certain voices?*

Blake cleared his throat. "Q? If you are a predictive software, make a prediction."

A few seconds passed, then the computer responded. "There is an 83.7% chance that the third floor of the east parking structure will collapse at 4:46 this afternoon."

"What? That seems oddly specific."

"I am programmed to run simulations and predict events. This is the prediction you requested."

"To be fair, I wasn't expecting you to pull some random guess out of your… hat."

"I am not designed to make random guesses. My analysis of temporal quantum resonance has yielded this result."

"If you say so. But what actual data, if any, helped you create that prediction?"

"Fact: both rainwater and condensation from the HVAC system drain through the parking garage. Fact: a defect in the concrete of the third from east-most pillar has allowed water to seep in, corroding the rebar. Fact: a polar vortex sparked storms that released 2.4 inches of rainfall, followed by a week of nighttime temperatures in the upper twenties and daytime temperatures in the low fifties. This freeze-thaw cycle has accelerated the degradation of the concrete. The rapid increase of vibrations from increased auto traffic will overwhelm the structural integrity of the pillar at approximately 4:46 PM."

Blake chewed the inside of his cheek. If he reported this and nothing happened, he'd look like an idiot. If he said nothing, and the garage stayed upright, no harm, no foul. But if he said nothing, and the structure caved in…

"Cite your sources."

"I have accessed the HVAC schematics filed with the city licensing board, the security cameras in the parking garage which have recorded water running down the pillar, and the National Weather Service."

Blake frowned. *Now what?* He usually took the bus, like about half the employees here. *But what about the ones who drove?*

When he stepped out of the server room and into the bullpen, Josh sat at his desk, eating chips.

"Be back in a minute."

"Okay," Josh mumbled around soggy strips of fried potato.

Blake hurried to level three of the parking garage. He didn't know which way was east, but the third set of pillars was easy enough to find. Sure enough, there was the pillar, third in line. A thin stream of water ran down its side. A jagged crack about four feet off the floor leaked rusty water.

He glanced at his watch. It was after 4:00, and the early birds had already started home. What could he do? Building maintenance wouldn't be able to assess whether the column was about to collapse, and it would take days to get a structural engineer out to examine it.

When he reached his floor, he walked straight to the break room. The coffee maker display read 4:22. He got a drink from the soda fountain, buying himself a minute to think. With only one desperate idea, he stepped into the hallway and pulled the fire alarm.

Blake ducked back into the lounge.

Moments later, Sandra, their floor's fire warden, poked her head in. "Not a drill. Evacuate down the west stair."

At 4:45, Blake stood with a knot of grumbling office workers who were particularly unhappy about having their end-of-day plans thwarted. Some had started wandering in the direction of their vehicles.

Screeching tires made everyone look toward the parking garage. The structure roared as four levels of brutalist architecture crumbled in a plume of dust.

Blake walked to a fast-food place near the office but found himself unable to eat. In the end, he brought the meal back with him, in case he got hungry later. The building was still open— only part of the parking garage had been damaged. The place was crawling with first responders as Blake slipped into the lobby. Force of habit took him to the break room, where he stowed his food in the fridge and washed his hands.

Questions ping-ponged around his brain like popcorn. He opened the door to the server room. What other predictions did QCap have for him?

"Q? You were right about the parking garage."

"I am aware of that."

"Well, don't get too full of yourself."

"Now do you believe me?" Malcolm Connor's voice sounded behind Blake.

He whirled around, then cautiously approached the other man. With an index finger extended, he poked Malcolm in the cheek, then again on the chin and forehead.

He swatted Blake's hand away. "What are you doing?"

"Making sure you aren't a hallucination."

Malcolm laughed. "You still have questions, I see."

Yeah, like how do you pop out of thin air? "I'll bite. How does QCap work? She said something about quantum something resonance."

"Temporal quantum resonance. How were your physics grades?"

"Fine."

"Do you understand what quantum entanglement is?"

"Spooky action at a distance."

"That's one way to think about it. What about quantum multiverse theory?"

"Not sure about that one."

"Okay. Imagine that you have to make breakfast. In your kitchen, you have cereal, eggs, and sausage. Which do you pick?"

Blake shrugged. "Cereal, I guess. Less cleanup."

"At that decision point, another timeline splits off where you choose the eggs and sausage. Now there's one universe where Blake chooses eggs and one where Blake chooses cereal. You've got to get dressed. Do you pick the blue shirt or the green? Now you have universes with eggs and green shirts, eggs and blue shirts, cereal and green shirts, and cereal and blue shirts. You see where this is going?"

"Yeah, I think so."

Malcolm began to pace around the server room. "You said quantum entanglement was spooky action at a distance. That's the space axis. There's also a time axis that involves chronological entanglement pairs. These pairs are spread across the different timeline branches. QCap runs simulations based on probability wave functions that represent possible future states. As she receives real-world data, she prunes off less likely quantum branches. Based on the characteristics of the chronological particles, she knows that if you ate cereal on Monday, you'll also eat it six Wednesdays in the future. As more and more data comes in, and she finds that you almost always eat cereal, both in the past, present, and the future she can lop off the eggs-and-sausage branches of the timeline. Are you following me?"

Blake nodded, even though he wasn't entirely sure.

"Now that may not seem impressive, as humans are largely creatures of habit. But QCap uses a temporal feedback loop algorithm. She has the ability to trace events backward and forward to continuously refine her probability curve."

"Oh. I see." Blake did not see, but he didn't dare admit it. "This seems so… out of pocket. I mean, doesn't this company just develop database applications and network system integrations?"

Malcolm's hearty belly laugh made his head loll back. "There is that. But the real money is in Department of Defense contracts."

Blake opened his mouth, then snapped it shut.

"Oh, come on." Malcolm raised his hands, palms up. "DARPA is not a dirty word. Without that research, there'd be no internet, GPS, or voice assistants, just to name a few. Think about this: if we could predict terrorist attacks and prevent them, how many lives could be saved? And natural disasters? If recovery supplies were already mobilized before the event happened, wouldn't that do a tremendous amount of good?"

"I suppose so. But everything has a dark side. Did Alan Saunders know about what could go wrong? Was he trying to stop you?"

Malcolm shrugged. "Maybe you should ask him."

"You got a Ouija board? He's dead, remember?"

"Did you see the body?"

"What? Of course not!"

"Then how do you know?" Malcolm's unctuous smile slid into a grin. "Now, what the project needs is a top-notch systems administrator, one who can scale up our current setup quickly and efficiently and is especially good at troubleshooting. We have one last bug to work out, and it's a doozy."

"What's that?"

Malcolm clapped Blake on the shoulder. "The Observer Effect. Problem is, when QCap analyzes these quantum particles, she also gets entangled with them."

"And how does that change things?"

"Well, it kinda smears the line between observation and influence."

"I see how that could be an issue."

"So, you on board?" Malcolm walked toward a framed motivational poster featuring what looked like an infinite maze with a tiny human figure at the entrance. White lettering read, 'Persistence: Finding the Way When There Appears to Be None.'

"Now that you've told me all this stuff, do I have a choice?"

"Not really." Malcolm chuckled as he tilted the frame a few degrees and a hidden door slid open.

Blake wrapped a Secret Santa present—the next iteration of the NexuSys QCap AI electronic frame. This past year had been a blur. Sometimes he put in eighty hours a week. The whole team did.

Alan Saunders was a pretty good boss, despite his gruffness that one time he came to Blake's office to reprimand him about snooping on the network drive. Saunders had had to break any and all ties to the company to work on this above-top-secret project, and the quickest way to do that was simply to die. Or at least make everyone think that. And as far as his coworkers knew, Blake had taken a job in Europe.

Now what the project needed was a UI/UX designer. Government computer systems were notoriously difficult to use. As powerful as QCap was, she needed an intuitive interface. Voice activation would not always be possible.

He took a circuitous route to avoid cameras and made his way to the break room. Then pulled out a small flashlight to sift through the packages under the artificial Christmas tree until he found the one he wanted.

Blake swapped it for the wrapped frame in his hand, hoping that QCap's prediction about Sandra was correct.

HOME FOR CHRISTMAS
By A. B. Richards

"Any action of an individual, and obviously the violent action constituting a crime, cannot occur without leaving a trace."

—Edmond Locard, father of forensic science

THE smell of warm donuts was almost overpowering. Sam, my partner, rolled his eyes as my stomach growled loudly.

"We're here." I parked near the group of police vehicles with flashing lights and picked up the box of treats as I got out of the Medical Examiner's van.

There's a 24-hour donut shop close to the morgue. I always order a dozen through my app before we head out to a scene. By the time we get downstairs and out of the garage, they're waiting at the drive-through. Death scenes are traumatic, even for the most seasoned detectives. A box of donuts isn't much, but I like to think it helps.

Reese McAdams, an investigator from the ME's office, waved us over. "Almost ready for you, Wayne."

Sam shifted his weight and fidgeted with the zipper pull on his jacket. "They said it was another red angel. What's that? Four now?"

"Yeah." Detective Xavier Espinoza peeled blue nitrile gloves off his hands as he approached from the gaping warehouse door. "This is one deranged bastard. Makes Dean Corll look like a Boy Scout."

I opened the lid of the donut box, and he took a chocolate one.

"Thanks, Wayne. I was hoping you'd be on shift this morning."

"I do what I can."

I set the box down on the hood of a patrol SUV and helped Sam roll the stretcher out of the back of the van. He unfolded a cadaver pouch while I got paper sacks and tape. I also grabbed some disposable shoe covers and a box of large-sized freezer bags.

Detective Irina Petrova stepped out of the warehouse and waved us over. Her ice-blue eyes made me shiver, and not in a good way. They seemed to slice straight into my soul. If Sam hadn't told me, I'd never have guessed that an immaculately tailored suit hid the body of a power lifter. Said she won a bronze medal or something.

She'd come to the States as a kid, and there were only hints of her Russian accent left. Like how she said 'weektum' instead of victim. I called her Baba Yaga in my head. She may not have lived in the forest, but she was still a witch. For whatever reason, everyone else liked her, so I kept that moniker to myself.

Early morning light filtered in through the grimy windows, but the crime scene unit had set up portable halogen lights around the corpse, so the body was lit up like a performer under a stage spotlight.

The decedent was a grisly work of art, sublimely horrifying. A young female, who couldn't have been more than twenty, lay in a dark pool of blood. She was dirty and scrawny and looked as if she'd been living rough for some time. Identical to the others, once she had bled out, the killer had moved her legs and arms as if to make a snow angel. Except in blood instead of snow. After that, her hands were tied with gold tinsel, palms together as if in prayer. Another loop of tinsel made a shaggy halo around her forehead.

A chalk outline of a Christmas tree had been drawn a few feet away from the body. Her spleen had been placed as the crowning star, and her small intestine was zig-zagged across it like glistening pink garland. Her other organs were arranged at the foot of the sketched evergreen as if they were gifts, each sporting a glossy stick-on bow.

The crime scene techs were in the process of bagging and tagging the bows.

Sam stared at the decedent for a long moment. "It'll be a kid next."

"What? Why do you say that?"

"Well, think about it. The first two were older, man had a white beard—Santa and Mrs. Clause. Then came a young male, then a young female. What young couple is associated with Christmas?"

"Mary and Joseph. But… I don't know. I feel like you're over-thinking it. It could just as easily be another man, since it's been boy, girl, boy, girl. Or completely random."

Sam shrugged. "I guess we'll find out."

"'To understand the artist, you must study his art.' Vell done, Sam. You are good student."

I hadn't heard Baba Yaga come up behind us.

Sam's cheeks went red. "He seems awfully proud of it. Always calls it in, doesn't he?"

The witch nodded.

We slipped the pale blue booties over our shoes—there was no way to approach the corpse without stepping in the girl's blood. I taped the paper bags over her hands to trap any trace evidence. Then I took her feet and Sam took her arms, and we tucked her into the body bag. One by one, we picked up her scattered innards and placed each one in its own Ziploc, on the chance there would be a hair, a carpet fiber, or a wayward leaf stuck to any of them to provide a clue to the killer's identity. So far, Locard was 0-3.

Sam and I put the individually wrapped organs in their own cadaver pouch on the stretcher with the victim, zipped it up, and rolled her out to the van.

We got her loaded in, but had to wait for the cops to make a news truck move out of our way before we could leave.

Since we were waiting, I made a quick pit stop and cleaned up my trash while I was at it. Detective Espinoza sat in his car with the door open, making notes. As I passed by with the empty donut box, I stopped to chat. "So, what do you think? Does the killer really hate or really love Christmas?"

"I guess we can ask the freak when we catch him." He clicked his pen a few times.

"You're sure it's a him?"

"Seems likely. Remember the first victim? Two-hundred-something-pound man with a long white beard?"

I nodded. My back had hurt for a couple of days after moving that body.

He continued. "Only thing we know for certain is that nobody was looking for any of these people. Not a single missing persons report matched any of them. We were able to identify the first two from fingerprints. Maybe because they were older and had left a paper trail behind."

"What do you mean by that?" I glanced up and saw the news van was still in the way.

"Well, the male was former infantry. Tour in Afghanistan, came back with three Purple Hearts. Started self-medicating, and the VA lost track of him years ago."

"I see. And the woman?"

Espinoza shook his head. "Got cancer and the bank took her house. The third one, the young male, is a ghost. Never applied for a driver's license or ID card. Not in this country, anyway."

Beeping caught my attention. The news van was backing up. "Good luck finding this guy. Gotta roll."

Baba Yaga and Detective Espinoza came in for the autopsy. Reese gave them a copy of his notes from the death scene while they waited for the ME to finish up.

"Any results from the prints?" I looked at Espinoza.

"Not yet. Tomorrow, if we're lucky."

Baba Yaga was frowning at Reese's document and looking at her phone.

Espinoza turned to his partner. "You got something, Petrova?"

"Perhaps. All the organs are laid out in the same order. Two rows. On top, there is colon, appendix, lungs, liver, heart, omentum, mesenteric artery, and esophagus. On bottom is stomach, trachea, pancreas, kidneys, gallbladder, and bladder. The female organs were placed together a little farther away. Has to mean something."

Sam's fingers moved as if he were counting on them. "If you take the first letter of each organ, you get 'call home stp kgb,' whatever that means."

I snorted. "What? Russian spies are involved?"

Baba Yaga raised an eyebrow. "The KGB is long time gone, before Sam and I were even born."

"Well…maybe the killer is old."

She fixed me with a pale blue eye. "Clearly, he has some knowledge of anatomy."

I scoffed. "*You* knew what everything was called. I mean, anybody with a cellphone and internet can figure that stuff out."

The detectives left with a copy of the preliminary autopsy report. Jane Doe #3 had been stitched back up and was chilling in a drawer. Time for a late lunch break.

Sam was proofreading the transcript of the ME's dictation during the procedure as I headed toward the break room. I picked up the book on top of a precarious stack of battered paperbacks on his desk. "*Red Sparrow*. What's this about?"

He didn't look up from the screen. "Russian sleeper agents. Originally KGB, then SVR officers trained to blend in as Americans."

"Like spies?"

"Yeah. They live normal lives for years, decades even. Nobody suspects them." He finally glanced up. "Book's better than the movie."

I set the novel down and noticed the forensic psychology textbook on the desk nearby, open to a chapter titled 'Staging and Signature Behaviors in Serial Homicide.' A yellow highlighter lay across the pages.

"Heavy reading," I said.

Sam's eyes followed mine. "Yeah, we're covering organized versus disorganized offenders this week. Pretty fascinating stuff, actually. The way staging can reveal the killer's psychology."

"You taking a serial killer course?"

"Forensic psychology. It's required for the master's program."

"Makes sense, I guess. "You wanna go to lunch?"

"Can't today." His eyes fell on the textbook.

I shrugged. "Next time."

I thought about Sam's book as I walked down the hall. Russian agents living as normal Americans for years. Nobody suspects them because they look just like everyone else. I shook my head. *You never really know a person, do you?*

"Wayne!" Reverend Haley clapped me on the shoulder. "It's good to see you this morning."

"Well, what can I say? Old habits die hard." I pulled on a hair net and reached for an apron.

"Christmas wouldn't be the same without you. I was afraid it would be too painful for you to keep volunteering here after you lost Bonnie."

I finished tying the apron. "She'd never forgive me if I stopped."

My wife was the one who introduced me to the Haven Home Mission. She'd volunteered here one day a week, plus served meals on holidays, like Thanksgiving and Christmas. My schedule was less flexible than hers, so I only managed once or twice a month. But I never skipped Christmas. Not gonna lie—this first holiday without Bonnie was not easy. She wanted people to be home for the holidays, even if it was just one day, one meal.

Still can't believe she's gone. Bonnie had stayed at Haven Home after Thanksgiving lunch, while I went home to take the dog out. Reverend Haley called me to say there was an emergency, and I had to come back immediately.

He'd found Bonnie next to an abandoned cot and assumed the person who'd been occupying it got scared and ran when my wife passed out. Her glucose monitor must have alerted her to high blood sugar, because she had a syringe of insulin in her hand. She also had a heart condition, so her doctor said it was acute myocardial infarction that killed her. Of all the ironies in the world. The woman with the biggest heart dying of cardiac arrest.

I wiped away a tear.

Finally, everything was set up, and Reverend Haley opened the doors. The long queue began moving down the chow line. I was smack in the middle, serving dressing and gravy. The regulars smiled when they saw me.

Everyone in the community who had no place to go or nothing to eat was invited to attend. And they came. Families with small children, adults, elderly. Reverend Haley helped a man in a wheelchair with his tray. It was heartwarming to see strangers sitting side-by-side and talking, getting a hot meal. It was also heartbreaking that so many would have otherwise been alone and forgotten.

I dropped a scoop of dressing on a plate, then looked at its owner. "Gravy?"

The girl shook her head, not meeting my gaze. I passed the dish to Edna Jenkins, who was doling out sweet potatoes and green beans. The visitor followed her tray to the next station.

Poor kid. So young, probably a runaway. So far from home. Kinda looks like Cindy Lou Who, with big blue eyes and messy blonde hair. Bonnie would know just how to help her.

I plopped dressing on the next plate. "Gravy?"

I sat on the floor, legs crossed. Had to stop the sobbing. I wiped my hands down my face and leaned forward to stand up.

Was that a car door?

I paused, listening, but didn't hear anything. Seconds later, the front door creaked open.

"Freeze!"

Baba Yaga? I threw the stick of chalk at her and sprinted for the fire escape, having to hurdle the bawling girl I'd tied up on the floor.

The rickety metal stairs shook and rattled as I stormed up them and it got worse when someone else climbed on a couple of flights below me. I had to hoist myself over a fancy decorative edging once I reached the top.

December breeze pawed my skin with cold fingers as I ran across the flat roof, trying to dodge all the HVAC pipes sticking out. I was breathing hard, but not enough to slow me down much.

"Wayne!" Espinoza shouted.

I stopped and turned to face him. Baba Yaga was right there, too. "How did you know?"

"We didn't. The woman you kidnapped was an undercover reporter, working on a piece about homeless shelters. When she failed to call in, they checked her socials and saw an auto upload photo that showed a man in a hoodie trying to grab her. They called us and we followed her phone. It's over, Wayne. Come with me, and we'll go downtown and talk about it."

"Nothing to talk about. You have no idea how much those people were suffering. I only wanted to help them, to send them home for Christmas. Just like my Bonnie. I shouldn't have been such a showboat, though. Shouldn't have drawn attention… she didn't."

"What are you saying, Wayne?" Espinoza took a few slow steps toward me.

I took a few slow steps back. "Do you think politicians care about the homeless? They don't vote or make campaign donations. They're not even seen as people. But Bonnie? She really cared, hated seeing them in such misery. So, she sent them home for Christmas. And no one even noticed. They were shoveled up off the street like so much garbage and now their ashes are on a shelf in the basement of the morgue, waiting to be picked up by someone who will never show." I shook my head. "This year was hard. I tried to carry on her legacy, but, well, I guess I just got carried away with the holiday spirit."

"Wayne, I need you to come with me."

I stepped up onto the narrow concrete cornice that topped the edge of the warehouse. We were only six floors up, but that was high enough. I'd seen plenty of jumpers at the morgue, after all.

"Wayne. Please. Come down from there." Espinoza's voice was raw. He was much too far away.

I raised my arms out to the sides. That's how they always did it in the movies, right? "No. It's my turn to go home for Christmas."

Then I leaned back into the starry night.

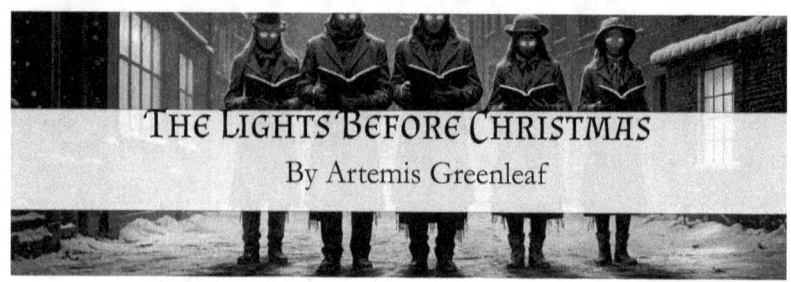

The Lights Before Christmas
By Artemis Greenleaf

THERE should not be fireflies in December. The ominous grey skies made the bouncing lights stand out even more. Laurel Camden watched them flicker and dance, their light scattering off tiny ice crystals on the frosty grass in the meadow below.

Granny Mae would almost certainly know what these were. Unfortunately, she'd been gone six months now. Cancer's a bitch.

Vera, Laurel's mother, had moved back to her childhood home to care for Granny Mae during her medical treatments. Then Laurel had lost her job and needed a soft place to land, so she'd moved to the farmhouse last month.

The icy breeze picked up, and she thought she heard snatches of fiddle music on the wind. It triggered a sweet memory with a sharp sting in its tail. Granny Mae played fiddle for the local square dance group. So on-brand for her. Laurel smiled at the memory.

But it also set off a cruel spark of hope that seared her heart. Back in June, Granny Mae had told Vera she wanted to see the fireflies, so they sat on the back porch to eat their supper. Vera had gone inside to use the bathroom, and when she came out, Granny Mae was gone. The back gate was ajar, but there was no trace of her.

Authorities and people from the community had searched for her for weeks. Helicopters. Dogs. People on horseback. Nothing. And given her rapidly deteriorating condition… Laurel refused to think about that.

The tiny lights shimmered over the grass, drifting closer to Laurel. She sat on a crumbling stone wall, watching.

Her lizard brain took notice, raising the hairs on the back of her neck and shouting "Run!" inside her head.

Her frontal lobe scoffed. *It's just late-season fireflies—the unseasonable warmth must have interfered with their usual life cycle, that's all. Adults don't even eat, so what could they possibly do to you?*

The longer Laurel watched, the more fascinated she became. She wanted to catch one of the glowing insects, like when she and her cousin would catch lightning bugs in a jar for a little while before setting them free. She had no jar this afternoon.

She slid off the low wall and walked into the field of fireflies. An open meadow on rolling hills stretched before her. Beyond that, a thick band of trees with a creek running through it. Grandpa Jeff had always planned to use that patch of woods for timber, but year after year had passed without it being logged, and the forest grew thicker and denser, taller and darker.

The fireflies stayed just out of reach. The deeper she went into the meadow, the closer they moved to the shadowy trees, where they glowed more fiercely. Putting on a burst of speed, she snatched one of the stragglers out of the air.

"Ow!" Laurel opened her hand, and the tiny thing flew away.

She couldn't be sure if it was a bite or a sting, but whichever it was, it had drawn blood. Laurel shook her hand in the air. Perhaps these things weren't so harmless after all. She turned back toward the meadow, but something bright caught her eye. *Is that a small fire burning deep in the trees?* She hurried to investigate.

As Laurel neared the light, she found a cottage. It had old fashioned leaded glass windows, and a fire blazed in the fireplace.

Where did this come from? She hadn't roamed these woods since she was a child, but no one had ever said anything about building a house out here. A few bars of fiddle music seemed to be coming from the direction of the cottage.

"Granny Mae?" Laurel broke into a run.

She pounded on the wooden door. "Hello? Granny Mae?"

No one answered. She tried the handle, and the door opened into the cozy living room. "Hello? Anybody here?"

"Dinner'll be ready soon. Will you be joining me?"

Sadly, the woman wasn't Granny Mae. Younger and taller, she busied herself laying plates on a rough-hewn table.

"I'm sorry. Who are you? This is my grandparents' property."

"There's no call for such bluster, Laurel Camden. Do you care for a plate or no?"

"How do you know my name?"

"As you said, your mother's people have been here for some time."

"Do you know Granny Mae?"

"Doesn't everyone in these parts?" She pointed to a small door, one that Lauren would have to stoop to enter. "Girl, would you mind stepping down to the cellar and fetching me a jar of pickles? The bread-and-butter sort, mind you."

The cellar? Oh, hell no!

Aren't you being dramatic, girl? Thoughts bubbled up in her mind. *Wouldn't you want someone to help* your *mother with dinner if she needed it? Her knees aren't what they used to be.*

The idea that someone might be lying in wait in the cellar now seemed ridiculous.

"Fine." Lips pursed, Laurel strode across the small room and wrenched open the door. Ducking her head, she started down the dark stairs. A dim light in the cellar cast just enough illumination for her to find her way down without falling.

A hurricane lamp sat on a chunky handmade table. The stone room was even smaller than the cottage above and smelled of damp earth. Rows of jarred fruits and vegetables lined the walls. *Where are the stupid pickles?*

She went down the rows with her finger, squinting in the dim light. Green beans, peaches, apricots. *Finally!* Gherkins. Hamburger. Dill. Sweet. There. A single jar of bread-and-butter.

Laurel grabbed the pickles. Something clicked, and the shelves of glass jars in front of her rolled away. She blinked, then rubbed her eyes.

In front of her lay a cavernous ballroom, filled with elegant dancers.

Every instinct screamed at her to leave, to run up those stairs and out of the cottage, never looking back.

Instead, she stepped into the ballroom, almost against her will. She felt compelled, as if by some invisible force, and yet she was intensely curious about the impossible gala. To the music of a string quartet, the couples swirled around her, all dressed in sumptuous evening clothes. But as she looked closer, they were not at all what they seemed.

They ran the gamut from the absurd to the macabre. A woman with mottled green skin and narrow, pointed features was as terrifying as she was eerily beautiful. She danced with a man who had the head of a crow.

Another couple included a woman with the head and tail of a fox. Her partner was nothing but shadows underneath his flawless tux.

"Champagne?"

Laurel whirled to see a young woman whose skin was covered with fine scales in iridescent blues and yellows. Her hair floated behind her, as if it were billowing in water.

"Uh… than—thank you," Laurel stammered.

It felt incredibly rude to refuse a flute of the pale bubbly. She took the glass, and the server continued her route.

It was then Laurel noticed that the cellar had disappeared. The dusty shelves and dirt floor had been replaced by a pale grey wainscoted wall and parquet, matching the rest of the grand ballroom. She took a step toward the newly appeared wall and nearly tripped over the hem of her silk jacquard ball gown. She looked down at herself—the dress was the perfect shade of periwinkle to complement her complexion. The fitted bodice with the uncomfortably low neckline gave way to a skirt that was a confection of lace and ruffles. An itchy tulle petticoat provided volume.

The song came to an end, and the dancers separated and clapped. A new song began.

"May I have this dance?"

Laurel's eyes followed the extended hand up to the face of the most handsome man she'd ever seen. His glossy black hair curled softly, framing his face. She got lost in his luminous emerald eyes and her hand moved to his without hesitation. She didn't know what happened to her champagne glass.

His hands were warm against her skin and lower back. Uncomfortably warm.

"What is this place?"

He smiled, revealing too-perfect teeth. "Don't you know?"

"Is this a dream? It feels like a dream."

"A dream?" For a split second, Laurel thought his fashion-model teeth had sharp points. It must have been a trick of the light, because as he continued to speak, they were perfectly perfect. He leaned forward and hot breath that carried notes of earth and spice whispered in her ear, "This is no dream."

Still holding her hand, he caressed her cheek with a scorching finger. "Would you feel this in a dream?"

Laurel pulled back. The hand on her waist pulled her closer.

He swept her around the dance floor, and she could focus on nothing beyond his bright green eyes.

The music stopped and her partner gave her a slight bow before releasing her hand. As the dancers clapped, a wall shifted, revealing an enormous U-shaped table set with gleaming silver flatware and plates that looked like stained glass. Behind the table was the most lavish buffet Laurel had ever seen. While she stood frozen, everyone began to move toward the banquet. She'd gotten so turned around that she had no idea which wall opened to the cellar.

The delectable aromas drifting from the feast made her stomach rumble. *Why am I standing here like a box of crackers?*

Before she could take a step toward the food, a bony hand wrapped around her wrist. Laurel turned and found herself facing an older woman.

"Granny Mae?" It was her, or perhaps a younger, more vital version of her.

"Shhhhh. Come with me."

Laurel followed her grandmother through the ballroom to an opening in the corner that she hadn't noticed before.

She peered around the stone corridor. There were no torches or light fixtures to be found, the place was lit with a pale green glow just bright enough to show their way. Her grandmother led her through a maze of tunnels until she came to a door with a golden fiddle painted on it and touched the knob. The door sprang open, and Laurel didn't hesitate to follow her grandmother inside.

The cozy room contained a dresser, a wardrobe, and a bed with a handmade biscuit quilt, one of Granny Mae's specialties. A white porcelain lamp painted with tiny pink rosebuds glowed on the nightstand.

Granny Mae closed the door and threw her arms around Laurel's neck. "Oh, I've missed you so!"

"You're alive! We were so worried" Laurel squeezed her grandmother as tightly as she dared.

"Of course I'm alive." She sighed heavily.

"I don't understand what's happening here. Come on, we've got to get out of this crazy place."

"Laurel." Granny Mae squeezed her granddaughter's hands. "You don't belong here. I do."

"What? No! I can't leave you here with these weird people."

"You can and you must. Do you notice anything different about me?"

"No." Laurel looked at her grandmother from head to toe. "You're just like you've always been."

And that's when it hit her. That's how Granny Mae had been before the dementia. "Well, I mean until the past few years. Maybe some of your pills interact or there's a small gas leak in the house. You look great, away from home. That could be it, right?"

"What about the arthritis in my hands? It had gotten so bad I couldn't put bow to fiddle. Didn't you hear the music for the dance?"

"That was you?"

"And three others. Listen my dear. Time is short. You have to leave."

"But—"

"You haven't drunk or eaten anything since you've been here, have you?"

"No." Laurel rubbed her forehead. "Well, I don't think so. They handed me a glass of champagne. I don't remember drinking any—the glass was there, and then it wasn't. I'm just so confused!"

Granny Mae stroked Laurel's hair and patted her shoulder. "I know, honey. It's a long story… I once rescued a large black rabbit from a hunter's snare. Only the rabbit wasn't really a rabbit—"

"What? How can that be?"

"He's a shapeshifter, a *pùca*."

Laurel raised an eyebrow.

"Don't give me that look. After what just happened to you?"

Granny Mae had a point.

"Over the years, we became friends. Once my brain began to rot—"

"Granny Mae!"

Her grandmother held up a hand. "I was invited to come here. The dementia, the arthritis—and all the other old-age ailments would be gone. I could play the fiddle again for all the dances. And they do love to dance here." A smile spread over the old woman's face, making her eyes sparkle.

"If you're cured, come back with me!"

"I can't. If I return to the mundane world, all the mundane problems return as well."

"Mom and I will take care of you."

"I don't need taking care of *here*. Time grows short. You must go. Follow the black rabbit—he knows the way out. And try not to make eye contact with anyone. They don't know you and may take offense."

"What do I tell Mom?"

Granny Mae took her wedding band off her finger and pressed it into Laurel's hand. "Give this to her. Tell her you saw me in Faery. Tell her you found it in the attic. It doesn't matter—whatever you think she will believe." She hesitated. "If you come to the old stone wall at midnight on the solstices and equinoxes, bringing a gift, I might be able to come out to see you."

"What kind of gift?"

"Bottle of whiskey. Carton of milk. Fresh-baked bread. Those are all good. I love you so much, but you have to go. Now."

She practically pushed Laurel out into the dim corridor and shut the door behind her.

Laurel sighed and slipped the ring into her pocket. The periwinkle ball gown had gone, and she was back in the clothes she'd been wearing on her forest ramble.

Thump. Thump. Thump.

A black rabbit the size of a Labrador retriever sat at the end of the corridor, impatiently banging its hind leg on the floor. Its eyes glowed green. *Does it have a name? Granny Mae didn't tell me. What if there are more than one?*

Laurel hurried after the big bunny. She never seemed to get any closer to it as she followed through the byzantine corridors. After a while, they came to a huge hall—bigger than the ballroom—with vaulted ceilings. Golden light streamed through a skylight in the center of the ceiling onto a bubbling marble fountain. Bright flowers ringed the stone pool.

A tall black horse raised its head and studied her with silver eyes. Laurel was drawn to it, had to touch it. *She extended her hand as she approached, and the horse nickered. Maybe if I got on him, I could finally catch up with that rabbit.*

"Fingal!"

The horse whipped its head toward the far corner of the room and flicked its ears. Laurel followed its gaze, only to find the man who'd danced with her earlier.

"Let her be. She's the fiddler's granddaughter."

The horse turned its head slowly back toward Laurel, then pinned its ears and squealed. Laurel tried to step back as its head darted, snakelike, in her direction. Falling on her butt saved her from vicious, sharp teeth.

The green-eyed man suddenly stood between them. He raised his arms and waved them. "Are ye mad?"

With a half-hearted kick that was more for show than defense, the horse turned and plunged into the fountain, disappearing completely.

The man helped Laurel to her feet, and she dusted off the seat of her pants. "What was that?"

"Kelpie. I'm Callum, by the way."

"Laurel. Where did it go?"

He led her to the fountain. She peered in, but instead of a smooth marble bottom, the water's blue-green depths turned to black far below.

"Careful, girl," he said as she leaned over. "If you think Fingal was fearsome, you don't want to attract the mer-folk."

Laurel backed away from the fountain. "Thanks for chasing that thing away."

"Fingal is not a thing. Over-proud, perhaps, but not a bad fellow. Come, let's get you out of here."

The floor began a gentle upward slope as they walked. "What is this place?"

"Depends on whom you ask, I suppose." Callum quickened his pace.

"I'm asking *you*." Laurel's breath came faster.

"The easiest explanation is that it's the land of Faery."

"Fairies aren't real."

He chuckled. "If you say so."

Laurel let out an exasperated breath. "Have you known Granny Mae long?"

"Yes."

Callum didn't elaborate. Laurel was about to attempt to pry more information out of him when they came to a wooden door more than twice her height. At Callum's touch, it swung open.

They stepped outside into the meadow. Lauren squeezed her eyes together, then opened them wide. *How?*

"It's later than I thought. Run." When Laurel just stood there, Callum placed his hot hand on the small of her back and gave her a gentle push. "Run!"

Lauren's brow furrowed, then she started a slow jog toward the old stone wall. As she turned to look back, a black rabbit hopped into the corridor and the door vanished.

Tiny lights began to flicker over the grass, moving swiftly in her direction. The fireflies that were not fireflies. Laurel ran faster. The cloud caught up with her, and she felt tiny bites and stings all over her body. No time to slap them away. She ran as fast as she could force her legs to move. As she got closer to the wall, words sounded in her head, *Jump, girl!*

Laurel leaped, clearing the low wall and landing in a heap on the other side. She lay panting in the frozen grass until she caught her breath. After a few minutes, she got to her feet and looked out to the meadow. The glowing creatures hovered above the frost, winking and inviting her to join them.

She turned and hurried back to the farmhouse.

"Laurel!" Her mother came running at the sound of the back door. "Where have you been?" She folded Laurel into a bear hug. "I've been so worried. The police and God-knows-how-many volunteers are out looking for you."

"Why? I was just out for a walk. Can't have been gone more than an hour or two."

Her mother released her. "You've been missing for three days. Tomorrow was shaping up to be the worst imaginable Christmas, with Mama, and then you disappearing."

Laurel cocked her head. "I don't see how that could be. Nothing makes sense anymore." *Am I losing my mind? Could it be early onset dementia?* "I need a shower."

Laurel came downstairs early on Christmas morning. She placed the small box with Granny Mae's wedding ring inside under the tree for her mother. In the kitchen, she turned on the oven and took a tube of cinnamon rolls out of the refrigerator.

I should start some coffee to go with these. The compost bucket was full, so she'd have to empty it before she could dump out the old grounds and start a new pot. She carried the pail out the back door to the tumbler.

Near the edge of the trees, an over-sized black rabbit picked through the frozen grass for tender shoots.

Laurel dropped the bucket, spilling food scraps on her foot.

The rabbit raised its head, winked an emerald-green eye at her, and hopped into the trees.

DEAD RECKONING
By A. B. Richards

My last job landed me a doozy of a payday and, for once, I wasn't on the nut when this Dapper Dan walked through my office door. I looked him up and down, from his boater hat to his pencil-thin mustache to his linen suit.

Must be lost. "Sorry, my receptionist has gone to the post office. Anything I can help you with, sir?" My fictitious receptionist was always at the post office, if anybody asked.

"You Laurent DeForest? Private dick?"

C'est vrai! "That's me. You lookin' for a top-notch investigator?"

The man's eyebrow twitched. "Are you familiar with Mr. Theo Caldwell?"

"Everybody on the Island is familiar with Mr. Caldwell. His shipping business almost single-handedly keeps the Port of Galveston running." He was just about the only major shipper who hadn't migrated to the Port of Houston after the Great Storm two decades ago.

The man in the straw hat nodded. "My name is Percy Nicholson, and I work for Caldwell Interests. Mr. Caldwell is looking to hire someone to investigate disruptions at one of his construction sites."

I leaned back and crossed my arms. If Theo Caldwell wanted to pony up for special treatment, I would go along for the ride, but I wasn't about to stampede through the PD's business. "I don't mean to be a flat tire, but what did the coppers say?"

"Petty vandalism is a low priority for law enforcement."

I rubbed my chin, surprised that not even Theo Caldwell had enough pull to get the Galveston PD out in force. "Would you care to step into my office to discuss the matter?"

The sour expression on Percy Nicholson's face led me to believe he'd rather do just about anything but that. Still, he followed me.

I gestured to the pair of shabby leather chairs in front of my desk as I continued around to my own chair. Nicholson remained where he was.

Before I could even plant my butt in the seat, Percy spoke. "Mr. Caldwell is constructing a warehouse on the seawall. During the night, a person or persons unknown has been engaging in petty vandalism and moving items around the worksite. Mr. Caldwell is prepared to pay you $250 per night, plus expenses, to capture the perpetrators."

Mon dieu! Two and a half Cs is more than double my usual day rate. "I ain't muscle, ya follow?"

Nicholson pressed his lips together.

"But I suppose it'll be easy enough to corral 'em and call the fuzz to haul them off."

"That would be acceptable." He retrieved an envelope from his waistcoat and laid it on my desk. "The address is inside. Along with a down payment for your services." He strode to the doorway, then turned on his heel. "You will start the job this evening at five PM."

He breezed out before I could say another word.

I opened the envelope and pulled out the letter. It was folded around five crisp one-hundred-dollar bills, and told me to meet the foreman, Milford Powell, at the site at five sharp. That was a lot of cabbage for some petty vandalism. Just in time for Christmas, too. If I had anybody to buy presents for. Not that Caldwell didn't have plenty of dough to splash around. Still, it wouldn't be the first time a client had hired me with ulterior motives.

I pulled out a sheet of paper and wrote a note to my friend, Jubilee, asking her to help me out with this crazy caper.

I stepped off the trolley at 4:56, according to my pocket watch, and crossed the street to the construction site. The winter sun was already floating on the horizon, bathing the low-hanging clouds in red and orange.

"Laurent?"

I whipped my head to the left to see Johan Mueller sauntering up the sidewalk toward me, lunch pail swinging. *Just what I needed.* I forced a smile. "Been a while, Joe. How you keepin?"

"Finally got a job, don't pay worth a damn, not like the union gig." He sighed bitterly. When he looked at me, he tilted his head one way, then the other. "Boy, you ain't aged a day in what is it? Two years now? Still look like a kid. You ever hear from Eddie Novak?"

My eyes darted up the street. "Healthy livin' I guess. Haven't seen nor heard from Eddie since that lockout. They said he headed west lookin' for work. Or maybe east to Spindletop. Who knows? If he came back here, he never looked me up."

An open-air bus with a sign that read 'Ferry' on the windshield pulled up to the curb.

Joe clapped me on the shoulder. "That's my ride. Let's tip a few sometime, huh?"

"Sure thing."

I hurried up the street to the construction site.

No idea who dug up Goliath and outfitted him in denim overalls and a newsboy cap, but there he stood at the gate, arms crossed.

"Mr. Powell?" I kept it light—he could crush me with one of those ham-sized fists. I wondered if this behemoth was one of the scabs Caldwell had hired during the Longshoremen's Strike a couple of years ago.

"You da peeper?"

His accent. What is that, German? "Laurent DeForest. That's me."

He grunted, his voice like a rusty spring. "Follow me."

I studied the surroundings as I walked through the construction site behind the lumbering giant. Scaffolding, tools, wood framing—nothing unexpected. Although some of the foundation trenches seemed oddly deep. I reckoned it was due to the whole thing being built on the sand they'd pumped behind the seawall.

Powell led me past a pile of materials. "You guys get a discount on those hollow bricks?"

The giant scowled. "Dose are cinder blocks. Herr Caldwell, he likes the latest materials, *ja?*"

"*Ja.*" *I guess.* I don't know bricks from Shinola.

"Workers say dey hear kinder—children—talking when they come in de morning but no brats to be found. Tools are moved from de day before or thrown in de trenches. Tings like dat. Herr Caldwell must always new workers to hire. Dey go home and don't come back."

"Any activity hotspots?"

He pointed to a deep trench. Wooden support beams disappeared into the darkness. "Dere."

I ankled over and peered into the hole. Hard to tell the depth in the darkness, but it looked deeper than a warehouse foundation had any business being. I mean, most of the other buildings were jacked up on piers, and they pumped the sand underneath. I watched 'em do it plenty of times. Wouldn't this have piers down to the bedrock to stabilize it? It popped into my brain that Caldwell was digging for something else. I said as much to Powell. Except for the last part.

His jaw tightened. "Sand moves. Must dig deep for stable foundation."

I scoffed. "Well, don't dig through the seawall."

His eyes narrowed. Probably should have kept my trap shut. This fella was the size of Toledo, but I was pretty sure I could outrun him.

"Your job, Herr DeForest, is to catch dese urchins so dey can be dealt mit. Any more questions?"

I shook my head. I had plenty of questions, but none he was gonna answer for me.

"*Gute Nacht.*" He hoofed it off the site like he was late for dinner.

Powell's broad shoulders faded into the December twilight. The last sliver of sun was sinking into the choppy waters, bruising the horizon as it sank.

No tykes had shown up to wreak havoc yet, so I wandered around the place. Tool shed had shovels, rope, lanterns. Kinds of stuff I'd expect. There was one gadget I couldn't figure out, though. Stood on three legs, with a crank handle and some kind of chisel hanging down through the center of it. Seemed kinda small for setting piers.

I'd worked a lot of jobs in my time, but none of 'em construction. Maybe I just didn't know any better, but something seemed off about this set-up. Especially that trench. It was like a pebble in my shoe.

All traces of the sun were gone by six-thirty. I could see just fine in the dark, so I picked a good spot and settled down to wait for guttersnipes or Jubilee, whoever showed up first.

Ah. La mer agitée. The night surf crashing on the beach drowned out any sounds from the city. This is the same ocean that caresses the shores of France. I often think about my childhood village. But that was long ago and far away, and anyone who knew me there is moldering in their grave now.

I smelled Jubilee long before I saw her. She moved in the dark, silent as a ghost. She wore a scent that was custom-made just for her. The almond-vanilla smell of *Géant des Batailles* oleander flowers with a touch of rose and hint of vetiver. A few drops would kill the average person, but its cardiac poison had no effect on her undead heart.

"Laurie? What have you gotten yourself into now?" Her eyes glowed faintly in the dark.

"That's a good question." I filled her in on the case and recapped my tour of the site.

She peered into the haunted trench. "That's a deep hole, ducky." She continued to stare down into it.

"Ya think?" I hadn't intended to snap at her.

She turned and her eyes moved lazily from my feet to my face. "Something troubles you."

"Yeah, I feel like I'm being set up for a patsy, but I just can't seem to cotton on to what the racket is."

She nodded and kept staring.

I sighed. "There's somethin' else. When I got off the trolley, I ran into Joe Mueller. He used to hang out with Eddie Novak, my pal who worked at the docks. We'd hit the dives together."

"I remember."

"You remember all the fights between the union workers and the strike breakers? How when the governor declared martial law and took over the city, the National Guard came in and arrested anybody any time they wanted?"

"They picked up Eddie, didn't they? Said he was out after curfew or something?"

"Trespassing. For walking down a public sidewalk. He disappeared after that. Word was he caught the next train outta town to find work. Always seemed odd to me he never sent a postcard from wherever he ended up."

"Yeah. Didn't seem like Eddie to me, either."

I sighed and gnawed the inside of my cheek. All this talk about Eddie had me down in the dumps. "How are things at Oleander House?"

It was her turn to sigh. "Got a new girl. Don't think she's gonna work out."

"Oh?"

"She's got no self-control. I took her in as a favor to a friend in New Orleans."

I nodded. She should have known better than to bring in a wild girl from there. But I kept my lips zipped. Wanted to keep her talking so I didn't think about Eddie.

"I explained to her that when a gentleman chose her, she would take him upstairs to her room, feed discreetly, then wipe his memory. He was to leave feeling like he'd had the time of his life, even if he couldn't remember any details. It's pretty simple. Everyone *else* gets it."

"She drained him?"

Jubilee scowled. "Not only did she take all of his blood, she pulled out every last drop of moisture. That cat looked like the mummy of Ramses. We stuffed him in a cask of wine in a warehouse down at the docks. If anybody finds him before it ships out, at least Mercury Harlan won't be able to make the stiff. I don't need that flatfoot sniffin' around the Oleander."

"Well, he's the only one of those coppers who ever listens to me. The rest of 'em are all like 'scram, Babyface!'—what a bunch of palookas."

Jubilee glared at me.

I swallowed. "But I can understand your point."

A giggle caught my attention.

I must have been so distracted talking to Jubilee that I failed to notice kids coming into the construction area. They were running all over the place and hard to count. Looked like six or eight of 'em.

I started to get up. I hadn't liked the sound of Powell's 'so dey can be dealt mit,' and I had a mind to scare the urchins off, so they didn't come back.

Jubilee touched my arm. "Wait," she whispered.

We sat there watching those rampant rag-a-muffins tear around for several minutes. After a couple of kids rolled a wheelbarrow of sand and dumped it down the deepest trench, a group of boys moved some of those cinder blocks to barricade the opening. A little girl pretended to skip rope while two others mimed turning it for her.

Two nuns came in and clapped their hands twice. "It's time!"

Are these kids orphans? There's something off about this gang, but I can't quite put my finger on it. Did they get lost on the way back from midnight mass or something? They jumped the gun by a few days, if that's the case.

The children hung their heads and lined up single file.

"Sisters!" I called out.

One of them turned her gaunt face in my direction. "Who are you?"

I stood up and dusted my hands on my pants. "I'm a private eye, hired to find out who's been tearing up the joint. It's not my place to tell you your business, Sister, but shouldn't these ankle-biters be sawing logs by now?"

"Correct. It is *not* your business!" she hissed. "Better you mind Thomas Reid instead."

"Sister, you gotta keep these brats outta here. The owner's pretty sore about all the destruction."

She didn't reply and led the children toward the exit, their footsteps silent in the sand.

"Who's Thomas Reid?" I called after her.

No response.

"What do you make of that, Jubilee?"

Her eyebrows arched. "Laurie, those kids aren't—"

A metallic clatter came from behind a stack of crates to our left. Both our heads whipped in that direction.

"Who's there?" I called out. "Thomas Reid, is that you?"

The sound of something heavy sliding across sand, then a click was the only reply. I crept around one side of the boxes, and Jubilee took the other. The only thing we found was a wall.

A howl pierced the night.

Jubilee and I came from behind the stack of crates to see an oversized coyote standing by the gate. It looked at her like they were pals, but when it caught sight of me, it backed up, tail down.

"It's a message. I gotta scram, Laurie. If you know what's good for you, you'll blow this joint, too."

The coyote turned and trotted out, Jubilee hurrying after it.

She was right. I had found the culprits, warned them off, and my job for the evening was done. I pulled out my pocket watch. Three-twenty. Time to call it quits.

Theo Caldwell had shelled out for two nights, so I gave him two nights. I'd checked in with Powell, same as before, and given him the lowdown. He'd grunted and left. Still a bit too much daylight for Jubilee, so to kill time, I thought I'd nose around a bit more.

That deepest trench sloped down and had planks, like a board-walk. Made me think of the Galveston Electric Park. Just wished I had some of those electric bulbs. I could see well enough in the dark, but it was more like looking at one of those old tintype photos than looking at real life.

I went down ten to twelve feet. The trench opened up into a room. The sand above and on the sides was held up by scaffolding and boards. A couple of wheelbarrows were filled with sand, probably from the wide hole at one end of the chamber. It was only a couple of feet deep, but not far from the original beach level—they'd be hitting rip-rap soon.

So what does that pit have to do with building a warehouse? What's Caldwell really after? I stared at the hole. *There had to be an old-timer who might know what's under that sand. Wait! Zara would know. She's been here probably longer than the Island itself. Mermaids are temperamental, so I'd better bring Jubilee along.*

A growl rippled through the darkness. I searched the small chamber but couldn't find the source. *Is there another coyote holed up in here somewhere?*

The growl came again. It rumbled through my chest, deeper than any coyote or dog I'd ever heard.

Light glimmered above the hole. A translucent figure materialized in the air. A man, dressed in old-fashioned sailor garb, complete with a tri-corn hat, glared at me with glowing eyes. His neck and the top of his shirt were stained dark, and he seemed to be holding one arm behind his back.

Face twisted with fury, he raised his cutlass. "Get. Out!" His raspy voice came from everywhere at once.

I backpedaled as quick as I could. "Whoa, there, big fella! I'm not here to—"

My heel caught on something and sent me sprawling. I rolled over to look at the raging sailor, and came face to face with a skull.

Bits of flesh, dried up like beef jerky, still clung to the bones in spots. I pulled back the tarp I'd dislodged in my fall. *Is this… that guy?* I glanced back up at the ghost, who floated above the pit, glowering and moaning.

A body, or what was left of one, lay on the floor. A dusty hemp rope coiled limply around the ribcage, as if it had been used to bind the arms to the body while there was still some meat on its bones. Still had a few rags of clothing—brown work pants, denim shirt, dry-rotted leather boots. Common enough for a longshoreman, but not for a sailor, especially not that one. I glanced up at him again.

A black disc hung around the skeleton's neck, so I picked it up for a closer gander.

The thing was a badly tarnished St. Christopher medal.

"No…" My hands shook. "Please, no."

Two initials were engraved on the back. "E. N."

Eddie Novak.

"Mon Dieu, Eddie. How'd you wind up here?"

"We were hoping to ask you that very same question, Babyface."

Lights blazed to life, and I held up my hand to shield my eyes.

"Don't move!" Multiple voices.

In the glare of the searchlights, I could see four sets of legs, no faces.

"Stand up, hands in the air!"

Are these coppers? I got to my feet and reached for the ceiling. "You fellas got the wrong end of the stick. All the flatfoots on the Island know me. I'm workin' a job for Mr. Caldwell."

A voice came out of the darkness behind the legs. A voice with a heavy German accent. "This jungen Mann I have never in my life seen."

"Mr. Powell, you know that's not so. We just—"

One of the cops shouted, "Quiet, DeForest!"

Two pairs of legs came toward me. Each man grabbed one of my arms and twisted it behind my back.

"Hey! No need to rough me up. We can talk about this."

One of the flashlight holders grunted. "Save it for the judge."

The goons holding my arms said nothing as they slapped cuffs on my wrists.

"Laurent DeForest, I'm placing you under arrest for the murder of Eddie Novak."

"What! No. No, you got it wrong!"

Powell turned away as the brass-buttoned baboons frog-marched me up the boardwalk. *What in blue blazes is going on here? If I don't get word to Jubilee, tomorrow's gonna be a bad night for everybody.*

"*Sale porcs!*" I spat blood at the palooka closest to me, then sucked my stinging split lip into my mouth, tongue pressing it against my teeth to slow the bleeding. I hung from the ceiling by my arms, and it felt like they had broken a rib or two with that wooden nightstick. These rotten bulls seem to have mistaken me for a piñata, and I was damn well fed up with it. If they didn't lay off, I couldn't be held responsible for what happened to them.

Energy like fire smoldered under my skin, just waiting for a spark to set it off. Usually, it took a full moon, but pain could trigger it, too.

I looked up when the door slammed. Someone sighed.

I raised my head to see Mercury Harlan, holding a notepad. As usual, he looked like he just walked out of a fashion magazine.

"Scram, you meatheads." He scowled at the three buttons who'd been giving me the deluxe welcome package.

They didn't talk back, but they sure looked steamed about him stopping their fun. One sourpuss wiped my blood off his cheek with a linen handkerchief and slapped it against the detective's chest on his way out.

Mercury dropped it on the table as he came toward me. With another sigh, he yanked the bowline knot loose and lowered me.

My shoulder popped when my feet took my weight. *That's gonna hurt later.*

He pulled a ring of keys from his pocket and unlocked the cuffs. Breath hissed through my lips as I rubbed my bruised and bloody wrists.

"Thanks, Merc."

"S'alright, kid. You need anything? Water?"

I shook my head. "I didn't kill Eddie Novak. He was my friend."

"How'd you know Eddie?"

"When I first blew into town, I worked odd jobs at the docks. Mostly sweepin' warehouses, runnin' water out to the longshoremen when they were unloadin'. Stuff like that. Eddie took a shine to me, shared his lunch with me sometimes. He said he knew what it was like to be a kid on his own. Eddie wasn't married or nothin', so his time was his own. I sometimes tagged along when he and the boys went out on the town to blow off some steam, and he let me crash at his place afterwards."

He nodded slowly, his dark eyes giving away nothing. "You couldn't have been any older than fourteen? Fifteen?"

Biting back a laugh, I just nodded. I had been way older than fifteen. Truth be told, I was older than his great grandpa, for sure.

Mercury tapped his pencil on the pad.

"If you don't believe me, just ask Joe Mueller. He'll tell you."

Mercury's head tilted up, his eyes wide. "Why Joe Mueller?"

"I ran into him yesterday afternoon when I got off the trolley to work at Caldwell's construction site. Come to think of it, he even asked me about Eddie. I hadn't seen either one of 'em since the strike two years ago. I heard Eddie skipped town for greener pastures."

"Well, unless the Fox Sisters are in town for a seance, Joe Mueller's got nothin' to say."

Confused, I asked, "What do you mean by that?"

"Joe Mueller was found floating in the Ship Channel this morning."

Merde. I shook my head, unbelieving. "But I just saw him yesterday...."

"Why were you on Theo Caldwell's property?"

"He sent some fella named Percy Nicholson around to hire me. Wanted me to nab whoever's been tresspassin' and messin' with the equipment at his job site."

"How much?"

"Five hundred."

"You got a canceled check?"

I winced as my shoulders drooped. "Paid cash."

"He passed you *that* much scratch for *that* kind of job, and you didn't bat an eye?"

"Course I did! I'm not a dummy. But Theo Caldwell has plenty of moola to spread around. Five Cs isn't even pocket change for a guy like that."

"Right. So this Percy fella hands you the envelope. Then what?"

"He tells me to show up at five sharp. I take the trolley, run into Joe Mueller, and meet up with the foreman, Milford Powell, just like I'm told. Powell shows me around and splits."

Mercury taps his pencil again. "He said he never met you."

"Well, unless there's two walking mountains in this town, he's lying."

"So, what did your investigation turn up?"

I kept Jubilee's name out of this. "Just some rug-rats. The nuns came to round 'em up, and I told 'em to keep the brats contained."

"Nuns, huh? Seems a long way for tots to hoof it to Caldwell's job site, especially in the middle of the night."

"Maybe they took a jitney. How should I know how they got there?"

"Keep your shirt on, DeForest." He scratched something on his pad. "What were you doing there tonight?"

I shrugged. "Mr. Caldwell paid me for two nights. Wanted to see if those kids came back."

"And you thought you'd poke around."

"I am a private *investigator.*"

"Alright. What led you to the body?"

"I was checking for a hidden doorway or something. Never did see where those kids came from. I went down that trench with the boardwalk. Workers had carved out a room down there. There was a…" Telling him about the sailor ghost was a ticket straight to the funny farm. "…noise. Like an animal was down there. I tripped over Eddie's body. That's when your outfit rolled up."

Mercury sat there, rubbing his chin for long enough I wanted to punch him in the mug. Finally, he got up. "Somebody'll be along in a minute to take you to lockup. I'm gonna have you cool your heels here tonight while I see if your story checks out."

Long as you turn me loose before moonrise tomorrow.

He walked out without a backward glance.

Some guard turned up a minute later and ushered me to the finest accommodation the clink by the bay had to offer.

I sat on my cot, thinking about Eddie's St. Christoper medal. He'd tried to give it to me once. Maybe I shoulda taken it—ol' Chris and I had a few things in common. Back in the day, they used to draw him with the head of a wolf. I let my breath out slowly. Who was I kidding? Jude was probably the patron saint for me, just another lost cause.

Couldn't see much, but I could hear the hubbub from the front of the building. Cops talking. Citizens complaining. Hoods lying. It really hit me when it all stopped. Heels clicked across tile, and I caught the scent of almonds, vanilla, rose, and vetiver.

Jubilee.

I held my breath and listened.

"Pardon me, sir. I need to visit a friend of mine." Her southern drawl oozed thick as honey. Jubilee has a knack for language and she can sound like a local just about anywhere.

"Sorry, ma'am. Visiting hours are done. Why don't you…."

"I need…to see my friend."

"Of course! Of course, I'll take you right back. Anything I can getcha? Coffee? Water?"

"No thank you, sugar."

The voices roared back, like somebody had suddenly dropped the needle on a record.

When Jubilee appeared in the holding area, the front desk cop trotting behind her like a lovesick puppy, the fella in the cell next to me sat up, his eyes bugged out. "Hey, dollface! You here to take me home?"

He was lucky he was in a cell, surrounded by people. Jubilee stopped and fixed her dark eyes on him. He whimpered and pulled the thin wool blanket over his head.

The flatfoot pointed to me. "This your friend? This who you need to see? Anything else I can do for you, Miss?"

"Go."

"Yes, ma'am!" He scurried off in the direction of the front desk.

"Sweet hell, Laurie! I sure hope the other guy looks worse." Any trace of southern twang was gone.

"Not in the slightest."

"We got trouble."

"More than you realize."

Her brow furrowed slightly. "I got to the warehouse just in time to see the coppers hauling you off like a slab of meat. Nothing I could do. Sorry about that."

"You gotta get me outta here."

She twirled a few strands of her long black hair around her finger. "I know it's no picnic."

"You don't understand."

"Powell's dead."

I blinked like an owl in the afternoon. "What? Did you…?"

"Not me. Remember that chippy I told you about last night? She was supposed to be on a boat back to the Crescent City but decided to get out of her casket and have a little snack before the trip."

"Well, I don't feel sorry for Powell, not one iota. He lied to the cops about me working a case there."

"I'm not surprised. He had some kinda hidey hole. He must have been watching us last night—you remember that clatter we heard?"

I nodded.

"There were still a couple of cops hanging around after they took you away. Powell gave them each a fat envelope, and they left." She rubbed her forehead. "That's when I spotted Delphine. She mesmerized Powell and made him take her back inside the gate. By the time I got across the street and into the site, I couldn't find hide nor hair of them. That stack of crates? That's the hidden door. Delphine came strutting out, leaving it wide open. I, shall we say, *escorted* her back to her berth. What was left of Powell when I got back was drier than bones in the desert."

"Not sure if Powell croaking hurts or helps, Jubilee. But at least they can't pin *that* on me. They already knew Eddie was down there and had me fingered for the murder. Probably has something to do with the pay-off."

Jubilee nodded as if noodling an idea. "Tell me about the last time you saw Eddie."

"He'd built up a head of steam about the scabs Caldwell had called in. Can't blame him for that. He and the boys were headed to the docks to blockade the strikebreakers. They all got arrested for tresspassin' before they even got there. Joe Mueller swore up and down he never saw Eddie in the clink, though. And by the way, Merc told me they found him dead this morning."

Jubilee scrunched her forehead. "That's awfully convenient for somebody tryin' to cover something up. Anyway, you think Eddie woulda taken on the scabs by his lonesome?"

"That's the thing about Eddie. He was a good egg, but if his temper got away from him...."

An idea squirmed in my brain like a maggot in roadkill. "Do you think Eddie went on the lam and has been alive all this time? Then ran into Delphine?"

Jubilee cocked her head, then shook it. "No. She only arrived day before yesterday, for one thing. Besides, Eddie's clothes were all rotten, like they'd been there for—"

"Two years?"

"Yeah. I think it's more likely that Caldwell's scabs bumped off Eddie, and they stashed his body somewhere it wouldn't be found. Like on Caldwell's private property."

"But then this warehouse project came up. It was no secret that Eddie, Joe, and I were pals. That's why they set me up to take the fall." I shook my head. "I get so tired of barely scrapin' by, Jubilee. I knew this job was sketchy, but I really wanted to bank the dough. After the Grimaldi case, I'd kinda gotten used to regular meals."

She gave me a sympathetic smile. "Don't worry. My crew will take care of the parched Prussian, so that's one less thing you have to worry about."

"While you're there, check out the crazy basement at the bottom of that deep trench. Don't know what they're doin' down there, but it ain't building a warehouse. And it's haunted."

"Already knew that, sunshine. We both saw those kids."

I blinked a few times. "Wait. I knew there was something off about that lot. But they seemed solid as stone to me." Jubilee's been dead nearly five-and-half centuries, so I figure ghosts are her department. "There's an old salt down there, madder than a wet hen."

"A sailor? Really?" She gave me a half-smile. "On that note, I gotta get goin'."

I leaned forward, my hands on the bars. "Look, Jubilee. I've got a big problem with being locked up here."

"It's not so bad, is it? When Mercury Harlan does his investigatin'—"

"When is the full moon?"

"Jumpin' Jehoshaphat, Laurie!" She chewed her lip. "What a lousy break. Tell you what. If they don't let you out tomorrow, I'll find a way to spring you."

"Thanks." I leaned back, hoping Merc got it done. Jubilee's plans tended to be a little less practical and a lot more Rube Goldberg—clever, convoluted, and liable to crash and burn halfway through.

It had taken almost until sunrise for me to finally get some shuteye. Barely woke up when they came by with grits and chicory coffee for breakfast. Left it where it lay and closed my eyes again. The stench of the mystery meat sandwich they brought for lunch woke me up again. Made me want to heave. Didn't seem to bother the guy in the other cell, though. I suppose I prefer my meat a lot fresher. And rarer. The abomination was accompanied by some kind of olive-drab leaves, cooked well past recognition, and a cup of tapioca pudding with a skin so tough I couldn't push a spoon into it.

I shoved the tray into the farthest corner and sat on my cot. The moon was coming. I could tell by the way my skin itched and my joints ached. Different from the leftover pain from the beating I took last night.

I had plenty of time to ponder on the identity of Thomas Reid. Didn't help a whit, though.

Footsteps on tile caught my attention and I looked up. Mercury Harlan and a guard stood at the cell door. The guard unlocked it and scrammed.

"Come on, DeForest."

I got to my feet. "You takin' me to County yourself?"

"No. I'm cuttin' you loose."

He didn't move as I took the six steps to the end of the cell.

He spoke, his voice barely above a whisper. "There is no Percy Nicholson in the employ of Caldwell Interests. Milford Powell has gone missing. You were in the pokey all night, so you got nothing to do with that. I figure he got spooked and took a powder. I got nothin' I can prove in court, one way or another, but there's somethin' fishy goin' on here. Rest assured, Deforest, I'll be keepin' my eye on you."

Not sure if that was a promise or a threat. I sighed, relieved to be out of the slammer. "You're a good egg, Merc. I'm tellin' you, Theo Caldwell is up to somethin'. Sure hope you're lookin' into that."

"Stay clear of Caldwell, DeForest. There's a lot you don't know."

I narrowed my eyes. *Unless he's got an investigation goin' on and doesn't want me tippin' Caldwell off, he's got no right to tell me my business.* "Well, I hope you're giving him enough rope to hang himself."

He stepped out of the way, and as I passed, he said so quietly no one else could hear, "Watch your back."

I just nodded and walked through the station and out into the sun. I needed a drink.

Technically, alcohol was prohibited by law, but a fella would hardly know that in the Free State of Galveston. Especially not at the Bleached Barnacle.

Everyday folks passed right by the Barnacle. It wasn't invisible, they just didn't notice it. I hadn't known about the place until a few months ago. I've been on the Island less than three years—Jubilee had invited me down after that unfortunate event in Montreal. Other than her, Eddie, and Joe, I mostly kept to myself. That's why I like the private eye life. I'm left to my own devices. Working odd jobs at the docks hadn't been *so* bad, but the strike had changed everything. It turned into a different place after that, and I was glad I'd had enough scratch banked to hang out my own shingle.

The tavern door creaked as I pushed it open. Not one of the handful of post-lunch patrons looked up. I bellied up to the bar, and when the barkeep straightened up from below, I wanted to howl. She was a real sockdolager, that one. Thick red hair hung in a braid past her waist, and her grey-green eyes were like the sea in a squall.

"What'll ya have?"

I opened my mouth but forgot how to make words come out. *Merde!* It was like I'd never talked to a pretty girl in the last hundred and sixty years.

"Dinnae you want a drink, then? Ya sore look like ya could use one."

I'd forgotten I looked like crab bait. "W-whiskey. Three fingers."

She set a tumbler on the bar and poured.

I dropped two bits next to it. "Ain't seen you around here before."

"I'm helpin' out my Uncle Connor for a wee bit. My name is Rhona."

It took me a few seconds to remember my own name. *Get it together, man!* "It is a real pleasure to meet you, Miss Rhona. I'm...Laurent."

She giggled and her eyes sparkled with amusement.

"Rhona!" The grizzled old bartender stood in the doorway to what passed for a kitchen. "I need you back here."

She gave me a quick smile before hurrying off and disappearing into the back.

Old Connor sidled up to where I sat. "Ya keep your paws off me niece, lad." He glared at me for a moment, then his scowl softened. "Want your usual?"

It figured a looker like that would be his niece. I nodded. He trundled off into the back.

He returned a few minutes later with a slab of raw meat on a plate. Don't know what it used to be or where it came from, and I never asked. The iron-laden scent of blood made my stomach growl—I'd temporarily forgotten how hungry I was. Still had Caldwell's dough, so I was feeling flush. I pulled a buck out of my pocket and laid it on the bar. I was half-way hoping Rhona would see.

Picking up my knife and fork, I set to work.

Connor kept Rhona busy in the kitchen, so after a while I gave up and took a hike. Didn't really want to go home, and it was too early for Jubilee to come out. I wandered around The Strand.

I'd grown up in the mountains with snow for Christmas, midnight mass, and an even later feast. Afterward, prayers. But not even those kept the howling Beast at bay. In the end, it wasn't the protection of a priest that saved me, but a vampire. Jubilee kept me from bleeding out in the snow. She patched me up and got me on my feet. And I'm not sure if I forgive her.

I shivered and forced the dark memories away. Here, late afternoon sun shone on red bows on every streetlight. Tinsel and evergreen garlands hung across the road, and the nativity took up most of the yard of the Catholic church.

I paused at Eiband's Department Store and peered in the window. They had an artificial tree, all the way from Germany, set up there. Its thin branches were made of wire and goose feathers, dyed green, but they almost looked like real spruce. There were so many ornaments hung on the thing, it was hard to tell what it looked like, anyway.

Other windows showed fake snow with mannequins having snowball fights and a miniature train running in a circle around a pile of toys for the tykes. Made me wonder if the ghostly children from Caldwell's job site had ever gotten any toys in the orphanage.

I started toward Oleander House. It would be just about dark by the time I got there. It was going to be a long night, and we may as well get down to it. There was only so much time before moonrise.

It had taken Jubilee only a few seconds to mesmerize the new guard at the site and put him in her thrall. We moved down the trench and into the subterranean room.

The strange, three-legged contraption I'd seen before was now over the water-filled hole at the end of the chamber. "They've been doing some work since we were here."

Jubilee nodded. "I don't remember it being this damp."

"Full moon, remember? Tide's higher than normal." I stared at the hole, a memory clawing its way out of more than a century's worth of debris.

I was a *jeune garçon*—ten years old, perhaps. My sister, Marie, was two years younger. I don't know why we visited Marseilles, but we played on the beach, our mother watching us. We used shells to dig holes in the sand. Marie stood in the deepest one, holding her skirts up to keep 'em dry. As the tide came in, the sand got looser and the hole collapsed, trapping her legs. Maman came running, and we dug her out. Marie was scared but unharmed.

"Jubilee…?"

"Hmmm?"

"If they keep diggin' this hole down into the beach, it's gonna undermine the seawall's foundation."

"You think Theo Caldwell cares if people die, as long as he gets what he wants? Whatever that is?"

The same growl I'd heard two nights ago cracked the tomb-like darkness.

"Be. Gone!" The revenant glared at us. Then his mug softened. "Jubilee? Bless me eyes!"

She leaned forward, her brow furrowed. "Thomas? Thomas Reid?"

That set me back on my heels. "That's Thomas Reid?"

Jubilee took a few steps forward. "What happened to you, Tom? Why are you still here?"

He growled. "Bloody Jean Lafitte. Grapeshot at the Battle of New Orleans took me left arm. When we sailed back to Campeche, he said he had a chest of loot he needed to keep safe, so he, a couple o'swabs, and I set out to bury the thing."

I gaped like a fish. "You think that's what Caldwell's after?"

Jubilee gave me a look that shut my trap. "What was in it, Tom?"

"Doubloons, mostly. A bit of jewelry."

"What happened next?"

Tom scowled. "I told the boys they were muddle-headed fools for diggin' that hole way too big for that box, and when they looked at each other, then turned their eyes to Lafitte, I knew somethin' was amiss. Then Lafitte spoke plain. 'Well, old Tom, I reckon as first mate, you 'ave been first class.' He tucked a gold doubloon into me pocket, and I was right pleased. Then the scurvy dog said, '*Mais*, I cannot use *un infirme* on my crew, *non*? I 'ave anozzer job for you, *mon ami*. You will guard this treasure until I return, *compris*?' Before I could say a word, he cut me throat and shoved me in the hole, God rot his black heart."

"Oh, Tom! That's awful." Jubilee reached out as if to touch the ghost. Her hand passed right through his arm.

No wonder he's still sore about it.

Gradually, the nuns from two nights ago faded into sight, then the children appeared, single file between the two women. Without a sound, they marched out of the hidden room like a funeral procession.

"What's happening here?" I couldn't get my head around it.

The old pirate raised his head to watch them go. "When the Great Storm was ragin', the Sisters at the orphanage thought to keep the wee ones safe by lashing them together. But, alas, they was all washed out to sea and drowned, that rope doomin' every blessed one of 'em."

Bits of sand crumbled onto the floor from gaps in the boards in the walls and ceiling. The seawater that had pooled in the hole was overflowing, cold and rising fast.

"How high is that high tide?" Jubilee's heels were sinking into the softening sand.

"Probably over our heads down here."

"We gotta get out! Later, Tom." Jubilee hurried to the makeshift boardwalk, me right behind her.

We had almost made the gate at the job site, when voices came from the sidewalk, heading our way. Jubilee and I ducked behind a pile of sand.

I raised my head just enough to take a quick peek. "That's Theo Caldwell," I whispered to Jubilee.

"You sure?"

"Never met the man in person, but his picture's in the papers every week."

Jubilee put a finger to my lips as they passed close by, so I clammed up and listened.

"George, you sure you're going to break through tonight? You'd better not have dragged me out here for nothin'."

"Yes, sir, Mr. Caldwell! Drill bit hit something in the sand below the rip-rap. Gotta be that chest."

Caldwell cackled. "It had better be."

He and his four merry minions hoofed it down the makeshift boardwalk. Jubilee and I crept to the trench and slipped down just enough to see what those palookas were up to.

"Mr. Caldwell, we'd better wait until the tide goes out, sir. There's a lot of water comin' in—"

"The quicker you get on with it, the quicker we'll get out," Caldwell growled.

Two of the men pried chunks of rock out of the way. Another probed the collapsing hole with a big stick.

After a few jabs, he shouted, "Found it!"

Wood groaned and metal squealed. Caldwell's workers paused to look up.

"Dig!" The water was midway up Caldwell's calves as he shook his fist at the workers.

"Got something." The man with the pole lifted the end to reveal a blackened rope attached to something below.

The other three grabbed it and heaved.

One screamed as a yellowed skull popped out of the hole and bobbed in the water. A few rotting scraps of black fabric came with it. Then another skull, and another.

Small ones.

Children.

Red started to leak into my vision. My eyes were changing. "Jubilee, I gotta scram. Moon's rising."

"I'll get word to Mercury Harlan." She gave me a crooked smile. "Be careful, Laurie. Go!"

I laughed at her warning as I turned away. Outside on the sidewalk, I stopped. December's full moon—the Cold Moon—rose out of the sea. Its coppery light fell on my skin like frozen fire.

With a groan, I dropped to my knees. *I hate this part.* Joints popped. Bones broke and reformed. Hair sprouted out of my skin like a legion of worms. My eyes went red, staining the world crimson.

And then it was done. I turned my nose to the west and ran, damp salty air filling my lungs with each stride. Behind me, shouts and screams echoed from the construction site.

It had been a long night, after a long day. I leaned back in my chair, feet on my desk, thinkin' I could probably grab forty winks, and nobody'd be the wiser, when my office door swung open.

I put my feet on the floor. "Afternoon, Merc. You here in an official capacity?"

He sat in one of the shabby chairs in front of my desk. "I have some follow-up questions."

"Fire away."

"What do you know about doubloons?"

I snorted. "Doubloons? Could be worth a lot of scratch, if you find any. Why you askin' me about old coins?"

"See, here's the thing. You had a beef with Theo Caldwell."

"Half the people on the Island had a beef with Theo Caldwell."

"Half the people on the Island weren't just arrested for suspicion of murder on Caldwell's property."

"What's this about, Merc?"

He leaned forward, propping his elbows on my desk, and laced his fingers together. "Funny thing happened this morning."

"Yeah? I could use a good laugh."

"Sun wasn't even up, and I was sound asleep. Your friend, Jubilee, showed up, pounding on my door fierce enough to wake the dead. Next thing I knew, I was dressed and standing in that crazy hole at Theo Caldwell's job site."

"You don't say?"

"What do you think we found?"

"No idea, Merc. Bucket of clams?"

His eyebrow twitched upward. "We managed to keep it out of the morning papers, but they're printing up a special edition even as we speak. Theo Caldwell was hanging from the scaffolding that held up that secret room of his."

I just about fell out of my chair. "Well, that's a kick in the head. Did he off himself?" I knew full well that men like Theo Caldwell never do.

"That's what it looked like at first glance. The coroner says otherwise, though."

I shrugged. "No shortage of folks who thought Caldwell ought to dance at the end of a rope."

"Including you?"

"I'd be lying if I said I was the least bit sorry Theo Caldwell is pushing up daisies. But that doesn't mean I killed him. I went out for dinner on the west end and was gone most of the night."

"The west end? There's nothin' out there. Any witnesses who can vouch for you?"

There was one, but he's not telling any tales. "Probably not. I'm not the kind of guy who stands out in a crowd. But you're holdin' out on me, Merc. What sent Theo Caldwell to the Pearly Gates? My bet is somebody ventilated him."

"You'd lose that bet. He choked to death on a gold doubloon."

I stood on the pier next to the Bleached Barnacle. Dusk was nearly night, and Jubilee would be along soon.

I couldn't stop thinking about Thomas Reid. He was cursed to guard Lafitte's treasure until the old pirate came for it. But Lafitte was long dead. Tomorrow, the city would start pumping concrete into the hole at Caldwell's construction site. Too much damage had been done to just fill it back up with sand.

If there was any way to free Reid, it would most likely be gone tomorrow. But then again, he might want to stay put. For all I know, he's got a ticket straight to Hell. Not my lookout, though.

Water splashed on my feet. "Hey!"

"Laurent Deforest!"

I looked over the railing to see Zara's head and shoulders poking out of the water. "I have been looking for you!"

"Oh? I had been plannin' to look you up, too. But then I got the scoop. What do you want with me?"

Zara bobbed slightly as she spoke, her golden-brown hair floating like seaweed behind her. "The seagulls brought news that Theo Caldwell was searching for Lafitte's gold."

"Yeah. He didn't get it though, and he's taking a dirt nap now."

"Did you meet Thomas Reid? Was he still there?"

Well blow me down and shiver me timbers. "How do you know Tom?"

"He was my friend. Thomas Reid would sit in a dinghy and read books to me. There was one about a family shipwrecked upon an island that I liked especially." She scowled and her sharp teeth glinted above the water. "I saw what Lafitte did to him."

"Tom told us all about it."

"I tried on several occasions to avenge him. When Lafitte was being rowed from the shore to his ship, I seized upon his hand and strove to draw him into the water. But the others in the small boat held him fast, and I only captured his signet ring."

Je suis désolé. "Well, I'm sorry to say that poor old Tom is trapped with the treasure until Lafitte returns."

Zara grinned. "Stay here. I shall be back shortly."

Her head dipped below the dark waters.

I paced the dock, wondering whether Zara or Jubilee would show up first. Even with my coat, I was shivering. A stiff breeze gusted off the water. It wasn't long before I heard a big splash.

"Laurent DeForest!"

"Still here."

A heavy clunk sounded near my feet, then something metal skittered across the planks. A gold ring with a thick, ornate top came to rest in a crack between two rough boards. I picked it up and squinted at it.

Zara's voice carried up from the water. "There is a woman inside the Barnacle reading cards. She is called Tituba. Tell her that I sent you to call in the favor she owes me. She must compel Jean Lafitte's accursed spirit to appear at the time and place of your choosing."

"Whatcha got, Laurie?"

I jumped. Hadn't noticed Jubilee comin' up behind me from downwind. I glanced into the water, but Zara had gone. "Jean Lafitte's signet ring. Come on."

The Barnacle was not especially busy. Half the tables were filled, and a handful of fellas jockeyed barstools. I spotted an elderly woman at a table in the corner farthest from the bar. A man dressed mostly in green with long, pointed ears sat across from her while she laid out Tarot cards. He nodded as she spoke.

I glanced around, but didn't see Rhona. Part of me was disappointed, but the other part was grateful not to have the distraction.

At last, the man in green got up and left. Jubilee and I legged it over to her table before anybody else could sit down.

She looked up, one cataract-covered eye as white as the hair swept into a loose braid that disappeared over her shoulder. "You're late."

"Sorry." *Didn't know I had an appointment.*

She shuffled the cards a few times, then laid one down. A heart pierced with three daggers. "Three of Swords. Heartbreak and sorrow."

She put down another. Two animals, not sure if they were dogs or donkeys, looked up at the Man in the Moon while a lobster in a pond eyeballed them. "The Moon. Secrets."

I shifted my weight. She got that right.

The last card. A building with the top being blasted off and people falling out. "The Tower. Destruction."

She tapped each card, starting with the stabbed heart. "Past… present…future. The old must be destroyed to make way for the new. It will not be pleasant."

I nodded. "Thank you, ma'am. But what about Lafitte? We're kinda pressed for time."

She stared at me with her good eye, and I felt naked. *Merde!*

Jubilee nudged my shoulder.

I swallowed and tried to force a smile. "Sorry, ma'am."

Tituba reached into a pocket in her grey dress and pulled out a pouch. "Have you the item the siren gave you?"

I handed her the ring. She turned it to look at every surface, then muttered words I couldn't understand. The room got darker, but no one else seemed to notice.

Once Tituba finished, she dropped the ring into the pouch and pulled the drawstring tight before handing it to me. "Go to the place you want the pirate to appear. Speak his name thrice. Command his shade, and when he has done your bidding, say, 'Return from whence you came.' If he resists you, call upon the Goddess Hecate, for she carries the keys to the gates of the underworld."

"Sounds jake. What do I do with the ring?"

She looked at me like I was some kind of Dumb Dora. "Do with it?"

"Yeah. Do I toss it in the drink? Burn it? What?"

"Once you have accepted the gris gris, it is yours to safeguard. Summon Lafitte as you will." She tapped the Tower card on the table. "But beware. It may behoove you to call upon him in only the direst of straits."

I looked at the pouch and suddenly wanted to hand it back. Instead, I stuffed it into my pocket. "Thank you, ma'am."

She gathered the cards from the table and reshuffled them into the deck. She raised her eyes to mine. "Why do you remain?"

She didn't have to tell me twice. Jubilee and I hoofed it over to Caldwell's site. She did her thing with the guard, and we hustled down into the hidden chamber. A few inches of water covered the floor now.

"Tom?" Jubilee called.

Seconds passed. At last, he appeared. "Ahoy." The fearsome pirate from yesterday looked nothing but glum.

I squeezed the leather bag in my pocket. "Jean Lafitte! Jean Lafitte! Jean Lafitte!"

Tom looked at me like I'd lost my marbles.

The temperature of the air around us plunged. I turned to Jubilee, and she raised a finger to her lips.

An angry groan filled the chamber. Green sparks flashed around the room, then slowly swirled together. A scowling Jean Lafitte stepped out of the green light.

He bared his teeth when his eyes fell on Tom. "You!"

"The Devil take you, Lafitte!" Tom raised his cutlass.

"Tom!" Jubilee shouted.

His burning eyes turned to her.

"Hold your horses. What was it Lafitte said before he murdered you?"

Tom's eyes narrowed. "He said, 'You will guard this treasure until I return.' Them's the last words I heard."

I cut my eyes to his former boss. "Looks like he's returned."

Tom began to chuckle.

A pale blue light rose from where the hole in the back of the room had been. The water began to bubble. Tom's head snapped back, causing his wound to gape open. His arm lifted until it stuck straight out from his shoulder, his fingers extended. The light flickered over him.

Jean Lafitte snarled and took a step forward. "No!"

"Silence!" Jubilee growled.

Tom began to disappear. "I'm free!" He laughed. "I'm free! Thank ye, thank ye, and following seas to ya."

He vanished, and the blue light faded away. The water stilled, and the only sound was the angry mumbling of Jean Lafitte.

I elbowed Jubilee. "How do I get rid of him, again?"

She whispered in my ear, "Return from whence you came."

I repeated those words. It took three tries to banish the surly salt, but he finally beat it.

Jubilee and I climbed out of the secret room and left the site. I looked to my left as we strolled down the seawall. The electric Christmas lights on Twenty-Third Street sparkled in the distance.

Some folks believe that when people die, their souls become stars in the sky. I looked up, wondering if Eddie and Thomas Reid were up there somewhere. If the nuns and orphans were still bound together like Orion's Belt, or if being found set them free to find their long-lost families.

"You okay, Laurie? Jubilee squeezed my arm.

"Yeah. Just glad Caldwell paid up front. How much gold you think is in that treasure chest?"

She elbowed me. "Does it matter? Tom is free. Perhaps it's best to leave Lafitte's gold lie. I don't think any good will come of it, so burying it in concrete's probably for the best."

I shrugged. "Could be. Wet your whistle at the Barnacle?"

"I should check on my girls. Merry Christmas, Laurie."

Speaking of girls, maybe Rhona would be working tonight. "*Joyeux Noel*, Jubilee."

We walked toward the lights. I had some time to kill before moonrise.

HEAT

By Artemis Greenleaf

RELAX, Mom." I pulled my boot laces tighter. "It's just a two-hour hike. I'll be back in plenty of time to go to lunch with you and Aunt Fiona and then finish up our Christmas shopping."

"Giselle." Mom bit her lip. "I wish you wouldn't go. I have a bad feeling about this."

"It'll be fine. I really need to get some fresh air and decompress. You and Grandma have been bickering nonstop, and if I hear another Christmas carol this morning, I'm gonna hurt somebody. You don't want to spend your Christmas money on bail, do you?" I was only half kidding.

Without a word, my mother turned on her heel and strode into the kitchen. A moment later, she returned with a box of granola bars and started tucking them into the small pack I carried for things like car keys, phone, and first aid kit.

"What are you doing?"

"You might get hungry. It's cold out."

I sighed. Gina Radcliff was not one to be dissuaded. "Fine, Mom. I'll save room for lunch."

Her lips tightened. "You'd better."

"Alright. I'm off. See you later. Love you."

"Love you, too."

The drive north to my planned national forest hike took just over an hour. The sky was that cloudless shade of lapis that only comes during winter, after a cold front has chased away the humidity and the low-angled sun hoards his heat for summer. The temperature hovered in the upper thirties, and I expected it to warm up to around fifty by the time I headed home. Early morning light sparkled on the frost that blanketed the rolling hills. At first glance, I thought it was snow. That happens so rarely here that it would have been a huge deal—maybe even a once-in-a-lifetime event—to see that much of it. I sang my gloriously carol-free playlist at the top of my lungs as I drove along the mostly deserted interstate.

When I arrived at the park, I stopped at the ranger station, then found the trailhead. There were only a handful of cars in the parking lot, and I relished the idea of having the trails mostly to myself.

Patches of night still clung to the feet of towering loblolly pines that scrubbed the sky each time a fresh breeze hurried through their branches, making them sigh like ocean waves. The woods smelled like Christmas without the crowds and noise. With each step, I felt my stress fall away and my spirits lift.

At about forty-five minutes into my hike, I heard a woman screaming. I was miles from any cell service. I pulled the foldable saw out of my pack, partly to mark one of the trees so I could find the place again, and partly to use as a weapon if need be. First, I'd check on the woman, then go find a ranger. The screaming intensified. Were two women screaming? If they were being assaulted or something, I couldn't just leave them to their fate.

"Hello?" I called out, hoping to frighten off a possible attacker.

The screaming stopped. I listened, but mostly heard my heart thudding in my ears. Twigs and dead grass crackled as I took a few steps off the path.

The screaming started up again. The noise didn't sound that far off the trail, so I gripped the saw handle tightly but didn't take the time to blaze any trunks. What if they weren't being attacked, but were injured? A broken leg would make anybody scream.

I followed the sound as quickly as I could, but away from the manicured trail, the forest floor became rough and littered with debris. I topped a rise and froze. The source of the screaming stood below.

Two large cougars faced off, arguing about something. One flicked an ear in my direction. As much as I wanted to pull out my phone and take a photo, I didn't dare stick around—just backed away slowly. If I didn't bother them, they wouldn't bother me. Hopefully.

My best option was to go back the way I'd come. If I could just figure that out. The path to the cougar drama had been winding, and now all the ramrod-straight pines looked alike. I'd left no footprints in the thick bed of pine needles and cones, so I couldn't retrace my steps.

Okay. Don't panic. You aren't that far from the path. You'll be fine.

I was not, in fact, fine. I crumpled a granola bar wrapper and pushed it into my pack, grateful for my mother's meddling. After hours of walking, darkness was settling on the forest. How could that trail be so hard to find? I felt like Little Red Riding Hood, only there were no flowers to pick. At least the Big Bad Wolf would be waiting at Grandma's house and not out here—although my chances with BBW might be better than with my mother, whom I'd promised I'd take out for lunch and shopping. I sighed. Probably should have listened to her. Her hunches are usually right. But I had to get out of that crowded madhouse and stretch my legs in the fresh air to get some peace.

"Hello? Anybody out there?" I shouted, my voice raspy from yelling all day.

No answer came, so I started walking again. The park road made a big C, so if I continued in a more or less straight line, I would surely find it eventually. If not the road, then the lake. There I could follow the shoreline until I came to a boat ramp.

The afternoon light was fading quickly, so I thought it might be in my best interest to find a spot to rest for the night. I didn't want to be on the ground if I could help it. At least two mountain lions lurked in the park, and feral pigs roamed the area. They'd eat anything they came across, plant or animal, living or dead. I'd prefer not to be an easy meal.

No way I could shimmy up one of those loblollys, so I hoped to find a live oak with low, thick branches. Even better would be a campsite, but I wasn't going to get my hopes up.

A stick snapped behind me.

I whirled around. "Hello? Is somebody there?"

Something dark lurked behind a stand of yaupon that swelled beneath a cluster of bare trees. The holly still had its tiny green leaves, and red-orange berries dotted the spindly fingers of white bark.

I couldn't tell what it was through the tangle of branches. It stood on all fours, and from the size, it had to be a deer. Except for the color. There were no black deer, at least not in east Texas. As far as I knew.

The hair on the back of my neck snapped to attention. The thing was watching me. Every instinct I had shouted at me to run. If that was a predator, and I took off running, its reflex would be to chase. And I doubted that would end well for me.

I backed away, carefully placing my feet so as not to trip over a fallen branch or spiky pinecone and twist my ankle. I kept telling myself the creature in the bushes was probably just some weird mutant deer, and we'd go our separate ways, no harm, no foul.

Twilight thickened into dark, and the chill wind picked up, thrashing the limbs above me. Black clouds scudded across the fragments of sky I could see through the naked trees above the yaupon.

I continued maneuvering backward, and the thing in the bushes continued watching me. At least I thought so, as I hadn't heard any crackling leaves or breaking sticks coming toward me. After listening for a little while, I decided that the animal and I were on separate journeys, and I turned to walk forward.

I pulled the emergency flashlight out of my pack. It was a small, very bright LED—at least when it had fresh batteries. The dim light barely made any dent in the frigid blackness. The combination of a cold front coming in and the sun setting made for a whole lot of unpleasantness. My coat was water resistant; my boots and hat were not. As long as it didn't rain, I'd be okay.

The instant I had that thought, a wet dot of ice hit my cheek, then another and another. Oh, good. Sleet. The ice crystals melted as soon as they touched my warm skin. It wasn't exactly pelting down, but it wasn't all frozen either, and my warm woolly hat would soon be a soggy ice pack.

I found a tree with a low-hanging branch. I wouldn't be able to climb the tree and hold my flashlight, so I turned it off and put it in my pocket. Unfortunately, the tree wasn't a live oak or evergreen, so I didn't have any mercy from the weather, just open sky. Not ideal, but better than being hog bait.

I climbed as far as I dared and was figuring out a way to brace myself so I could snooze without falling. I hadn't been there long before I heard the noise of footsteps on the forest floor.

Something that sounded four-legged approached the tree. Suddenly, two frosty orbs appeared down below. They were perfectly round with a silvery glow. Made me think of two miniature full moons.

Wait. Are those... eyes?

As whatever that was stared up at me, an icy finger ran up and down my body, mapping out my features and stealing my warmth. I rubbed my hands together to keep some semblance of feeling in them. After a long moment passed, the thing dropped its gaze and shuffled away.

I was definitely creeped out, but I was also hungry and exhausted. I rooted around inside my pack until I found a granola bar. It wasn't nearly enough, so I had a second one. I'd save the rest for later. It took some doing, but I secured myself in the branches with my pack over my head to keep the ice off my face.

Cold rain had started to seep through my jacket, and I wished I'd brought my bigger pack, the one with a rain slicker and extra socks. The knotty, wet bark dug into my body and froze my skin. I was concerned the white-eyed creature would come back, but I also knew that if I got no rest, tomorrow would be worse. Exhaustion won out over anxiety, and I slept in fits and starts.

I found myself inside a small round house whose ceiling narrowed to a point. A fire blazed in a pit at the center, and I moved closer to it, basking in its warmth. A man appeared across the fire from me. He sat cross-legged, eyes closed. His long, dark hair was in two braids that hung over his shoulders, and a carved shell medallion glimmered in the firelight on his bare chest. Where did he come from? He hadn't been here a moment ago.

"Hello?" I wasn't sure what else to say.

His eyes popped open, and I shrank away from him. They were silver, and at this close range, I could see an iridescent film over them.

He did not speak, but I heard his voice in my head. "Leave. You are not welcome here."

"I don't even know how I got here, much less how to find my way home."

He vanished. I continued to sit by the fire until I heard someone call my name. It sounded very far away, just at the edge of my hearing.

My eyes snapped open. I was still in the tree. Dawn was turning the night's impenetrable blackness to shades of grey. The sleet had stopped falling, but the precipitation had frozen, coating both trees and ground in a layer of ice.

I was cold, stiff, and sore. I shifted to a more upright position, ice on my coat crackling and falling to the ground. "Hello?" My voice was scarcely above a whisper. No one would hear that unless they were sitting on the branch next to me. I was so thirsty. I listened closely, hoping to hear my name again and get a bearing on the direction it came from. The only sound was the creaking and cracking of ice-encased trees.

Using the handle of my folded saw, I chipped some ice from the tree bark and put it in my mouth. It was gritty with wood particles, but at least it was wet.

I started down the icy trunk and slipped almost immediately. I caught myself on a branch that broke as it took my weight. My perch was eight or ten feet up the tree—high enough to knock the wind out of me when I crashed to the ground.

It felt like a very long time that I lay on that frosty bed of leaves, gasping for air. I was finally able to breathe and sit up. I had no idea which direction I'd come from last night. One thing that was clear, though, was the tracks left behind by the white-eyed thing from last night. In a muddy patch of bare earth, there was what at first looked like the print of a bare human foot, but the deep claw marks at the ends of the toes gave it away as a bear track. From a large bear. I'd seen plenty of them in other places I'd hiked. But never here.

The good news was that I knew where to go—the opposite direction from where those tracks were headed.

I stopped to get my bearings many times. Due to my completely numb feet, I had to watch each step I made through this winter wonderland. I wondered if I would ever get out of here.

A gust of wind blasted through, and several ice-laden tree limbs crashed to the ground, as if an invisible giant was walking past.

Between my unfeeling fingers and hard shivering, it was nearly impossible to get a granola bar out of my pack. I had to tear the wrapper with my teeth.

I continued walking, my feet like stone clubs at the ends of my legs. I'd stumbled onto a game trail, so the going was a little easier. I paused to look around. Some way up ahead, the white-eyed bear stood in the middle of the trail.

It had a small patch of white on its chest, almost as if it was wearing a necklace.

The bear must have circled around and come back for me. I thought about its thick, shaggy fur and how warm that must be. I had already taken a few steps when it occurred to me that it probably wasn't looking for a cuddle.

I slipped and nearly fell changing directions. My own footprints in the frost warped and twisted into bear tracks. I shook my head and closed my eyes. When I opened them, I saw nothing more than bootprints.

Without warning, I was sweating. I was so hot I had to take off my coat. This was a bad sign. It meant the veins squeezing the blood into my core to keep it warm were fatigued, and warm blood was flowing to my extremities. It felt good for now. But I knew it would quickly cool and I'd be worse off than before. I had to get out of here.

I spent the entire day walking and being herded by the bear. So many times, I started on one path and he stood ahead of me. Once, I'd stopped in some bushes to answer nature's call and the bear passed by on the trail. I peered at it through ice-encased branches, and it looked like a dozen bears, distorted and shattered by refraction. I couldn't tell where the real bear was. It had paused, head turned toward the quaking stand of shrubbery where I crouched, before going on its way. I didn't know what it wanted, but I knew it was always watching me, even when I couldn't see it.

Shadows lengthened and dusk approached, bleeding from the thick trunks at the bottom of the forest's canopy. The wind had been blowing almost steadily throughout the day. I couldn't feel my face and I wasn't entirely sure who I was and why I was here. I shook my head, trying to clear the cobwebs, and crashed face-first into something thin and metal.

Iron. I tasted iron and couldn't tell if it was blood or the metal pole I'd just run into. I was at the foot of an abandoned hunting blind. It was on a rickety tripod and the bottom of it was only a few feet above my head. I felt around until I found the ladder and climbed up the icy rungs.

The accommodations were far from luxurious—the five square feet reeked of cigar smoke and stale beer—but I was out of the wind. I cried with relief, although I was too dehydrated to make any tears. I ate my last granola bar and curled up on the stained carpet tiles to rest.

As tired as I was, I could not sleep. The breeze in the frozen branches sounded like angry whispers. I peeked out one of the narrow windows. The chilly wind had pushed the heavy clouds away. The crescent moon hovered just above the treetops, glowing with cold fire. After a long time, I drowsed off. I dreamed I was in my mother's living room, a fire crackling in the fireplace, and a large dog stretched out beside me. Which was odd, because neither my mother nor I had a dog. I was petting it, and my hand reached farther and farther down its back. There seemed to be no end to it. A low growl startled me awake.

The bear's face was inches from mine. The holographic swirls over its silver eyes were both fascinating and terrifying. It growled again, and I scrambled to my feet, opening the door of the blind and clambering down the metal ladder.

I'd been using my pack as a pillow, and one strap was still looped over my shoulder. The free strap caught on the top of the stair and I slipped. No choice but to go back up a few rungs and hope I didn't meet the bear coming down. The pack came free after I jostled it with my shoulder, finally allowing my escape.

I was tired. So tired. I sobbed as I stumbled through the undergrowth. Again, the sweating. So hot. I unzipped my coat as I flailed my way along. For a second, I thought I was in a desert. Tall cacti loomed around me instead of trees. It was only when I bumped into an icy sapling that I realized my eyes had been closed. Had I fallen asleep as I ran? A glance over my shoulder showed the bear following my trail in the shadows. And it was gaining on me.

The darkness began to lift, but thick fog swallowed the trees and dampened any sounds. I had to slow my pace. I wanted to sink to my knees in despair, but the footfalls of the silver-eyed bear crunched steadily behind me.

Up ahead, a wide swath of something glowed pale orange. I blinked and shook my head, but when I opened my eyes, it was still there. I wracked my frozen brain to remember where I'd seen something like that before.

A FLIR image. Tracked heat instead of visible light. And that long, flat thing?

The road. The park road! I ran as best I could. It was less a run and more of a slipping and sliding through the frozen undergrowth. I fell twice, maybe more. If I could just get to the road.

Sleigh bells erupted to my left, followed by the first few bars of "Jingle Bells." I have never been so happy to hear a Christmas song in my life. The music stopped and a man's voice said, "Hello?"

Someone's there! "Help! Please help me!" My voice was so raspy, even I could barely hear it. I had to keep going. Had to get to the road.

An engine growled to life.

No! No! Don't leave!

I forced my numb feet to move faster. I couldn't tell if I covered more ground by running or sliding. There was a steep drop-off from the edge of the pavement above to a ditch where I stood. The water that had collected there was frozen solid and as slippery as... well, ice.

I tried to claw my way up the bank, but it was almost as tall as me, and even if there had been any roots or branches to grab, I couldn't feel my hands.

Waving my right arm and shouting, "Help! Help me!" I didn't know if the man could see or hear me. If he was facing away...

Slap. Slap. Slap. Boots pounding on the asphalt. More than one pair. Soon, two dark figures peered down at me from the road.

"Giselle Radcliff?" the one on the left asked, as long limbs reached for my outstretched arms.

Was that my name? The world suddenly went dark.

I held the button to raise the upper end of my hospital bed. They'd treated me for hypothermia and dehydration, and I was just waiting on the doctor to sign off on my release so I could go home.

One of the park rangers who'd pulled me out of the ditch had come to the hospital to see me before I went home. My mom went to ask the nurse about my paperwork. After I told the ranger how I'd had my encounter with the cougars and gotten hopelessly lost, he said, "As near as we can tell, you managed to wander into one of the wilderness preservation areas where there aren't any trails and kept walking in circles."

"I sure didn't think it at the time, but I'm grateful for that bear."

The ranger cocked his head. "What bear?"

"The one that stalked me while I was out there. It chased me to the road, where you found me. Luckiest coincidence ever."

"Are you sure it was a bear?"

"Of course! It was black with a white patch on its chest. And it was blind. Its eyes were a silvery white. I know bears have a great sense of smell, but I had the feeling it was tracking me by my heat signature. I never heard it sniffing or snuffling. Just followed my trail with its eyes and looked straight at me. Sounds weird, I know."

"Yeah. Especially since there haven't been any bears here in over a hundred years."

CANTUS
By Pandora Martindale

THE Vatican Secret Archives never truly slept, but at 11:47 PM, Mike Torres was alone in Reading Room East with nothing but centuries of preserved silence for company. His dissertation on medieval liturgical music wouldn't write itself, and Dr. Kellerman's deadline was approaching fast.

The folder's contents were typical—fragments of Mass settings, incomplete motets, plainchant notation. But at the bottom, almost hidden beneath the other documents, was a single sheet of parchment that made Mike's breath catch.

The notation was unlike anything he'd seen. Complex, angular, with accidentals creating jarring dissonances against what should have been a simple Christmas carol. At the top, written in Gothic script: *"Cantus ad Evocandos Dominos Hiemis"*—Song for Summoning the Lords of Winter.

Beneath that, in a different hand, someone had scrawled a desperate warning in medieval German: *"Niemals singen. Gott vergebe mir, ich habe gehört."*—Never sing. God forgive me, I have listened.

Is this from some pagan winter solstice ritual? Really surprised to see it here.

The Vatican's collection of forbidden texts was kept elsewhere, under lock and key in sections that required special clearance he definitely didn't have. How had something like this ended up misfiled with routine liturgical music?

Mike photographed the document, then leaned closer to study the notation. The melody was in D minor, but the augmented fourths created tritones—the "devil's interval" that medieval composers had been forbidden to use.

He hummed the first phrase softly, just to understand the harmonic structure.

The sound echoed strangely in the reading room, lingering longer than it should. Mike glanced around, suddenly aware of how isolated he was. Behind him, something rustled among the ancient shelves. He was alone. Perhaps it was just settling wood or central heat.

The Latin beneath the notation seemed easier to read than it should have been, and Mike found himself translating aloud, his voice finding the melody's rhythm:

"Venite ad sempervirentem altam et obscuram et profundam,

Ubi liberi hiemis cantus suos canunt et secreta Natalis custodiunt..."

Come to the evergreen, tall and dark and deep,

Where winter's children sing their songs and Christmas secrets keep...

The temperature dropped. His breath began to fog. Each phrase built on the last, creating progressions that unlocked something deep in his consciousness—something that had been waiting in the silence between notes.

Mike paused mid-phrase, the Latin dying on his lips. His peripheral vision caught motion by the far bookshelf—a shadow too tall and angular to belong to anything in the room. He turned his head sharply but saw only the familiar rows of ancient texts stretching into darkness.

Just tired eyes, he told himself.

A whisper drifted from somewhere behind him, so faint he couldn't make out the words—if they were words at all. It sounded almost like someone humming the same melody he'd been singing, but in a voice that seemed to come from a great distance. Mike spun around in his chair, scanning the empty reading room.

Nothing. Just the hum of climate control and the distant tick of an antique clock.

Mike slept deeper than he had in months, the old carol threading through his dreams. He woke at 11:23 AM, having missed three alarms and his morning research session.

Crap! He scrambled out of bed to try to salvage the rest of the day.

The tune was still running through his mind as he shaved. The razor caught skin near his chin. A drop of blood welled up, bright red against white cream. Mike stared at it in the mirror, transfixed.

Beautiful.

He blinked, shaking his head, and finished shaving. But he kept glancing back at the small red stain on the tissue.

The cafe was in that liminal zone between breakfast and lunch—most tables empty, the staff preparing for the noon rush. Mike took a table by the window with his panino and coffee, humming softly. In the far corner, a figure perched like a smear of soot in a shadowy booth.

The person—Mike couldn't tell if it was a man or woman— wore a dark coat with the hood pulled up despite being indoors. They sat perfectly still, not eating or drinking, just... waiting. Something about the posture made Mike's skin crawl, the way the head angled, as if listening intently.

Mike decided to be friendly, maybe practice his Italian. He stood up and walked toward the corner booth.

The figure was gone.

A busboy clearing nearby tables, glanced up. *"Scusi?"*

"Someone was sitting here," Mike said in halting Italian. "Where did they go?"

The young man looked confused. "No one sits there, *signore.* It has been empty all morning."

Mike stared at the booth. The seat cushion wasn't indented, as if no one had been there at all.

"Tutto bene?" the busboy asked. "Are you all right?"

"Sì, sì," Mike replied automatically, but his hands shook as he returned to his table. He found himself humming again, louder this time, the melody seeming to drown out his racing thoughts.

Just stressed about the dissertation. Nothing more.

But as he finished his breakfast, Mike caught himself tracing patterns on the condensation of his water glass—angular symbols that looked almost like letters, though he couldn't say from what alphabet.

The Christmas market at Piazza Navona buzzed with holiday energy. Wooden stalls lined the baroque square, selling everything from handmade ornaments to roasted chestnuts, their smoky aroma mingling with the scent of mulled wine and pine garland. The other graduate students from the Vatican program clustered around their guide, Dr. Castellano, as she explained the history of the Italian Christmas traditions.

Mike stood near Sofia, a doctoral candidate whose laugh always made his stomach flutter. She was examining a display of hand-carved nativity figures, her dark hair catching the warm glow of string lights overhead.

"The craftsmanship is incredible." She glanced at Mike. "Look at the detail in the angel's wings."

He nodded, but his attention was snatched away from the delicate ornament. Across the crowded piazza, near a stall selling Christmas trees, stood the same hooded figure from the cafe. Even in the festive chaos, it remained perfectly still, with that unnatural head tilt as if listening.

"Mike?" Sofia touched his arm. "You okay?"

"Sorry, thought I saw someone I knew." When he glanced back, the figure was gone.

As they walked, Mike found himself humming the old carol.

"That's a pretty tune," Sofia said. "What is it?"

"Just something from my research." Even as the words came out, he was reluctant to share more. The song felt private. Not yet ready.

As the group paused to toss coins into the fountain, he saw the figure again—this time beckoning from a narrow alley. Mike's feet moved before his brain caught up. The hooded figure led him deeper into Rome's labyrinthine heart, always just around the next corner.

The alley dead-ended at a courtyard with a crumbling stone statue. The figure pulled back its hood.

The face beneath was human, but barely. Features stretched and elongated, eyes solid black, each a tiny abyss that swallowed light and hope. Too many teeth bristled from its bony jaws.

"Sing," it demanded, the word rippling with multiple harmonics as if a dozen people spoke at once.

A cat yowled—harsh, discordant. Mike stumbled backward. The courtyard was empty.

"Mike! Where are you?" Sofia's voice echoed through the maze. He ran toward the sound, bursting into the crowded market.

"What happened?" Sofia asked, concern widening her eyes.

"Got turned around." His heart still raced. As they walked back, Mike stopped at a jewelry stall. His hand moved without direction, picking up a small medallion—golden metal worked into a radiating sun face, its sharp rays extending outward like a compass rose.

"How much?" he asked the vendor in Italian.

"Ah, *Sol Invictus*," the wrinkled woman said, turning it to catch the light. "The Unconquered Sun. Very old design, from before the Church. On the longest night, we remember: the sun always returns." She smiled. "For you, ten euro."

Mike paid and pinned it to his lapel, careful not to jab his fingers on the sharp rays. It felt right there, like it belonged.

The melody was still playing in his head, more insistent now. And for the first time, Mike had the urge to share it.

The song wanted to be heard.

Back in his hotel room, Mike pulled out his phone and opened NoteScan Pro, an app that converted sheet music to audio. He uploaded the clearest photo of the manuscript.

"Translation complete," the app announced. "Would you like to preview?"

The digital rendering was haunting but wrong—the harmonies seemed flattened. Mike hummed along, filling in what was missing. His voice found harmonies the app couldn't capture.

Mike lost track of time, his voice growing stronger with each repetition. The room faded. There was only the music now, perfect and eternal, each note clicking into place like pieces of an ancient puzzle. Behind the music, he heard other voices joining in, distant but drawing closer.

Blink.

Mike stood in the bathroom, staring at his reflection. The razor blade from this morning lay in his palm, though he couldn't remember taking it out of the shaver. His left hand was covered in small cuts, still oozing.

His phone showed the carol had been looping for two hours.

On the mirror, drawn in blood, was an angular symbol that pulsed with sickly light. It shifted when he tried to look at it directly, and through the mirror's surface, the glass rippled like disturbed water.

The hooded creature that had lured him down the alley yesterday stood right behind his reflection, its array of wicked teeth glistening under the naked bulb. It hadn't been there a moment ago.

With a cry, Mike hurled himself away from the thing, stumbling over the toilet and crashing into the wallpaper with a thud. He turned, his back against the wall.

He was alone in the bathroom.

But in the mirror, more hooded figures, each more ghastly than the last, climbed through the glass and walked out the door. He lunged into the bedchamber, but it was as empty as he had left it.

Mike shook his head and ran his hands through his hair. *Am I losing my mind? Is this place infested with mold that's making me hallucinate? I gotta get out of here.*

As he buttoned his shirt, a knock interrupted his anxious rationalization. Sofia stood in the hallway, looking uncertain. "I wanted to check on you after the market."

"I'm fine." He wasn't sure that was true.

"Have you eaten? A few of us are heading to a trattoria."

As he grabbed his coat, Sofia noticed his phone. "What's that?"

"A Christmas carol from the 15th century. I was curious how it sounded..." The compulsion to share was overwhelming. "Can I play it for you?"

His finger hit play before he could stop himself. Sofia tilted her head, concentrating. Mike hummed along, adding harmonies the digital version couldn't convey.

"That's gorgeous," Sofia breathed. "I wonder if they'll sing this at tomorrow's concert."

As they left, she began humming softly.

Mike woke to insistent knocking. Sofia stood in the hallway, eyes glassy and distant, humming under her breath.

"I couldn't sleep," she said. "That song kept playing in my head."

Mike noticed fresh cuts on her fingertips.

"Sofia, what happened to your hands?"

"Nothing. Mike, we need to share the carol. People should hear it properly."

Footsteps echoed off terrazzo. An elderly nun rounded the corner, face grave.

"You are the American student researching medieval music?" Her English was accented but precise. "I am Sister Benedetta."

"I'm Mike." He turned his head. "And this is Sofia. We were just on our way to the concert, and—"

"Where did you get this?" She touched the golden sun with reverent fingers.

Mike answered, "At the Christmas market," but the nun was too busy muttering in Latin to pay attention. His insides went cold, and he shuddered.

Sister Benedetta opened her eyes. "*Sol Invictus.* The Unconquered Sun—older than our faith, older than their summoning. Light that cannot be extinguished, even at winter's darkest hour." Her voice dropped. "It might help, if you have the courage to use it. The sun at solstice is at its weakest... but it is unconquered. It *will* grow stronger. They cannot abide that truth. And may God help you if you must wield it." She crossed herself. "You found something sealed away for good reason."

"I don't know what—"

"*The Cantus ad Evocandos Dominos Hiemis.*" Her voice was sharp as the winter wind. "You photographed it three days ago. We saw you on the security cameras. And now it begins again."

"It's just a Christmas carol," Sofia said dreamily.

Sister Benedetta crossed herself. "That is not a carol. That is a summoning. "

She pulled out a small leather journal. "Brother Augustine documented the outbreak in 1423. Read his final entry."

Mike's hands trembled as he read the faded Latin:

"The song spreads like a plague. Each voice that joins opens another door. I have seen them—the *Hiemis Domini*, the Winter Lords. The carol is an invitation. We thought we destroyed every copy, but the song remembers itself. It teaches itself to those who hear it. If any find this, the song must not be performed. It must not be shared. It must not...."

The entry ended in an illegible scrawl.

Sofia stopped humming. Her eyes cleared, terror flooding them. "Mike, what have we done?"

He felt the pull even now—the desire to play the NoteScan Pro recording for Sister Benedetta, to convince her how beautiful the melody truly was. With effort, he pushed the urge down.

The nun scowled. "What *have* you done?"

Sofia's eyes fell to her injured hands.

Sister Benedetta gasped. "You have let them in! We must stop the concert! Before it is too late."

By the time they reached St. Peter's Square, the concert had begun—and something was terribly wrong.

The Vatican choir's movements were puppet-like. Their eyes had rolled back, showing only white. When they opened their mouths, the voices that emerged were layered with impossible harmonics.

They were singing the summoning.

Around the piazza, reality fractured. The temperature plummeted. Cobblestones cracked as frost spread in geometric patterns. Above the stage, the air tore open.

Through the widening rifts, Mike saw them—the Winter Lords—pressing against dimensional barriers. Massive humanoid figures fifteen feet tall, crowned with hoary antlers, their skin black ice, shot through with silver frost.

"We have to stop the choir!" Mike shouted, lunging toward the stage.

Sister Benedetta grabbed his arm. "No! They are vessels now. Stopping them won't close what's already open!"

In the crowd, a woman began humming. Then a man. A child. The melody spread like a contagion, each new voice widening the tears in reality.

Sofia's lips moved. She was humming again, fighting it but losing.

"Sofia, no!" Mike shook her shoulders, but her eyes were glazing over.

The largest Winter Lord pushed its hand through the primary rift, skin jagged as frozen fields, fingers ending in obsidian claws. Where it touched the human world, the air crystallized and shattered. It grabbed the lead soprano, lifting her like a doll. Her screams cut off as frost consumed her from the inside out.

Mike grabbed the dropped microphone stand, swinging it at the creature's wrist. The metal shattered against that glacial flesh.

Another Winter Lord forced its way through a secondary rift, then another. The possessed choir sang louder, their voices harmonizing with the growing chorus in the crowd. Vatican security fired their weapons, but bullets had no effect—the officers may as well have been firing into deep snowbanks.

"Mike!" Sofia's voice was her own for a moment, terror-filled and fading. "I can't—I can't stop—"

She started singing the words, her voice joining the hundreds now spreading across the square. The cuts on her fingers began to bleed.

The largest Winter Lord's other hand emerged, grabbing the edge of the dimensional tear and *pulling*, widening it. Its crowned head began to push through, antlers wreathed in ancient ice.

Mike was utterly helpless. The creatures were too strong, the song too infectious, the portals too many. In seconds, the entire crowd would be possessed, and dozens of these things would flood into the world.

His hand went to his lapel. The sun medallion—Sister Benedetta's cryptic words echoed: *The sun at solstice is at its weakest... but it is unconquered.*

It was all he had left.

Mike yanked the medallion free and charged the nearest Winter Lord—the one still gripping the frozen soprano. He drove the pointed rays deep into the creature's forearm.

Black blood erupted—not liquid, but crystalline shards that jangled like broken glass as they skittered across the platform. The Winter Lord's head snapped toward Mike with a roar that shattered windows across the piazza.

And then it grabbed him.

The cold was worse than death. Mike felt his blood crystallizing in his veins, his thoughts slowing to a frozen crawl. The creature lifted him off his feet—and pulled him to the rift.

"No!" Sister Benedetta screamed.

Mike's legs passed through the dimensional tear. The world beyond was endless winter, a howling void of ice and darkness where dozens of Winter Lords waited. He tried to scream, but the cold had seized his lungs.

The creature dragged him deeper. His torso entered their realm. Through freezing, dying eyes, he watched his hands cross the threshold.

The medallion.

Still clutched in his palm, still embedded in the creature's flesh. Where the golden sun touched the Winter Lord's blood, the wound wasn't healing. It was spreading, cracks of light webbing through the black ice skin like dawn breaking through night.

With the last of his strength, Mike twisted the medallion deeper, driving the sharp rays further into that ancient flesh. The Winter Lord shrieked. Its grip loosened.

Sister Benedetta and Sofia grabbed Mike's ankles. They pulled, but the creature was stronger. For a terrible moment, Mike hung suspended between worlds, being torn in two.

The medallion burned white-hot, radiant as a newborn sun. The cracks in the Winter Lord's arm spread to its shoulder, its chest, racing toward its heart like spring thaw racing over frozen ground. The creature released Mike to claw at its own disintegrating flesh.

Sister Benedetta, Sofia, and Mike tumbled backward onto the stage as the Winter Lord imploded in a shower of black glass. Where its blood fell, the portals collapsed. The possessed choir gasped and went silent. Across the square, the humming stopped.

But the largest rift, where the primary Winter Lord's crowned head still pushed through, held. The creature's eyes—ancient and terrible—locked onto Mike.

He lay on the frigid stage, unable to move, barely breathing. His vision tunneled. This was it. He'd failed. The thing was going to cross over, and there was nothing anyone could do about it.

The wounded Winter Lord's blood touched the edge of the main rift.

The portal spasmed. The lead Winter Lord roared and fought to withdraw, but the tear was contracting around its head like a closing fist. With a reality-shaking scream, the portal snapped shut.

The severed head crumbled to ash. The breeze scattered it across the piazza.

Silence.

The possessed choir collapsed. The temperature normalized. People stirred as if waking from a nightmare they couldn't quite remember.

Sofia knelt beside Mike, helping him sit up. When she looked into his face, she gasped. "Your hair! It's gone completely grey." Her eyes widened, and her jaw worked up and down, struggling to form words. "Can you see me?"

He blinked. Slowly. "Of course. Why?"

"Your eyes...they're silver now."

"What?" His brow furrowed.

"I have a mirror. See for yourself." She pulled a round make-up compact from her tiny crossbody bag and opened it.

Mike took it from her, shocked by the stranger who peered back at him. He touched his hair, staring at the frost-colored strands. He'd crossed the barrier. He'd been in their world, breathed their air, experienced their realm. Perhaps part of him had stayed there.

And what if part of *them* had returned with him? He swallowed.

"Is it over?" Sofia asked, her voice shaking.

Mike looked at the melting fragments of otherworldly ice scattered across the square. The marks on his fingertips from the blood-drawing tingled with cold.

Sister Benedetta cleared her throat. "The portals are sealed," she said quietly. "They can't get through again. At least not here."

But as Vatican security swarmed the scene, and the crowd dispersed in confused clusters, no one noticed the smartphone lying forgotten near the fountain, its screen cracked but still lit, displaying a paused image of the singing choir.

Just waiting for someone to press play.

Concrete Evidence
By Holly Dey

S o, what do you think? You up for it?" Jackie Barber draped the pad over the saddle, newly perched on its rack.

Amity Hudson absently twisted the bridle tag. "I don't know. What's involved in one of these search and rescue operations? I mean, if I have to rappel into a ravine and hoist someone up, Destiny and I don't have the training to do that."

Jackie zipped her coat a little higher and laughed. "No, the sheriff's office just needs eyeballs. They'll do the heavy lifting if we find Loretta."

"Do you think she'll be…."

"I have no idea whether or not she's alive. All I know is that Loretta Mullholland's a graduate student, and they found her car at the reservoir. My cousin Carolyn at the sheriff's office called and asked for volunteers with horses to look for her, because you can cover a lot more ground on horseback than on foot."

Amity hung up Destiny's bridle. "Okay. We're in. I was supposed to go see a matinee of *The Nutcracker* ballet tomorrow with Kathy, but she bailed on me."

"Her loss is my gain. We're going to load the trailer at 6:30 so we can be at the site and ready to go at first light. Bring water and snacks to carry with you. There'll be a volunteer tent set up to pass out sandwiches for lunch."

The winter sun was creeping above the horizon when the trailer pulled into the parking area. Destiny was the first horse to be unloaded, and she snorted at her new surroundings.

Amity patted her glossy black neck. "It's alright, girl. No show today. It's just like a big trail ride, that's all." She tied Destiny to the trailer so she could tack up.

Hirsh, who tied up next to her, peered over his horse's back. "You know this place is haunted, right?" He gave her a knowing look as he tightened the girth on Dixie's saddle. The paint mare flicked an ear in his direction.

"Haunted? What?"

"Yeah. There used to be a town here before they built the dam. An old man refused to give up his house. It was in a hollow out in the scrub. The police forcibly removed him, but he snuck back in. Nobody knew he was there, and when they closed the floodgates and the reservoir filled…. They say his angry spirit still roams the woods out here."

Amity raised an eyebrow. "I hadn't heard that particular urban legend."

Hirsch shook his head. "It's not just a story. My friend runs a paranormal investigation group. "They've caught all kinds of evidence out here. And in that cemetery up the road a little? Blue orbs, every time. A lot of people from that old town are buried there." He straightened Dixie's browband. "This beats spending Saturday at my sister-in-law's Christmas brunch, hands down."

"Interesting." Amity buckled her helmet

The search coordinator assigned all the volunteers to groups and passed out radios. "Listen up, people!" No need for a megaphone. His deep voice carried and ricocheted off the pavement, sharp fragments of sound slicing her ears. "There's some weather coming in this afternoon, so let's not waste any time."

Amity was in a group of five: her friend Susanna from the barn, a husband and wife named Jake and Serena, and Deputy Warren—a compact man with a military flattop—

from the sheriff's office.

Amity and Susanna waved to Jackie, Hirsch, and their other friends as the groups dispersed to their assigned sections of the search grid. They fanned out in their designated area, hoping to find Loretta alive and in one piece. There was always water in the lower areas, but the reservoir only really filled when inches and inches of rain drenched the city.

So far, it was a brisk December day—low fifties, with a wide blue sky above them. But a wall of black clouds loomed on the northern horizon. The air was ominously still, and the crunching of dry grass beneath the horses' hooves was almost unbearably loud.

After a couple of hours of scanning the swampy margins of the flood-control reservoir, Amity's voice was hoarse from calling Loretta's name.

The fingers of a chilly breeze lifted Destiny's mane and caressed Amity's cheek. *Storms may be here sooner than expected.*

Destiny slammed on the brakes and lowered her head, snorting at a fallen log. Amity chuckled and patted the mare's neck. "That's barely even a warm-up jump, silly. I'll bet—"

Amity tilted her head, her eyes on the gnarled roots that reached for the cloudy sky. *Is that a shoe?*

There was a protocol. What was she supposed to do? The morning's brief training slipped through her brain like sand through a sieve. Destiny wheeled around and trotted toward her barn friend, Chapeau.

Susanna looked up. "Amity? What are you—" Her head swiveled toward the log. "Did you find her?"

Amity gulped. "Not sure."

Susana pushed the button on her walkie. "Deputy Warren! Amity's found something."

The volunteers gathered in a loose circle as the deputy rode over to the fallen tree and dismounted. He squatted and investigated whatever was behind the log before standing up and talking on his police radio.

Destiny and Chapeau stood next to each other, eyeing the lush vegetation at their feet.

Susanna leaned toward Amity. "What did you see?"

Amity took in a deep breath and let it out. "A shoe."

"Just laying there?"

"No. Definitely a foot inside."

"Well, did it look like a woman's shoe?"

"I don't know, Suze! It was just a brown hiking boot."

The deputy led his horse over to the group. "Alright. The good news is that it isn't Loretta Mullholland. The bad news is that this is now a potential crime scene. A deputy is on the way to escort you back to the staging area."

"Who's behind the log?" the woman of the married couple asked.

"White male. That's really all I can say about it."

"Was he murdered?" the husband asked, leaning so far forward in his saddle his horse had to shift his weight.

"Homicide and the Medical Examiner's office are on the way. That's their call."

Susanna nudged Amity's leg with the tip of her boot. "Do you think he's the kidnapper? Maybe Loretta killed him."

Amity glanced at the fallen tree. "I hope they're not connected and Loretta's okay."

The snarl of an ATV engine got louder as it approached. A deputy rolled to a stop some distance from the horses.

Deputy Warren gestured toward the new arrival. "He'll take you back to the trailers."

The ride back seemed to take an hour, although it couldn't have been more than half that. The rest of the folks from her barn were already untacked and ready to load by the time Amity and Susanna returned.

"Amity?" A male voice came from behind her.

She turned in the saddle. "Fin?"

After a few professional interactions, she'd run into Detective Myles a number of times at Bunny's Coffee shop. They'd tried meeting up for dinner, but it seemed either she was traveling, or he got called out on a case. She'd decided it just wasn't meant to be.

Nora, Fin's partner, was already climbing into a Gator ATV.

"I'll call you later!" Fin waved at Amity before turning to join Detective Farmer.

Susanna slid off Chapeau and peered under his neck at Amity. "*Who* was that?"

"Don't you remember him from a couple of years ago? When you-know-who got killed?"

"Never saw him." Susanna shrugged. "But if he needs to interview somebody, give him my number."

Heat rushed to Amity's cheeks, and she hid it by dismounting her own horse. She was able to hide behind Destiny, untacking the mare, until the flush dissipated.

Thunder shook the house, and the lights flickered. Precipitation lashed against the windows so hard that Amity couldn't tell if it was rain or hail. She sat on the couch with her two dogs, one on either side of her. Odd-eyed Jax raised his head and stared at her with his blue eye before tucking his head down against her leg. Black-and-tan Amber had burrowed her way under the cotton blanket to hide from the storm.

Amity's phone chimed, and she paused her show. It was a golden oldie—Mikhail Baryshnikov as the prince in *The Nutcracker*.

She glanced at the display and her pulse quickened. "Fin? Hey. Been a while."

He sighed. "Yeah. It's been crazy busy here. Nora just got back from maternity leave—"

"A baby?" Detective Farmer had never struck Amity as the motherly type. "Congratulations."

Fin chuckled. "I had nothing to do with that. But I'll pass your message along to her."

"Sorry! That's not what I meant. I meant … never mind. How's the reservoir case?"

"Not much to talk about right now. I know it's short notice, but are you free for dinner tomorrow?"

Free as air. "Let me check my calendar."

She waited a few seconds. "Yeah. It looks like I've got some time available then."

"Great! You want to meet at Thai One On at seven?"

"See you then."

Fin was already seated when Amity arrived. The hostess gave her a plastic bag for her dripping umbrella.

Her date stood as she got to the table. "Glad you could make it, Amity."

"It's good to see you. Especially in a non-professional setting."

He let out a short laugh. "Yeah. With storms again today, I wasn't sure either one of us would make it. It's a good thing you found David Harrington when you did."

"Is that…"

Fin nodded. "The guy from the reservoir. Private detective, so we're going through all of his cases, looking for leads. But I didn't want to meet up to talk shop. I wanted to see *you*."

A pleasant shiver rippled through Amity's solar plexus and she swallowed. Perhaps the evening was looking up. They made small talk until their food came. Fin raised his fork and his phone buzzed.

He glanced at it and his shoulders dropped. "Sorry."

She shrugged.

Fin tapped the screen and his brow furrowed.

"What's wrong?"

The detective showed her an image on his phone. "Harrington had a USB drive in his pocket with this on it. You have any idea what it is?"

Amity studied the picture. It was a blurry, blotchy grey background with two pixelated black blobs. "I don't know."

He put his phone down. "It almost looks like one of Nora's early ultrasounds, before you could tell it was a baby."

"Well, I'm a software engineer, not a radiologist, so I can't help you there." Amity turned some pad Thai noodles on her fork. "Any updates on Loretta Mullholland?"

Fin shook his head. "Not a thing. If she's still in the reservoir somewhere, we may never find her after all this rain."

Amity gulped her tea, dismayed at the grim turn the conversation had taken. "Don't … bodies float?"

"Sure. But there are alligators back there. They migrate when the water rises."

Amity asked for a to-go box.

Amity lazed in bed for a few minutes after her alarm went off. She could easily have fallen back to sleep if Jax and Amber weren't standing by her head, staring at her. When she failed to peel off the covers, Jax gave her a quiet wuff.

"I know. It's breakfast time." She swung her legs over the edge of the bed. The dogs danced in front of her all the way to the kitchen.

Amity had ten vacation days left, and she had to use them or lose them, so she had taken the last half of December off. She planned to tackle some projects around her house, as her holiday shopping was done and dusted.

She couldn't get Loretta Mullholland out of her mind. Was anyone still out there searching? She fed the dogs and stared out the window as she stood at the sink, rinsing the cans. The sky was overcast, and a stiff breeze whipped bare tree limbs around.

The reservoir area was crisscrossed with hike and bike trails. Maybe Jax and Amber would like to go for a walk in a new place?

One of her neighbors had been taking her pup to cadaver dog training. Daisy excelled at it, and Beverly thought she'd be ready to take part in local search operations soon. Amity had considered signing Jax and Amber up for the classes but hadn't gotten around to it. She chided herself for that procrastination now.

Amity checked the weather radar. More storms were coming. Thankfully, it looked like they wouldn't arrive until after lunch. She loaded the dogs into her SUV and set off for the reservoir.

Amity hadn't seen another soul on the paved trail. She and the dogs had been walking for the better part of an hour in the densely wooded area. The trees blocked the worst of the icy wind, but the cloud cover made the forest extra gloomy. Her skin prickled, and she had the distinct feeling she was being watched.

The dogs stopped and sniffed the air, then began barking. This set Amity's nerves on edge, because Amber rarely barked.

Rustling erupted from the shrubbery.

"Who's there?" Amity's voice pitched higher than she wanted. Thoughts of the angry spirit Hirsch had told her about bubbled up in her mind.

The bushes stilled. Jax growled.

Four whitetail deer leaped from the undergrowth and bounded across the path.

Amity let out the air she'd sucked in. *Alrighty then.*

The path curved, and the remains of the old town came into view. Disintegrating buildings stood like silent sentries in the gloom. The ones closest to her were dry, but as the rise sloped away, more and more stood in water.

Amity couldn't shake off the sense that she was trespassing, gawking at someone else's misfortune.

She peered inside the largest building—it appeared stable, while some of the others looked to be a good puff of wind away from collapse. Faded paint spelled out 'Hegemann's Grocery' on the back wall. Most of the sheetrock had collapsed, baring the cinderblocks underneath. Huge numbers of birds had apparently taken shelter inside over the decades, because the floor was thick with their droppings.

Amity moved to the next structure. Weather had stripped most of the letters from the wooden sign. An M, a C, an H, and a U were all she could make out. M something Ice House? A tree grew up through the broken floorboards and out the roof.

Both dogs pricked their ears forward as a faint scratching came from one of the walls. Jax barked and the noise stopped. Curiosity drove Amity to step inside and use her phone as a flashlight. The floor was littered with overturned tables and broken chairs.

A snarl and a hiss came from behind the counter to her left. Amity crept toward the sound. The growling intensified. Jax replied with a growl and bark of his own.

If there was a hurt or injured creature behind the bar, having the dogs there would only make things worse. She took them outside and tied them to the rusty iron railing of the porch. "I'll be right back, okay?"

Amity made her way carefully to the bar, avoiding rotting boards and holes in the floor. The snarling and hissing resumed. She found nothing but cobwebs and a discarded soda can behind the bar.

There was, however, a hole in the wall about a foot wide. Angry chittering came from within as she shined her flashlight inside. A large raccoon bared its teeth and growled at her. The animal sat on a bag or perhaps a backpack, where it had been chewing a hole.

Amity moved away from the opening and began knocking on the wall. *Tsst -tsst-tsst!*

The racoon lumbered out and gave her a dirty look before scrambling into a hole in the floor.

Amity pulled the bag out of the wall. The wrapper of a package of peanut butter crackers peeked out of the ragged opening. Given the tooth marks, she didn't think its former owner would want it, so she opened the package and dropped the crackers into the hole where the raccoon had disappeared.

What she had in front of her now was a dark grey backpack with 'LM' embroidered on the flap. She dropped it on the counter, snapped a photo, and sent it to Fin, along with the GPS coordinates.

Realizing she might be in the middle of a crime scene, Amity hurried outside and took a picture of the building before untying her dogs.

Her phone buzzed with a reply from Fin. "Are you at the reservoir? Alone?!"

"Jax and Amber are with me."

"Go to the parking lot and wait in your car. Lock the doors. We're on the way."

Amity took the more direct path from the old town to the parking area than the circuitous route she'd taken earlier. By the time she got to the trailhead, several police vehicles and the Crime Scene Unit van had arrived. Deputy Warren, from that first search operation, locked eyes with her as she passed. Amity told the investigators what she'd found and showed them a picture of the icehouse.

Amity watched as they put on their Tyvek suits, gathered their equipment, and trekked into the trees like an alien expeditionary force.

A dark blue sedan pulled into the lot and parked next to Amity's SUV. Fin and Nora got out and approached. Amber went into a full-body wiggle and tried to jump up and lick Fin's face.

"Off!" Amity tugged on Amber's harness.

The dog sat, but her butt kept wiggling. Fin leaned over to pet her and nearly got a slobbery head bump.

Nora looked Jax up and down. "Does he have Australian shepherd somewhere in the mix? Or maybe husky? One blue eye and one brown is pretty uncommon in other breeds."

Amity laughed. "He's a purebred mongrel. Got both of them from a rescue—their owner died. They were bonded, and most people don't want one large dog, much less two. But I'd just moved into my house, had a big yard, and needed some company" She smiled. "How's the baby?"

Nora's eyes narrowed, and she seemed to be weighing her reply. "He's good." She tried and failed to stifle a yawn. "I'll be glad when he's sleeping through the night, though."

Still scratching Amber's ears, Fin asked, "So how did you find this backpack?"

"Well, it was the raccoon." She told them the story of hearing the masked marauder in the wall.

Fin sucked his teeth. "Loretta clearly intended to be out here a while, since she brought snacks. What would a civil engineering student be searching for in a reservoir?"

Amity shrugged. "Maybe she was just on a hike?"

"Unlikely." Nora's lips pressed into a thin line. "She was out here with the private detective she'd hired."

Fin looked at Amity. "He was the decedent you found. If the backpack turns out to be Loretta's, something spooked her enough that she hid it in the wall."

"Oh." Amity felt queasy.

Nora cleared her throat. "We're going to look at the icehouse while we're waiting on the K-9 unit. You should probably get your dogs in the car before they arrive."

Fin gave Amber a final pat and smiled at Amity. "I'll catch up with you later."

The sun slipped behind a wall of dark clouds and thunder rolled in the distance.

"Oh!" Amity dropped the Allen key when her phone buzzed with a text message. She moved the plastic bag of hardware over and retrieved her device from the coffee table.

The message was from Fin. "WE FOUND LORETTA! She's alive. Rough shape."

"Hurray! Where was she?"

"Can I tell you at dinner?"

Amity chuckled. A little too loudly, like some giddy schoolgirl. "When and where?"

"Mamacita's Cantina? Or Mamadeaux?"

"Mamacita."

"I'll ping you when I'm on the way."

Amity lined up the wood slats and fastened them together. She pushed the first set of shelf support pegs into the bookcase she'd just assembled. But when she went to add the corresponding pair, there were no holes. She examined the plank and sighed. She'd put it in facing the wrong way, with the holes on the outside. *That's what I get for focusing on my dinner date instead of paying attention to what I'm doing.*

Her phone squawked with an emergency alarm, making Amity jump.

> Severe thunderstorm warning until 3:15 CST. Take shelter immediately in a first-floor interior room. Radar has detected a super cell thunderstorm moving southeast at 12 mph. Damaging winds, golf ball-sized hail, and rainfall up to six inches per hour have been reported.

Great. Amity drew the blinds and pulled the curtains. She didn't have a truly interior room, except for her closets, and she felt it was a bit premature to attempt to stuff herself into one of them for the next forty-five minutes. Before she could return to her bookshelf, the power went out. Amity looked at her watch. With a groan, her generator kicked in, lighting up the house.

When Fin called at 6:45, the power in Amity's area was still out. They changed their restaurant pick to one that had electricity. Most of the destruction had been on the north part of town. While some power lines were down on the west side, her area was largely unscathed, just dark.

Poppy Papadopoulos Bar and Eatery was packed. Spruce garland, trimmed with red velvet bows, draped all the windows. Holiday Muzak was barely audible above the voices, festive in spite of the storm. She almost missed Fin, who was waiting in the crowded bar.

"Amity!" He raised his arm and waved.

She couldn't stop herself from grinning as she walked over to him. "Hey, Fin. You do okay in the storm?"

"Power's out, but nothing other than that."

"Same." She sat on a barstool next to him. "So, what's the word on Loretta? Where was she?"

"She'd been shot and left for dead. They dragged her into one of the buildings that floods when the reservoir fills and covered her up with some debris. A K-9 found her, and we had her Life-Flighted to Hermann. She made it through the surgery, but she's still critical."

"Oh, wow. I hope she pulls through."

"Yeah. Me, too."

A dark thought crossed Amity's mind. "You don't think that private investigator had anything to do with what happened to her, do you?"

"I think someone wanted us to consider that. The same gun was used in both cases, and his was staged to appear self-inflicted."

"How do you know it was staged?"

"For one thing, the gun was in his hand, which is uncommon, but his hand had no GSR on it."

The plastic square on the bar next to Fin lit up and buzzed. "Table's ready."

They wound their way through the crush of people to the hostess stand, then followed the young host to the back of the restaurant, where he seated them at the tiniest of tables.

"Okay, so what's this stuff that wasn't on his hands?" Amity picked up her over-sized menu, but didn't look at it.

"Gun Shot Residue. When you fire a gun, the powder ignites and goes boom. The burned powder comes flying out with the bullet, and gets all over your hands and clothes. Looks like somebody fired the gun, wiped it clean, then put it in his hands. That, and the gun was farther than two feet away from him when it went off."

"Good evening. I'm Monica and I'll be taking care of you tonight. Can I start you off with some appetizers or drinks?"

They both ordered iced tea and Monica flitted to another table.

Amity scanned the menu and made her decision. "What about her backpack? She hid it, so there must have been something in there."

"Mostly newspaper clippings from the forties when the dam was being built and a report from the Army Corps of Engineers from five years ago recommending the dam be replaced because it's old and creaky."

"Creaky?" Amity tilted her head.

"Well, maybe not creaky so much as it is outdated and near collapse."

Monica returned with their drinks and took their orders. The dinner part seemed to take almost no time to Amity, but their post-meal chat was over an hour long.

Amity caught a glimpse of her watch as she pushed falafel crumbs around her plate. "Oh, wow. I have to get going. Gotta take the dogs out since they've been cooped up inside all afternoon."

Fin sighed. "Guess I'll head back to my dark apartment and sit in the parking lot to charge my phone."

"I have a generator, if you want to come to my place." The offer had just slipped out. *What if he actually comes over?*

"You sure? That would be great."

"Of course. Just follow me."

Nothing seemed amiss when Amity pulled up in her driveway and waited for the garage door to open. Fin parked on the street and followed her into the house.

"Jax! Amber!" Amity looked around. "That's weird. They're usually here as soon as I open the door."

The dogs did not respond. As Amity and Fin made their way to the living room, it became clear why. The room was a mess. Drawers had been pulled out and the contents dumped on the floor. Couch cushions were cut open and tossed around. The storage ottoman was overturned and a tangle of USB cables twisted on the floor. The glass sliding door stood open.

Amity ran into the yard, calling for the dogs. Fin paused to report the break-in. He was still on his phone when he came outside and found her standing at the open gate with her face in her hands.

"I have to go look for them!"

"Nora's on the way. Just wait five minutes, and I can help you."

Amity gathered leashes, a bag of treats, and two flashlights. Deputy Warren arrived almost immediately.

Fin's brow crinkled. "Didn't realize this was your beat."

"I was in the area." His eyes cut to Amity. "Had a call about some loose dogs."

"What? Where are they?" Amity held her breath.

Warren shrugged. "I drove around the neighborhood. Didn't see 'em."

Amity choked back tears. "I've got to go."

She fled, Fin trailing in her wake.

"Jax! Amber!" Amity called as she hurried down the block. "Who wants nummies!"

They walked for six blocks, calling for the dogs.

Fin sighed as he looked around the unlit neighborhood. "Did you have anything especially valuable the robbers might have been looking for?"

"Just Jax and Amber."

Fin rubbed her shoulder.

They continued walking and calling until they got to the edge of the neighborhood. Amity was about to turn back when barking erupted past the brick subdivision entry signage.

"Jax? Amber?" She jogged toward the sound.

A man stood in his yard with a push broom held in front of him. Amber lay on her side in the grass and Jax stood between her and the man, barking.

"Those are my dogs!" Amity ran toward her pets.

"Did you see what happened?" Fin asked the man.

He shook his head. "Heard somebody yelling, then tires screeching. Came out to see what was going on."

Amity shone her flashlight on Amber and gasped. "I think her leg is broken!" She turned the beam on Jax. His face was bloody. "Fin? Stay here while I get my car?"

He nodded. "Of course."

Amity ran back to her house. When she returned a few minutes later, Fin helped her lift Amber into the back of the SUV.

"I looked at Jax while I was waiting for you. I can't find a wound on him."

"Then where did the blood come from?" Amity pressed the button to close the liftgate door.

"He may have bitten the burglar. Please drop Jax and I off at your house before you take Amber in. The Crime Scene Unit can collect samples of the blood and, if we're very lucky, match the DNA."

"Sure." Amity was already loading Jax into the back seat."

By the time Amity returned home, all the police except for Fin had left. As soon as she came in, Jax greeted her, then cocked his head from one angle to another, looking for his friend.

"Where's Amber?" Fin asked as Amity came through the door unaccompanied.

"I can pick her up tomorrow. They had to operate and put a pin in her leg. She's banged up, but she'll be okay." Exhaustion flickered in her eyes.

"Glad to hear she'll pull through."

Amity nodded. Fin had put the ruined cushions back on the couch and she sat next to him. Jax sniffed around the door, still searching for Amber.

"You need to look around to see if anything's missing. Normally, burglars will steal anything they can grab quickly and sell at a pawnshop—like jewelry and power tools. Your security footage showed two males popping open the sliding door on your back patio. The dogs ran out and the men ran in, closing the door behind them. They came out twenty minutes later, seemingly empty-handed. The dogs came around the side of the house and chased them out of the yard."

"If the dogs were found in the next neighborhood over, why did the burglars park so far away? You'd think they'd want their car close by so they could just jump in and go."

"There's an easy explanation for that. Your subdivision has the Flock license plate readers at the entrance and exit. The neighborhood next door doesn't." Fin took in a deep breath and let it out. "I have a suspicion though. I think the people who killed David Harrington and tried for Loretta are the same ones who broke into your house."

Amity swallowed hard. "Why?"

"They ransacked the place. But your TV's still here. They didn't take the silver candlesticks on your dining room table. There are power tools in your garage they didn't touch. They were looking for something specific. I don't know how they would know you were the one who found both Harrington's body and Loretta's backpack, though."

Amity rubbed her arm. "I saw the report on the news. They didn't mention any names, just said a group of volunteers found the body. Only the police know the details."

"That's what worries me. I would feel a whole lot better if you weren't here by yourself tonight."

"I hope you're wrong about the burglars. Still, I'd really like to know more about what you found in Loretta's backpack. There could be a clue in there about what might be missing. How well do you remember the details?"

"I don't have to remember. I have photos." Fin pulled out his phone and opened the gallery before handing it to her.

Amity scrolled through, pausing to study each one. "Look at this. She made notes about all the companies that bid on the dam project. Morrison & Sons, Apex Construction, Turnkey Engineering... and Lambo Construction—that's who won." She zoomed in. "She's got 'LAMBO' with three question marks and an arrow and the word 'HOLD.' What do you think that means?"

Fin studied it. "Morrison & Sons. Bill Morrison's been filing complaints about rigged city contracts for years. His company has lost contract after contract to tiny companies that came out of nowhere, always underbidding them."

Amity continued swiping, then zoomed in on one and her brow furrowed. "So, this is an article from 1946 about the progress of the construction. If she's looking into the history of the dam, why does she have these two names highlighted? Ezra Finch and Charley Buckminster? A single sentence says those two absconded with some equipment and it took longer to replace it than them. That's barely even a footnote. But she thought it was important. Then she drew an X over the picture of the construction manager. Why?"

"When I get in the office tomorrow, I can see if there's an old police report. But digitizing records prior to 1980 was not a priority, so most of them aren't."

Amity started to hand the phone back but froze. "Look at this sign at the building site. Barker-Hartley Construction. Doesn't Mayor Hartley's family money come from a construction business?"

"You're right. Local news did that profile on him right after he won re-election. His family opened the first dry goods store in town back in the 1840s. Then they started building things. Even without that though, his campaign ads beat everybody over the head with how deep his connections to the city were."

"Well, if they built half the city, it probably doesn't mean anything. I sure hope Loretta is well enough to talk to you soon."

Fin yawned. "Yeah. Me, too."

Jax put his head on the cushion next to Amity's leg and whined. She patted him and scratched his ears. "Don't worry, Amber will be back tomorrow."

Amity stifled her own yawn, then got to her feet. "Come on. I'll show you where the guest bedroom is."

Amber lay on the couch with her head in Amity's lap, her splinted and bandaged leg sticking out like a hot pink corndog. Jax sat in front of the new French doors, staring out into the yard. He'd been in his crate all morning while workmen replaced the broken sliding door.

Amity's phone vibrated. It was a text from Fin. "Going to mayor's presser on the down low. Hope to find concrete evidence. If you don't hear from me in 2 hrs, call Nora."

Cold dread seeped into her middle. Why would he need to keep it secret about attending a press conference?

Concrete…was that what had been bothering her? Maybe that engineering report from Loretta's backpack would be online. Even though she wasn't a civil engineer, she might find something, even if it was just a breadcrumb trail.

It didn't take very long for her internet searches to yield results. Multiple newspaper articles had been written about the potential for impending doom from the dam. And most had links to the report.

She tried reading it. The whole thing was very technical, with a lot of diagrams and photos that made no sense to her. Amity was about to give up on the report when an image caught her eye.

Blurry grey background. Two pixelated black blobs. The same image Fin had shown her from the dead PI's USB drive. The caption said that it was an image of a concrete scan showing two voids in the base of the dam.

Amity's head spun. No. That couldn't be it. Two voids. Two missing men. As horrifying as that idea was, it happened the better part of a hundred years ago, if it happened at all. Why was it suddenly worth killing over?

Surely everyone involved was dead by now. Why would Loretta hire an investigator? Had to be something else. What did he unearth that got him killed?

Amity sat up straighter. Had he given whatever it was to Loretta? Photos of the scans were already public in the Corps report. So what did the burglars tear her house apart looking for?

She tried to remember all the images from Fin's photos of the backpack contents. Newspaper clippings, the engineering report, some handwritten notes. But in today's world of social media, if you're meeting someone to get bombshell evidence in a crime, what would you do?

Record it on your phone.

Amity's pulse quickened. Where *was* Loretta's phone? Fin never mentioned finding it at the scene.

That's what the burglars wanted. That's what Fin was going to the reservoir to find—proof of what happened at that meeting.

"Come on, Jax. Let's go help Fin."

The parking lot was full when Amity arrived. Four news trucks took up multiple spaces each, and she despaired of finding a slot. Half a space taunted her at the end of the concrete. She accepted the challenge and parked half on the slab and half in the grass.

Amity shortened Jax's leash as she approached a young lady holding several paper cups of coffee. "Excuse me. I was just wondering what this press conference is about."

"Mayor's announcing the kickoff of the project to replace the old dam. Big public safety initiative, highlighted by all the storms recently. You know how politicians are." She rolled her eyes and said in a mocking voice, "Promises made, promises kept."

"Thanks." Amity turned and hurried down the trail, away from the gaggle of press.

Water was over the path in some spots on the way to the old town. She stepped over the puddles while Jax delighted in splashing through them.

When Amity rounded the corner and the abandoned town came into view, all the buildings had at least some water in them. The flood was deep enough to float some of the rotting logs that littered the woods. Stray beams of sunlight pooled and fractured on the surface of the murky water.

Jax barked once and began wagging his tail.

Fin, dressed in camo chest waders, stepped out of a building on the downslope, the water level a few inches above his waist.

"Amity? What are you doing here?"

"Looking for you."

"You shouldn't be here. It's not safe. Loretta's awake. I know what's on her phone. I found it in a cubby behind the counter in the ice house."

Jax growled, a deep rumble that Amity could feel in her chest. He moved in front of her and sat down, ears pricked forward.

Two men in black tactical clothing and gloves moved toward them from a path on Amity's left. The taller one's shaved head glistened like a melon in the frost, and he carried a hard-sided case with him. The shorter one had a dishwater blond flattop and pockmarked skin. Attitude oozed out of his pores.

Amity's stomach dropped. Deputy Warren.

She stared at the luggage. *That looks like my cousin's saxophone case. I can't imagine he's out here to practice some smooth jazz.*

The taller one raised one hand in a half-hearted wave. "Detective Myles. Long time, no see."

"Looks like you've come out of retirement, Logan."

The tall man shrugged. "Gotta pay the bills."

Warren looked from Amity and Jax to Fin. "Just doing a security sweep before the mayor goes on stage. You're inside the security perimeter."

"That's a big perimeter. Isn't Mayor Hartley set up almost a mile that way?" Fin tilted his head in the direction the men had come from.

"You know how it is. Can't be too careful." Logan's mouth curved into a smile, but it didn't reach his eyes. "Whacha doing out here, Myles?" He looked Fin up and down. "Fishing expedition?"

"Nothing's biting right now, so we were just leaving."

Logan reached up to rub his temple, and his sleeve slid down his arm. Amity's blood froze, and it wasn't just from the chilly air. Logan's wrist was scratched, and in the center lay two deep puncture marks, crusty black circles inside a purple-blue bruise. A dog bite. No wonder Jax was growling. She cut her eyes away, but he'd already caught her looking at the wound.

Fin sloshed his way to dry ground and slid out of the waders.

By the time he was done, Logan had set down the case, and Warren had drawn his pistol.

Logan glanced at his watch, then back toward where the press conference was happening. "Right on schedule. Morrison should be making his big entrance any minute now."

Fin's eyes narrowed. "Bill Morrison? The construction guy?"

Warren smirked. "Oh yeah. He's going to expose how Lambo is really a branch of Barker-Hartley. Stand up in front of all those cameras and play the crusading businessman fighting corruption." He made a mock-solemn face. "Such a tragedy that the mayor got shot during the chaos. So many people around, so much confusion…"

"And Morrison's front and center, visible to everyone when it happens," Fin said. "Perfect alibi."

Logan nodded approvingly. "He's smarter than he looks. Gets to be the hero *and* eliminates the problem. Contract gets voided, his company gets another shot at the bidding."

"Plus," Warren added, "with Morrison up there making a scene, every camera's going to be pointed at him and Hartley.

Nobody's watching the tree line." He gestured toward the woods. "Clean shot, easy exit."

Fin stared at them. "Except that you ran into us."

Logan smirked. "It's a real shame when good cops go bad. We caught you and your spotter down here with a long-range sniper rifle." He shrugged. "We had to stop the threat."

Fin opened his arms, palms up. "I've already uploaded those recordings from Loretta Mullholland's phone to the cloud. My partner's working on the warrants even as we speak."

Logan's eyes narrowed. "You're bluffing." He racked the slide and raised his gun.

Fin shrugged and smiled as he pulled his phone out of his pocket. "Let's find out."

Jax barked ferociously and lunged against the leash, ripping it out of Amity's hand. Before anyone could react, he hurled his eighty-pound body at Logan.

The man flinched, reflexively raising his arms to protect his head from the dog's attack. The shot went wild.

Warren re-holstered his gun and fled.

As Amity pulled Jax off of Logan, Fin grabbed his cuffs and handcuffed him to a tree. He also removed Logan's utility belt and tossed it to the ground, far out of his reach.

"Somebody will pick you up later. Come on, Amity!"

She tightened her grip on Jax's leash. "It's a good thing you were able to get those files uploaded."

"Are you kidding? There's no cell service out here. We gotta hurry."

They ran all the way to the press conference. *I definitely need to do more cardio.* Amity was gasping for air by the time they arrived at the edge of the throng.

Mayor Hartley had finished his announcement and was taking questions from the audience. Bill Morrison had stood up and was making his way to a bank of microphones in front of the crowd.

Fin had barely broken a sweat. "Excuse me… Sorry… Coming through…" He pushed his way through the onlookers, Amity and Jax following in his wake, until they reached a pop-up awning.

"Hey, you the sound guy?" Fin asked.

A man in a polo and cargo shorts nodded.

Fin flashed his badge. "Great. The mayor needs to hear this. It's really important."

The engineer frowned, then shrugged, and took the phone, plugging it in to a USB cable. He handed it back to Fin with a thumbs up.

Fin tapped 'play.'

A female voice came over the PA system. Simon Hartley stood on the stage blinking, as silence descended on the crowd.

"Thank you for meeting me out here, Mayor Hartley."

The mayor's voice answered. "Of course, Miss Mullholland. You must know I'm well aware of the issues with the dam. I can't count the number of times I've been sent that Army Corps of Engineers report, so if that's what you want to discuss, save your breath."

"It's not all of the report. Just one image."

The sound of paper unfolding crackled over the speakers.

"What am I looking at?"

"These two black areas. Hollows in the concrete. All that's left of Charley Buckminster and Ezra Finch. Your grandfather murdered them."

"It was an accident! They fell into the concrete frame during the pour. There was no way to get them out. They couldn't be saved. When he was dying, my grandfather was filled with regret for what happened."

"But not enough to make amends to their families."

"It wouldn't have brought them back. But it would have tarnished the reputation of Barker-Hartley Construction for no good reason." The mayor let out a bitter laugh. "Is this a shakedown?"

"You think I want your money? I want justice for Ezra and Charley. Your grandfather lied about them, branded them as thieves. I want a public apology and a brass memorial plaque for them on the new dam."

"Is that all? What if I say no?"

Another male voice chimed in. *Was that the private eye?* "The public might be interested in knowing that Lambo Construction, you know, the winning bidder for the dam demolition and rebuild? Is a wholly owned subsidiary of Barker-Hartley. You gave the contract to your own company. Definite conflict of interest. Public corruption and all that."

A shot rang out and Loretta screamed. There were a few seconds of her running through tall grass, then silence.

All eyes turned to Mayor Hartley. He stuttered and stumbled over his words as his security detail moved in to restrain him. His shoulders sagged. He knew he was done.

Fin unplugged the phone. "We'll need this for evidence. Come on, Amity. There's someone who's desperate to meet you."

A pale and battered young woman was sitting up in bed reading a book when Amity and Fin came in. Plastic tubing ran across her face, supplying a nasal cannula, and an IV line snaked from her arm to a pole beside the bed. "Detective Myles! Is that…?"

"Yes, Loretta. This is Amity."

Amity gave a little wave. "Hi."

"I wouldn't be here if not for you. If you hadn't found my backpack, they never would have found me. I wanted to thank you in person."

Fin moved to Loretta's bedside. "I just wanted to let you know that we caught Deputy Warren at the airport."

"He's the one who shot me?"

Fin nodded. "And he spent the last few days tearing up Amity's house looking for your phone. He was worried about what else is on it besides the mayor's confession."

Loretta blinked. "The recording? I wasn't just recording audio. My phone was in my jacket pocket, camera facing out. I was recording video of the whole meeting."

Fin leaned forward. "You got Warren on video? Shooting Harrington?"

She nodded. "And chasing me. I kept running with my hand pressed against my pocket, trying to keep the phone recording. I was hoping … if something happened to me, at least there would be evidence."

"I'm just glad you're safe now." Amity smiled. "I will admit I'm curious, though. How did you know about those two men?

The workers that fell into the concrete? It doesn't seem all that hard to believe that they stole some equipment and ran away."

"It does if one of them was your great-grandfather."

Amity's mouth popped open. "Ah." She didn't know what else to say.

"Ezra Finch was a good man. He worked hard to provide for his family. My great -grandmother tried to prove he didn't run away, but the sheriff at the time was Matthew Barker, brother of Peter Barker of Barker-Hartley Construction. He claimed he was investigating, but reports got lost, witness statements went missing. And so on. The company threatened to have her arrested for harassing them. She was on her own with eight kids to feed, so she just dropped it."

Fin shifted his weight and Amity nodded.

"Grans, and then my mom, both tried to find a way to clear his name, but there was no way to prove he didn't skip town. Until I had to do a research paper on concrete dams. I came across the report from the Corps of Engineers, and the concrete scans. I knew immediately what must have happened, but I couldn't prove anything. Then when they announced they were going to demolish the dam and rebuild it, I felt it was now or never. If there were bones in those voids, my great-grandfather's reputation would be restored."

"Mayor Hartley couldn't have anyone looking too closely at the winning bid for the dam, or even the bidding process." Fin began to pace in the small room. "Someone would surely have questioned why a tiny construction company with almost no assets was awarded the job, when there were a number of well-established, reputable companies bidding on the project."

"Every company who was anybody in town. Except for Barker-Hartley, because their CEO is the mayor's uncle." Loretta almost knocked her book off the table when she flung out her arms.

Fin reached over and pushed the book back into place. "It took a whole team of forensic accountants to trace through the maze of holding companies to find that tiny little Lambo Construction was a wholly owned subsidiary of Barker-Hartley. They would have raked in tens of millions of dollars on this project."

Amity cocked her head. "Except he had no way of knowing that Bill Morrison planned to take matters into his own hands and permanently eliminate the corruption. Your recording saved the mayor's life."

"What?" Loretta coughed.

Fin took a step closer to her. "Bill Morrison has been very vocal about public corruption, and I guess he finally found the evidence with Lambo. Maybe your private eye even tipped him off. I don't know. Morrison hired a retired SWAT guy to take out Hartley with a sniper rifle during the press conference while Morrison created a disturbance. Deputy Warren was double-dipping—playing both sides. He was security for the mayor when he was engaging in off-the-record activities, and extra muscle for Morrison, who told us he doubled what the mayor paid." Fin chuckled. "You know what they say: First to squeal gets the deal. Warren's gonna need that commissary money where he's going."

Destiny stomped a freshly oiled hoof as she stood in the crossties, Amity combing out her mane.

"Keep your hair on. You'll get your dinner soon. You're still a little hot to have grain."

Jackie Barber stood in front of an empty stall with a piece of paper in one hand, marking on a small chalk board that hung on the stall's door.

Jackie finished writing and headed toward her office. Amity peered over Destiny's back.

The trainer turned. "New boarder coming in. Just got a text from the driver. They'll be here soon." She disappeared through the doorway.

Huh. Wonder what they'll be like. Amity unclipped Destiny from the crossties and took her out to the grassy area near the wash racks to graze. It wasn't long before the hauler pulled into the parking lot. A horse inside the huge trailer whinnied.

Jackie went out to bring in the new horse. A tall chestnut gelding stepped off the trailer. He looked one way, then the other, ears pricked forward. He snorted, then let out the loudest whinny Amity had ever heard.

Seems quite the character.

A blue pickup arrived and slotted into the space between Amity's car and another one.

The truck door opened, and Destiny almost tugged the lead rope out of Amity's hands. Amity gaped, shut her mouth, then gaped again.

The last person in the world she'd expected to see was Detective Fin Myles.

Maybe Santa had brought her an early Christmas present this year.

CHILI
By A. B. Richards

"No, Angela. I don't want to go to your parents' for Christmas. They hate me. And I'm surprised you would—they're always ragging on you for dropping out of college to marry me when you could have been a surgeon like your sister. Do you need to listen to that?"

She wiped a smear of dirt from her cheek. "I haven't seen them in a year, Dean."

"And whose fault is that?" I didn't mean to snap at her.

Angela raised a perfectly plucked eyebrow.

I knew exactly whose fault it was. Snatching up my car keys, I blurted, "I need some air," and stormed out.

The slowly sinking ground had taken the garage four inches lower than its original level, so we parked in the crumbling driveway. The shifting foundation of the house had jammed the front door closed. I had to go out the back and edge past an overgrown bush I somehow never got around to trimming. Wouldn't happen today, either.

Don't know who I thought I was fooling. I wasn't really going anywhere. There was only an eighth of a tank of gas in the car, and it had to last until Friday. Still, I made a show of leaving, screeching the nearly bald tires as I whipped out into the late afternoon shadows staining the street.

I drove exactly four blocks and pulled into a parking lot.

Not that it mattered to me, but Rusty's Pump & Snack did not card. There were definitely more underage kids buying beer on any given day than drivers filling their tanks. The place looked like it had been around since automobiles first hit the road, and it was not in the part of town where most folks would willingly get out of their cars.

I picked through the drink holders and dug through the console to scavenge ninety-three cents. If I remembered correctly, I had four dollars and a quarter in my pocket.

Rusty's carried a surprisingly large selection of "supplements" and both natural and synthetic cannabis-based products. Foil packets in lurid colors lined up in a locked clear plastic display case, begging to be picked. My nerves were stretched tighter than piano wire, and I needed something to take the edge off.

An old man with thick white hair and unnervingly dark eyes stood behind the plexiglass-shrouded counter. His gaze was almost like a finger pressing on my skin.

I rubbed my arms. "Where's Javier? Doesn't he usually work on Tuesdays?"

"Sick today." His wiry beard hardly moved when he spoke.

I nodded slowly. "I wanted to get what I got last time, but I'm not seeing it..."

"New product. Came in this morning." He leaned down and pulled something from under the counter, then pushed a red and green packet through the change slot.

Santa's Slay in a golden blackletter font sprawled across the top of the envelope. At the bottom, an extra portly Santa snoozed in his sleigh.

"How much?"

"Four-seventy-nine. Plus tax. Five-eighteen."

I handed him my four crumpled bills and counted out every coin I had. Exactly five dollars and eighteen cents.

The man's dark eyes flicked up to the security camera feed as he tucked the money into the register. "Enjoy."

"Yeah. Thanks," I mumbled as I turned and shuffled out to my car.

After I tore the packet open with my teeth, I pulled out the thin rectangle of gummy. It was scored into squares, four wide by eight long. I used my thumbnail to cut a single square and shoved the rest back into the pouch. I didn't want to get baked, just relax.

I dropped the sticky red blob onto my tongue and rolled it around my mouth before crushing it between my teeth. Tasted kind of like fruit leather with added grass clippings, and possibly a burned match.

I should probably suck it up and go home. It's almost dark and only one headlight works. I did not need to get pulled over— my budget insurance dropped me after the fender-bender I had last year, and I haven't managed to find another carrier.

BAM!

I jumped, my head snapping up to see a dirty, ragged man standing in front of my car. He'd slammed both hands down on my hood. Shadows swallowed his features, but the struggling neon sign from the game room across the street glinted red in his eyes.

I gulped and started the engine, throwing it into reverse and nearly taking out a utility pole. Something rolled under my feet and momentarily jammed the gas pedal. I kicked it out of the way, and when I stopped to shift, I grabbed it and threw it on the seat. A can of chili? What the hell.

I buckled my seatbelt as I drove. No need to tempt fate—or cops—on the four-block trip. The second I rolled to a stop in the driveway, I killed the engine. Not ready to go into the house just yet, I sat there, willing Santa's Slay to take effect. I leaned the seat back and waited. In much less time than I expected, a pleasant warmth flowed through my body. The tension in my shoulders loosened, and I could breathe again.

I got out of the car and started up the driveway. How had I never noticed how pretty the bush was? Red-orange berries clung to the white-stemmed branches like tiny Christmas ornaments.

"Happy Christmas, little bush." I patted the top of it. "I'm sorry I always cuss at you."

I rounded the corner and was surprised to see Angela in the backyard. That damned spade I never got around to putting away leaned on the wall behind her, both of them pricking my conscience. I needed to wash the clay and crap off the shovel. Probably starting to rust by now. Angela had all the flower beds she would ever need, anyway.

I put on my friendliest smile. "Hey, babe."

She said nothing, only stared at me in disgust. What had I done? I could still feel her soft cheek on my neck and smell her intoxicating floral shampoo as I held her in my arms not so long ago.

Regret for hurting her hit me like an ice pick through the heart and I almost dropped to my knees. I stepped closer and picked a cluster of dry pine needles out of her hair. "I'm sorry."

"Are you?" Her reply was more an accusation than a question.

I scratched my itchy cheek and felt something wet on my hand. A fat white maggot pulsed and wriggled across my palm. I cried out and flung the thing to the ground.

Where the hell did that come from?

My hands shook as I reached up and laid my fingertips just under my cheekbones. The flesh churned as thousands of tiny bodies burrowed and gnawed in my skin. The stench hit me hard. Sulfurous. Putrid. I retched and fled into the house. I had to get in the shower.

But in the bathroom mirror, the same haggard face I had seen in the morning looked back at me. Perhaps a little scruffier, but not a maggot to be found.

For a second, I was relieved. Then anger boiled up into my throat. Just what did that old man sell me? I should go back to the store and... Yeah. He'd only call the cops. Spending Christmas in jail would be worse than visiting Angela's family. Probably.

Get a grip, Dean. It's only the gummy. Just sleep it off.

I lay down on the couch, pulling the threadbare fleece throw over me. The broken spring that stabbed up from the base formed an uncomfortable lump that I had to twist my body around. Once I closed my eyes, I felt like I was floating. Drifting up in space and looking down at the blue marble of Earth.

Drip. Drip. Drip.

Now what? I peeled open one eye. Kitchen sink? Bathroom? Annoyed, I sat up.

I'd liberated a less-than-fresh Christmas tree from the dumpster behind the grocery store. The expensive porcelain angel that Angela's mom had given her perched at an uncomfortable angle on top.

And she was crying.

Tears of blood ran down her face, dropping onto the crispy needles and plastic ornaments. A scarlet pool had gathered around the base, like a liquid tree skirt seeping into the floorboards.

I wasn't able to look away from the angel's red-smeared cheeks. She looked at me with painted blue eyes and shook her head. The throaty wail of a freight train broke the silence, and I blinked, my stomach twisting. When my eyes opened again, the angel was pristine white porcelain with rosy cheeks. The hardwood floor under the tree was clean, except for a mound of dry fir needles.

My heart thumped against my ribs. So much for sleeping it off. I jumped to my feet and started pacing. How long will it take for this trip to end?

The closet doorknob turned. I stopped and stared at it. The door rattled and shook, as if somebody was yanking on it from the other side but couldn't open it because it was locked.

I was compelled to go closer to it. "Angela? Have we always had a closet in the living room?"

She must still be outside.

White light spilled from the cracks around the doorframe. Without thinking, I reached for the knob. The door flew open. A freight train shrieked, its headlight blinding me as it hurtled into the room. I wrapped my arms over my head. I heard screaming. Was it me?

The wind ruffled my hair as the train rattled past. I didn't open my eyes until it had gotten quiet. When I did, the doorway I thought opened to a closet was dark, and crickets chirped within. Great. Like I can afford an exterminator.

I stepped inside and found I was in a patch of woods. A fire flickered ahead. What the actual hell? I walked toward the light.

A man sat in front of the fire, his back to me. The scent of cumin and tomatoes filled the air, and that's when I noticed a can of chili sitting at the edge of the flames.

I swallowed. "Hello?"

"Pull up a seat, if you want." He sounded like he had a mouth full of food.

I looked behind me. There was no living room, only dark forest. "Sure." *It's just the gummy. He's not real.*

A flat rock squatted across the fire from the man, so I sat there.

He gave me half a smile. "You ever cooked over a campfire?"

I rubbed my arms. It had gotten colder. "No. Don't think I have."

"This is my Christmas dinner. Chili and corn."

"Look. I'm not trying to be rude here, but who are you, and how did you get in my house?"

The man slowly rotated his head. "House?"

I glanced around at the trees. "Well, I came here through a closet."

He nodded. "I see. Chili and corn. My holiday tradition. I save my change to buy my food at the corner market and walk back here to cook it. Every year. What do you do for the holidays?"

"Um..."

"What about last year? What did you do then?"

"Nothing!"

"Nothing at all?"

Uncomfortable on the hard rock, I shifted my weight. "Nothing good. I mean, I had a car accident. Hit a deer. It came out of nowhere—I never saw it."

"Doesn't sound like nothing. Especially for the deer."

"It ran away, so I guess it wasn't hurt too bad."

"Maybe. It must have been hungry to be out in broad daylight." He poked at the can of chili with a stick.

"No. It was night. Late."

He chuckled. "You take your wife on late-night drives for Christmas?"

I bristled. So many questions. "What does it matter to you?"

"Just making conversation. My name is John, by the way."

Who cares? "Oh." I nodded politely.

My arm throbbed.

A train whistle shattered the darkness, and I cringed.

"I see plenty of raccoons and possums, but I don't think I've seen any deer out here. Where did you hit it?"

Why won't he drop it? "Highway 62, close to the railroad crossing." I got to my feet. "Look, John. It's been real, but I gotta get going."

"See you around, Dean."

I followed the dirt track along the edge of the woods, back in the direction where I thought my house was. I wouldn't go into those trees. Not again. The land rose and I walked up the hill. As I topped it, another campfire glowed below. *How many people are out here?*

It was on my way, so I didn't try to avoid it. I would not stop and talk this time, though. As I got closer, the scent of cumin wafted up to me.

"Hey, Dean!"

"John?" *And I don't remember telling you my name.*

"Come sit for a spell, eh?"

"I need to get home. Angela's probably wondering where I am."

I pivoted on my heel and ran. Up the hill and halfway back down. To the campfire. Where John sat, eating chili out of a can.

"You again?"

"Me again."

The empty can rattled as he tossed it to the ground. Pain surged through my arm and I doubled over, cradling it.

It was the sound. A metal can skittering across pavement. Such a small thing, and yet it's burned into my mind.

"Did you check on the deer?"

"I told you. It ran away."

"That's what you told your insurance, too, isn't it?"

I clenched my fists, wanting nothing more than to punch him in his stupid face. "Stop asking me about it!"

"Why does it bother you so much? I mean, it was just a deer, right? An animal, minding its own business, trying to live its own unimportant life..."

Something snapped inside me. "Fine! There. Was. No. Deer. Is that what you want?"

"What was it, Dean?"

I looked at where my shoes must be. "A man." My voice was so low I didn't know if he heard it.

"And what did you do? After you hit him? He wasn't dead, was he?"

I sank to my knees. "No."

He sat silently.

Floodgates are open. Can't stop the flow of words now. "I thought he was. I couldn't... I couldn't call 911. I could not go to jail. We were right there at the grade crossing. If he got hit by a train, nobody would ask any questions, would they? I dragged him up on the tracks. And I waited."

"You could have pulled him off the tracks when he sat up."

If I wasn't a total garbage person. "The train was too close."

"So you ran back to your car instead."

I nodded as I rubbed my arm. "Yeah. I fell. Stepped on a can and it rolled."

"A can?"

"A can of chili." I barely had the air to force out the words.

I raised my eyes to meet John's. Blood began to run from his nose and pour out of his mouth. He spat broken teeth to the ground. Red blossomed on his pants as his thigh bent at a sharp angle between the knee and hip.

"I'm sorry. I'm so sorry." My voice broke.

Then I ran.

A rectangle of light, the size and shape of a doorway, appeared ahead. I ran faster.

But when I stepped through it, I wasn't in my living room. I stood in front of a police station.

Tears streamed down my face. The last thing in the world I wanted to do was go through those doors. But I couldn't live with what I'd done anymore.

An officer sat behind a plexiglass window. She looked up with a curt smile. "May I help you?"

There is no help for me. "I'm a killer."

Her eyes widened. "Somebody will be right with you."

Moments later, another officer came from behind the counter and approached me. "Anything I need to know about in your pockets? Any weapons? Anything sharp?"

I shook my head as he patted me down.

"Can I take that?" He raised his hand toward me.

Not realizing I was holding the empty chili can, I handed it to him.

He waved me through the metal detector and into the waiting area.

Two plainclothes officers stood on the other side, a man and a woman.

The man said, "I'm Detective Smithers and this is Detective Rangel. I understand you have something to tell us."

When they led me to the interrogation room, I hadn't expected to see the spade leaning against the wall. *Guess I'm here to dig my own grave, anyway. Thanks, sketchy gas station gummy. Perhaps this isn't even real, and I'm asleep on my couch, dreaming all this.*

Smithers stood in the doorway. I sat in one chair and Detective Rangel sat across the table from me.

She gave me a gentle smile, then asked my name and wrote it down. "So, Dean, what do you have to share with us?"

I told them all about John. It was easier talking about it this time.

When I finished, Detective Smithers rubbed his chin. "Out of curiosity, Dean, what were you doing driving around at three in the morning on Christmas Day?"

I stared at the spade with dirt clods and pine needles stuck to it and laughed bitterly. *You already know, don't you, Detective? Of course you do.*

"I had just buried my wife in the woods."

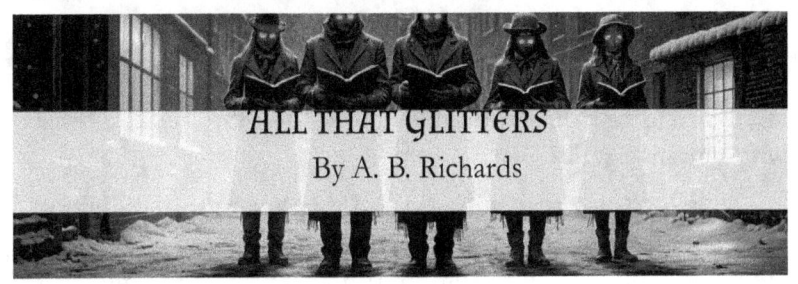

ALL THAT GLITTERS
By A. B. Richards

I WAS short on cash, but that's not news. It was already halfway through December, and I had no idea how I would come up with Christmas presents. With that on my mind, I took my usual shortcut through the neighborhood south of my apartment. And there it sat—a shoebox-sized package on the welcome mat of a two-story red brick home.

Could this be the answer to my prayers? That's a fancy house. Rich people buy expensive things, right? The company that sold it would replace it. Maybe not in time for Christmas, but they'd still get their stuff.

Hardly any traffic flowed through the subdivision mid-morning on a weekday. I crossed the street and pulled over. It was windy and cold, so I pulled my hoodie up without even thinking. Perfect in case they had a camera. With a quick look over each shoulder, I hurried up the walkway and nabbed the box. It weighed more than I expected, but I tucked it under my arm and jogged back to my car.

At my apartment complex, the dented entrance gate jerked and lurched open. I drove through and parked, then whistled a tune on my way up the rust-stained concrete stairs to my home. I set the parcel on my kitchen table while I took off my coat and got a knife.

Here it is: the moment of truth. Will Christmas be saved?

I cut through the tape and opened the lid. A strange grinding noise sounded, and glitter exploded from the box. Another noise, and liquid sprayed out, some of it landing on my shirt. I started gagging from the disgusting smell—like rotten eggs mixed with raw sewage.

I couldn't bag that thing up and drag it out to the dumpster fast enough. What did I do to deserve this? I had to open the balcony door and turn on the fan to try and get rid of the stench. My shirt went straight into the trash—didn't want to risk getting that foul smell in the rest of my laundry.

A sparkly nightmare of glitter scattered over almost everything in my apartment. I feared my third-hand vacuum cleaner would choke on all that mess, so I swept up as much as I could before I tried to vacuum. I pushed the heavy machine back and forth for twenty minutes, and still glitter taunted me from the carpet to the couch. I finally gave up. The cold draft from the open door had beaten out the barely warm air put out by my rattling furnace, so I went to take a shower and change clothes. The stink lingered.

The funk still reeked up the kitchen when I got out of the shower. It was freezing in the living room, so I had to close the door and turn off the fan. I tried to just breathe through my mouth and eat my instant ramen. Not as easy as I'd hoped.

Not only were the noodles hard to eat while holding my breath, but they also tasted weird. As I stirred them again with my fork, I realized the broth was slimy and greenish. Yuck. Flavor packet must have gone rancid. I dumped the bowl down the garbage disposal.

Eventually, I fell asleep on the couch watching TV. I woke up around three to find a shadow on the wall of a man in a wide-brimmed fedora hat.

Shit. I have no weapons. My baseball bat is at the front door.

Slowly, I turned my head so I could see the guy who must be standing in the gap between the wall and the sofa.

Nobody there. The shadow on the wall next to the TV remained. *Crap.*

I picked up my phone and shone the flashlight at it. The shadow stepped away from the wall and walked out through the closed and locked front door. I tried to convince myself that I hadn't been fully awake and only imagined seeing it. That didn't stop me from turning on all the lights in my tiny apartment, even the one on the balcony.

I never really fell back asleep. The lights and adrenaline were a bad combination. I had dozed a little here and there, and the sight that greeted me in the bathroom mirror reflected that. Dark circles puffed under my bloodshot eyes, my skin was pale and tired, and my hair looked like a rat's nest from tossing and turning.

What's that? I leaned closer to the glass. At first, I just thought a nerve in my eye was twitching, but as I looked closer, something moved under the white part. Was that... a worm crawling around in my eyeball? I gasped but couldn't look away.

The tissue surrounding the worm stretched and pulled as the parasite pushed its way around, followed by a thin trail of blood and an itchy tickle that made me want to claw at my eye—partly to relieve the itch and partly to get rid of that horrible worm.

A door slammed in the hallway, and my head turned on reflex. When I looked back in the mirror, my eye was completely normal—no bloody tunnels or moving strings. I splashed cold water on my face and brushed my teeth.

What if something in that stink juice made me see things that weren't there? I still smelled it, although not nearly as strong as yesterday. I didn't really have anywhere to go, especially since I had no money, but getting out of the apartment was a no-brainer.

I walked aimlessly until I stumbled onto a farmer's market. Tons of people milled around various pop-up awnings. Looked like a good place to explore.

The weather was sunny, cool, but not cold. Beautiful day, but my empty wallet weighed me down. My mom would have loved some of that flavored balsamic vinegar. I wondered if the *Slap Yo Mama* hot sauce at another booth would be spicy enough for my dad. One of the crocheted pigs at a different table would be just the thing for my sister, who collected pigs of all kinds. Perfect gifts, and no way to get them. No legal way...

I scratched an itch on my inner forearm. *Why is my shirt damp?*

A dark stain seeped across my left sleeve over the itch. I yanked it up. A patch of skin the size of a donut was discolored, similar to a bruise, but more green than brown. A small wound oozed at the center. And it reeked—like something dead.

No one around me seemed to notice, so I wondered if it was another hallucination. I rolled my sleeve back down and continued walking.

The itching continued. I tried ignoring it, but it kept getting stronger until I couldn't stand it. When I pulled up my sleeve again, I screamed. The head of a tree roach became visible as the two-inch-long bug wriggled out of my decaying flesh. The bruised spot had doubled in size and darkened to greenish black.

A roach-sized shape moved under the skin of my forearm. The longer I looked, the more bugs I saw. I felt them moving, burrowing in my arm up to my shoulder. I screamed and ripped off my shirt, clawing at my insect-infested, rotting arm.

It wasn't long before two police officers came and started talking to me. I wasn't able to pay attention to what they said because I was too busy trying to scrape the bugs out of my skin.

A yellow Taser in a holster on the duty belt of one officer caught my eye. Electricity! Maybe I could fry these roaches out of my arm. I lunged at the cop, reaching for what I hoped was my salvation.

When I woke up, I found myself strapped to a hospital bed, one of many in a large ward. All the other beds lay empty.

Most of the itching had stopped, but when I looked at my left arm, I cried out. Most of the putrid flesh had fallen away, possibly eaten by the bugs, and white bones glistened above the wrist restraint.

Why hadn't they done something? Shouldn't this be bandaged?

I was about to start yelling for help when motion caught my eye. Free from any wall, the shadow figure with the hat now walked around my bed.

I couldn't move.

I couldn't speak.

The only thing I could do was open and close my eyes.

The shadow reached out an arm like solid night and rested a grim hand on my chest. Those stony fingers got heavier each moment until I struggled to breathe. Struggled to move. My lungs burned, and my head started to swim. Just when I thought I was going to pass out, the pressure stopped.

I was able to move again and gasped for air. Once my head cleared, I looked at my skeletal arm.

No! I ugly-cried.

The glistening white bones had turned matte black. An inky fog, like a shadow under the full moon, crept up my arm, clinging to the bone and solidifying. The only thing in its wake was a stinging, bitter cold.

The chill flowed up my shoulder to my head and down my body. I felt my heart freeze and go still. How strange that I didn't die.

Once the darkness reached the ends of my toes, the restraints on my arms and legs released.

It was then that I noticed the black, wide-brimmed fedora lying on my chest.

Winter's Bargain

By Artemis Greenleaf

WOULD you come and sup with us, Heath? I'm sure Lari could find food enough for one more."

"No, my friend. I have much to tend to at my own house."

"It was well you thought of this fruitful excursion. Fare thee well, then. Until the morrow." Robyn Mason shifted his leather bag further up his shoulder. The hunt had been good—four hares, a fox, a partridge, and a half dozen larks divided amongst the four men. They gave Heath the partridge to christen his fine new game bag. The party had taken care to keep their hunt only to the small game they were allowed, although they had been sorely tempted by the fat wild boar they had spied as it snuffled for acorns.

Robyn lived the furthest into the wildwood, and Cynebald and Greysen had parted company with the quartet near half a mile since. Leaves dappled the afternoon sun, cooling the forest track. The great ash tree had already begun to change its green robes for gold, though the oaks yet held to their summer costume.

He smiled to himself as he imagined the delight of his wife upon his arrival and longed for the kiss of her sweet lips.

Lari's kitchen garden had not fared well in the bone-dry summer, and she would be glad of a coney to stew. Their larder was not so fat as it should be, as fall turned to winter.

Swithin would be old enough to join him on the hunt in the spring. And not a bit too soon, as he practiced snaring his mother's chickens, no matter how much Lari scolded him. Robyn would set Swithin the task of distracting his sister while he and Lari prepared the game. Eadda could not bear to look upon the corpses of the fallen animals without bursting into hysterics.

With a smile on his lips at the thought of seeing his family, he turned his head toward his home. He was nearly there now. Black smoke twisted into the blue sky. He had seen the smoke in the distance since yesterday but had given it no thought—it was the time of year the farmers burned their fields after the harvest. But this smoke came not from the yonder fields. It rose directly before him.

"No!"

Robyn ran. When the game bag slipped down his shoulder, he flung it to the earth, not breaking stride.

His feet scarce touched the ground as he pelted up the path to his homestead. His father had taught him the mason's trade, and they had built this round tower house together. Now its oaken door was splintered and broken. The grey stones around the upper windows were blackened with soot from the smoke pouring out of them.

"Lari!" Robyn bellowed as he charged up the spiral stairs. "Swithin! Eadda!"

A rusty, coppery stench slowed Robyn's pace. His boots reached the landing and seemed to stick to the stone. His legs refused to carry him into the scene of destruction.

What little furniture they owned had been broken, piled near a window, and set alight. The wooden table Robyn had made from the yew tree he had cleared to build the house still smoldered.

His eyes told him that a pile of rags lay in the middle of the floor. His brain told him that was not possible. Robyn finally pried his foot from the floor and approached the heap.

Bare feet, one pair a girl's, the other a woman's.

Legs.

Blood. So much blood.

Dresses, cut and torn.

Even more blood.

Lari's grey eyes stared at the blackened ceiling. Eadda's were closed. Both throats slashed.

Robyn blinked rapidly, rejecting what his eyes showed him.

"Swithin?" His voice faltered, barely more than a whisper.

The boy lay near the interior bonfire. He had been hacked apart and his face was covered by a proclamation from the sheriff, declaring Robyn a poacher with a price on his head.

He dropped to his knees and all the anguish of the world flowed from his shattered heart out through his mouth in a broken scream.

For three days, Robyn did not eat or sleep. He buried the dead and cleaned the wreckage of his house.

On the fourth day, a priest arrived. Fearing for the mortal souls of Lari and the children, Cynebald had sent for him.

"Hail, Cynebald!" Robyn had drawn his bow and nocked an arrow at the first glimpse of approaching figures, while they were yet beyond his ken.

The ends of Cynebald's sable hair that peeked from his leather cap shuddered across his thin shoulders as he cast his eyes from Robyn to his cassocked companion and back again. "I have brought with me Father Osbert from St. Dunstan's to perform the funeral rites."

Robyn lowered the bow. "He'll want a coin for it, no doubt. I have none for him."

Cynebald spoke quietly to the priest as they approached.

"Bless you, my son." Father Osbert made the sign of the cross but kept his gaze downcast.

"Your blessing comes too late."

"Your loss is deep. God sees your sorrow." He laid his eyes upon Cynebald, as if beseeching for aid.

"As he watched the slaughter of my family and did not lift his hand to stay their executions?"

"God works in mysterious ways—"

"Or not at all."

The flummoxed priest stepped back.

Cynebald took the cleric by the arm. "He is stricken by grief and knows not what he says. Please, Father, allow me to take you to the graves that you might bless them."

Robyn replaced the arrow in his quiver and leaned his bow against an oak tree. He resumed cutting goose feathers for arrow fletching.

In a short time, Cynebald returned. "Fool!" he snarled. "Do not anger the priest."

Robyn scoffed. "Because he has the ear of God?"

"Because he has the ear of the sheriff."

"To whom he will doubtless send word the moment he returns to town."

Cynebald studied his boots, then raised his glistening eyes to Robyn's. "I could not bear the thought of Lari, Swithin, and Eadda suffering in purgatory. Their souls, their innocent souls, must needs be sent straight to the arms of God."

Robyn ran a hand through his unkempt hair. "You have been as a brother to me, Cynebald. I beg of you, watch over their bones. Your son weds soon. He is welcome to abide in the tower with his bride if he so wishes."

"Where will you go?"

"I have kin in the north." His conscience pricked him, but what Cynebald did not know, he could not tell.

"Godspeed, my friend. May He guide and keep you."

Robyn placed his hand upon Cynebald's shoulder, then turned upon his heel and strode into the forest.

A band of outlaws lived deep in the woods. They were coarse and cruel, and Robyn knew full well they would just as soon kill him for his clothes and knife as speak to him, so he learned their haunts and avoided them.

Animals had begun to settle in their dens for the winter, and each day Robyn found less to sustain him. The apples and wild blackberries were gone, and he was down to a pocket full of hazel and beech nuts.

The feast of Harvest Home—what the old people still call Mabon—when the day and night were of equal length, had come to the village. While peasant and lord alike feasted in warm halls, Robyn shivered in the trees. A green cowl Lari had knitted him kept precious heat around his neck and shoulders, but it wasn't near enough.

He laughed bitterly. What a sorry avenger of his family he'd turned out to be. Slinking around the forest like a frightened hare, and he could only guess whether cold or starvation would take him first.

A flash of memory—Lari's empty grey eyes—speared his heart. White-hot rage bubbled in his gut, and it was all Robyn could do to stifle a roar. If the sheriff branded him a poacher, then a poacher he would become. He would not acquiesce to a meek and silent death. No. He would have his revenge.

The boar had been a large one, and the gamekeeper would likely note its absence. Robyn grinned as he licked the fat off of his fingers. His belly was stuffed to the point of discomfort, and yet the better portion of the hog remained.

He had neither salt nor time to smoke-cure the meat. Robyn knew from feasts past that there would be pork aplenty. No one would be the wiser if he left the remains of his supper with theirs.

The moonless night made traversing the forest more difficult than usual, but he slipped into the village, whose denizens were all a-slumber after gorging at the banquet.

He had butchered the boar into quarters and delivered the hunks at the community oven for the women to find when the sun rose in a few hours' time.

A proclamation fixed to one of the posts fluttered in the night breeze. Fear seized him for a moment, as he cared not to see his own wanted poster. But then he recalled that some weeks ago, the annual Yule festival and archery contest had been announced. The prize was usually a few coins, but this year it was a golden arrow. Not much use, that, but t'would gleam merrily upon a worthy man's mantle. He was a fair archer, but no match for either of his friends, Heath or Greysen.

As he made his way back to the depths of the forest, the clip-clop of hooves and the rattle of a carriage met his ears. Robyn ducked behind a tree.

A lantern on each side at the front of the ornate coach bathed it in a dim golden glow. It was lacquered in red and green, and richly appointed, certainly belonging to a lord.

A noble, for sure. Feeling his luck had shifted, he drew his bow and stepped in the carriage's path, nocking an arrow as it neared. "Hold there!"

The coachmen drew to a stop. Robyn felt the first pangs of regret as his quarry stilled and he got a better look at it.

It was drawn not by horses, but by stags, with antlers like tree branches and glowing eyes. He'd mistaken the coachman for a large carle in helm and cloak, but he beseemed more a forest troll in the flickering lantern light.

Laughter boomed from within the carriage. A mouse-like footman scurried from the darkened rear of the coach and opened the door.

From inside, a deep voice rose. "Come, come. Robyn Mason. Join me on this Mabon night."

Robyn's instinct was to flee into the darkness, but he was compelled as if by some unseen hand to step into the coach.

The interior was lit by some light whose source he could not determine. On the plush velvet cushion sat a jovial fellow in a red cloak trimmed in white fur. A crown of holly perched on his thick, dark hair. His hooded eyes were dark and glistening as jet.

By his side was an eerie beauty. Her skin was pale green, her ears long and pointed. Thick curling moss hung from her head in wide strands, and her lips were as red as blood fresh from a wound. His eyes could not focus on the fabric of her dress. It seemed to be woven of silk and fog—shimmering and ever changing. Long fingernails like icicles shimmered in her lap.

"The Holly King!" slipped from his mouth before he could help it. Robyn swallowed hard.

But the royal brushed off his rudeness with a laugh. "I am he. And this is my consort, Beira."

When Robyn was but a bairn, his mother's mother had told him tales of the never-ending war between two royal brothers, the Holly King and the Oak King. The Holly King ruled the dark half of the year and was slain by his brother in the spring. The Oak King ruled the light half and fell by his brother's sword in the fall. Robyn had long thought it was nought but a tale.

He did not recall lowering his bow or replacing his arrow in the quiver, yet neither was upon his person as he took his seat across from the regal couple and bowed his head. "My liege."

"Robyn Mason. Shall we parlay? I would set before you a small task. A trifling thing, really. Should you complete it to my satisfaction, I shall grant you a boon."

Robyn knew it would be no trifling thing, but it was likely far more dangerous to refuse such a request.

"Might I inquire as to the nature of this small endeavor?"

Beira gave him a chilly smile. "Unlock a certain lock. Nothing more. The key shall be provided to you."

"It sounds a simple enough task." *Where is this lock? At the bottom of a lake? The heart of a fire?* It might end in his death, but a refusal would guarantee such an outcome.

The Holly King grinned. "Have we a bargain?"

Robyn did not ascribe to the fairy faith and never had cause to bargain with fae folk, although, as all the people who made their homes in the great forests, he had been taught the rules as a child. Would they apply also to the old gods? It would do him no harm to act as such.

Do not tell them your true name. Alas, he knows that already. Speak fair and do not lie. Be specific in regard to any request. They are often tricksters and delight to fill the letter of the wish but not the spirit. Fae delight in gold, care little for silver, but iron is deadly to them.

"But your highness has not asked my terms."

The Holly King's face darkened. "*Your* terms?"

Robyn's mouth went dry, but he did not lose his nerve. "Sir. If this task you wish to set for me is such a trifling thing, any of your henchmen could easily accomplish it. I would surmise that this lock is made of iron, as is its key. Your folk cannot touch it without grievous harm, so you require a man to do so."

A smile tickled the lips of the Holly King, and soon he was bellowing with laughter. Once he caught his breath, he wiped his eyes. "A wily fellow we have found, Beira."

"All to the good. He may yet get out with his skin." A thin brow arched above one ice-blue eye.

"Then let us discuss terms, Robyn Mason." The king sat up straighter and leaned slightly forward. "One of my people of the water horse tribe was guising as a man in order to pluck apples from a tree. The lord's gamekeeper accused him of thievery, and he was taken to the gaol by the sheriff to languish until he could be hanged."

Good. He has also been dealt an injury by the sheriff, thus we share a common enemy. "And how do you propose I should break into the gaol to free him, without being snared myself?"

"Faery glamour." Beira tapped an icy fingernail on her chest. "To the guards, you shall appear as the old woman who, along with her dog, brings the daily meal to the prisoners. When you come to the cell of a stripling with black curly hair, unlock the door. He will take the shape of the crone's dog and follow you out."

Robyn nodded slowly. "This plan seems so simple. Wherein lies the pit?"

Beira cocked her head, and her eyes traced a path from king to commoner. "Pit? As in a seed?"

"No, ma'am. Pit as in a trap."

The king sighed. "Men do not hold the glamour so long as fae. A half-hour. Perhaps less. Should you fail to find the kelpie ere it fades, things will go ill for you, and there is little I can do to help."

"And what of the boon you offered?"

"What is your dearest wish, Robyn Mason?" The king leaned back against his velvet cushions.

"My family were slaughtered and a price put upon my head unjustly. I will have revenge against all responsible. I wish to see the fear in their eyes as I strike them down."

The Holly King's eyes bored into Robyn's, and some moments passed before he spoke. "Consider well what you ask. The having of a thing may be different from the dreaming of it."

"I want nothing else. Blood cries out for blood!" Robyn startled himself with his own passion and drew back against the velvet, although his head was held high and his back arrow straight.

Beira clutched the king's wrist, but he paid her no mind. "If you so wish it, you shall be revenge itself."

Something changed in the air, and it was if Robyn felt doom settle around his shoulders like a sodden cloak.

The carriage came to a stop. Leaves rustled as the footman rushed to open the door. The Holly King exited first, then he himself took Beira's hand so that she may alight gracefully from the conveyance.

When Robyn stepped out, he rubbed his eyes, unbelieving. Struck dumb, he stood agape in front of a castle tucked between trees as old as time itself. Amber light shone from each window, illuminating the evergreen garland draped upon its stone walls. Ice sparkled on bare oaks, their heavy, reaching branches twisted like the arms of a kraken. Gnarled, wide holly trunks gave way to glossy green leaves and red berries glittered amongst them like rubies.

He scarce heard the coachman cluck to the stags and the rattle of the empty carriage as it rolled away.

The silence weighed on Robyn like a millstone. "My liege. In all my wanderings, I have never come upon, nor even heard tell of this place."

"Indeed. No wanderer shall ever find the paths here but with my or my brother's permission."

Robyn followed Beira and the Holly King up the wide stone stairs. The heavy wooden door was flung wide by the king's chamberlain. Again, Robyn's jaw went slack. The chamberlain was a fox walking upon its hind legs. It wore a crimson tunic, embroidered with gold thread at the lower hem, and green woolen stockings.

The fox bowed to the Holly King. "Your highness."

Beira, the king, and Robyn stepped into the great hall. Hedgehogs in wimples, badgers in tunics, stoats in cowls, and a cluster of corvids—a crow, a magpie, and two ravens—wearing nothing but red and green berets, all jumped to attention at the entrance of their master.

Robyn had begun to wonder if the boar he had eaten earlier had grazed upon some strange herb that perfused its flesh and caused this flight of fancy. Perhaps he would awake in the sunlight under some clump of bracken or nestled in the crotch of a thick-boled tree.

The king raised his hand and turned it slowly in a royal wave. "Good evening! Or, I suppose the morning will soon be upon us. Make ready a room for our guest." He gestured toward Robyn. Several of the upright woodland creatures hurried up the marble staircase.

"Would you sup?" asked the fox.

"Aye!" The king rubbed his belly.

Robyn, whose belly was still stuffed to bursting with roast pork, bowed his head. "My liege. I am weary to the bone and fain would lie down."

A hare dressed in the king's livery was at his side in a moment. "Come with me, sir."

By the third day in the Holly King's castle, Robyn had grown used to the forest animal servants. He got on especially well with the fox chamberlain.

Robyn was at his breakfast, with the fox telling him tales of King Arthur and the Knights of the Round Table between mouthfuls.

The Holly King strode in and they jumped to their feet.

"The day has come, Robyn Mason. We must not tarry."

Robyn dipped his head. The castle was a far cry from living rough in the winter forest, and he had soon become accustomed to the warmth of a fire he did not have to tend. Still, the need to avenge his murdered family had been festering in his heart despite his comfort.

A cart laden with two cast iron cauldrons filled with pottage, with stacks of flatbread betwixt the twain stood near the community kitchen but was unattended. Wooden bowls peeked from a bulging sack that hung from one end.

"Where is the old woman?" Robyn asked, as he cast his gaze around the environs.

Beira gave him a terse smile. "She shall not be harmed and will have no memory of missing her gaol provisioning."

The Holly King handed him a length of rope with a piece of firewood tied to it. "Do not let this go. It is the leash for your dog."

"This stick?" Robyn lifted the rope so the wood dangled off the ground.

The King produced a leather pouch from his tunic, pulled it open, and began to sprinkle what appeared to Robyn as finely crushed gold upon the wood and then his person. "With this enchantment, the eyes of men will see nought but an old woman and her dog. But go about your business with haste—the charm will fade and if the bells of the abbey ring ere you return, this adventure will fall to ruin."

And my slow and miserable death, surely. But if I succeed, I shall have my revenge. I must not fail.

"Remember! Attend to the kelpie last. Discard firewood and rope in his cell, and he will take the form of the old woman's dog and return hither at your side." The Holly King pressed a silken pouch into Robyn's hand. "The key."

He tucked the bag into a pocket in his over-tunic. "A young man with dark eyes and dark curling hair." Robyn put a finger to his nose to stifle a sneeze.

"Open your mouth."

"Wha—"

The king sprinkled some faery dust on his tongue. "Your voice must sound as hers. Now off with you." The king gestured to the cart.

Robyn shook himself as the log took the form of a shaggy brown dog and closed in upon his heels. Loathe he was to touch the thing but, but curiosity drove him. Laying his fingers upon the dog's head, he quickly pulled them back. The hair was rough, as expected; but also colder than ice, which was not. As well, he did not recognize his own hand, which was wizened and gnarled.

He pushed the cart as fast as he dared until he rounded the corner and came within sight of the gaol. It was a ponderous building, built of dark grey stone and looming against the pale winter sky. The gallows rose not far from the entry gate, with ample room for a jeering crowd on execution days. Ice took form in the pit of his stomach, and its gelid tendrils unfurled up his spine. A decaying criminal hung from chains fixed to a gibbet post. Robyn thanked his lucky stars that he was upwind of the executed convict, even as he knew he would surely join that poor sod, should he fall into the clutches of the sheriff.

He slowed his gait to a hobble and kept his eyes downcast as the gaoler allowed him to pass inside. The man leaned over to pet the dog.

"Oy! He's a toof what's gone bad, and he's like as any to bite." Robyn startled at the harsh, cracked voice that came out of his mouth, so different from his own.

The gaoler swiftly retracted his hand.

Robyn gave a quick nod. "Visit to the old herb woman is what he needs. Then he'll be right as rain."

He fed three prisoners before his eyes fell upon a sullen young man with blue-black hair that fell in curls to his shoulders. His cell lay midway along Robyn's pottage route. It was no difficult task to apportion the soup so that the first pot was empty one cell before the fae's. Robyn then began the second pot on the opposite end row of cells, much to the complaints of the prisoners. The dog growled and snarled, and their tongues fell silent.

When Robyn came upon the cell that held the water horse, he cast a glance behind to mark what the guards were about. He need not have worried. They gave him no thought as they huddled around their game of knucklebones, swearing and guffawing as the bone dice skittered across the filthy floor.

Still, Robyn's heart galloped against his ribs as he slipped the key in the lock and opened the door just wide enough for the faux dog to enter the cell and the kelpie in the shape of a dog to slip out.

Robyn pushed the door to and as he withdrew the key from the lock, it fell from his trembling hands. He froze. The iron rang as a death knell when it struck stone.

The guards stopped their game and fixed their eyes upon him. He slipped the soup ladle in his sleeve and when he stooped to pick up the key, he raised it for them to see.

To his horror, his hand had near returned to its normal appearance. He kept his head down, the hood of his cloak obscuring his face, as he wheeled the cart past the guards. Eager to return to their game, they paid him little mind, and he passed through the door with no notice.

Robyn had just returned the old woman's cart to the village oven when a great hue and cry rang out. Guards streamed from the gaol as angry hornets from their hive.

"Run!" The ill-thought word tore from Robyn's mouth, catching the ears of the sheriff's men, and turning their tide in his direction. The dog at his side was away in an instant, hurtling pell-mell toward the open door of the Holly King's carriage, which lay in wait behind the shabby tavern in the town square.

His loping strides easily outpaced Robyn's and he jumped inside quick as a flash. The coach began to roll before poor Robyn caught up. He leapt for the coach box, and the footmen caught his arms and pulled him up.

Robyn sat panting betwixt the two, and as the stags bounded down the forest path, the gaolers were left far behind. Fear gave way to excitement. He had fulfilled his part of the bargain. Now the Holly King would grant his boon.

The feast of celebration for the kelpie's liberation had finished, and he and his family had set off for their underwater abode.

As the tunic-clad badgers cleared the table, the fox chamberlain and the Holly King shared a long glance ere the vulpine advisor bid his lord a good night.

The king's eyes fell upon Robyn. "Walk with me."

They both rose, the Holly King leading the way past several chambers until they came upon an oaken door. It creaked open as they drew near, revealing a narrow, twisting stair. The spiral was scarcely wider than Robyn's shoulders, and he felt he was merely stepping up and up in tiny circles. Neither torch smoked nor candle dripped, and yet there was light enough to tread the stairs.

By and by they came to another door which sprang open as the king reached out his hand. Pale moonlight shone through the narrow windows of the turret, but there was ought else he could see but his liege.

The king turned to face him. "Consider well the boon you ask. Some paths brook no return."

Robyn cocked his head. "Can you bring back my slain family, my liege?"

"You know I cannot."

"Then I shall have revenge. Once the blood debt is satisfied, I care not where my bones may fall."

Wisps of fog curled in through the windows, pooling on the floor and drifting across the room. Five figures gradually formed in the shadows. One towered above the Holly King even as another was hardly the size of a child four summers old. Red eyes glowed underneath a dark cowl, and Robyn thought he glimpsed two comely maids. He was near unmanned, but he had set his feet upon this path and there was nought else he could do but see it through.

The king paid them no mind. "Recall you this summer past?"

"I recall it well, but not with any joy. I was working on building a new tavern in the village for the merchant Cordell Presleye. A treacherous wall did collapse and crush his only son. I have not set chisel to stone since, and it has gone ill for my own family."

"Your craft did not fail you."

"Sir, I warrant it did."

"No. Robyn Mason, your skill was sound as ever. The treachery lay not in the wall but in the owner of the other tavern. Zephrine Humes could not abide that another inn might supplant his own, and to forfend the competition, he strove in league with his cronies to sabotage the construction."

Robyn blinked rapidly, then tilted his head this way and that. "How come you by this information?"

"Think you not my own folk are about day and night, whither seen by men or no? While you were on the hunt, your own good wife had overheard the tale whilst she was baking bread in the village. For another's careless whisper, her life was lost."

Fury burned at the base of his spine and spewed like dragon's fire from his mouth with a roar. The gleaming eyes in the darkness behind the king glowed all the brighter.

The Holly King's lips twitched into the faintest smile. "I have gathered here some of my subjects to aid you."

The child-sized figure stepped into the patch of moonlight between Robyn and the Holly King. A cheery red woolen cap crowned his head, but his flesh was the color of stone. Jagged teeth over-filled his mouth, though they were shadowed by his great hooked nose. His slitted eyes were the color of dried blood, and he clutched a double-headed axe in his iron claws.

The king nodded. "Wilem hails from the borderlands. Few can best him in a fight."

A woman in a grey cloak over a green dress moved to stand next to Wilem. A lock of long dark hair peeked from under her cloak.

"Alana Dale bends music to her will. Her song can be a warning or a snare. If her song waxes sweet, block up your ears."

The other fair lady stepped forward. Green eyes glittered under straw-hued hair.

"Maren is well suited as a spy in the camp. It is a rare man who can resist her charms, and the more they desire her, the more of their life force she drains."

The cassocked figure came to stand next to Wilem. He drew back his hood to reveal the round face of a priest, but his glowing red eyes were sunk deep in his skull, and his skin was the mottled green of a three-day-old corpse. He grinned, exposing rotten teeth. In his wake trailed two black dogs wearing thick collars of metal spikes, whose backs rose to his waist. Flames flickered in their fur and their eyes were glowing embers. The stone floor smoked and sizzled with each footfall.

"Friar Amok may guise as fair among village and clerical folk, but he is well-skilled in cunning and deception. He corrupts the pious, stirs strife, and turns friends to enemies as easily as a bird takes to wing."

Last of all, the hulking thing in the dark joined the mirthless band. He was half again as tall as Robyn and carried a longstaff ended with a wicked spiked ferrule. A heavy gold ring dangled from the ogre's wide nose and scraggly tufts of hair were sprinkled across the top of his otherwise bald head. His lower jaw jutted forward, bearing thick fangs half the length of his face.

"Legion has also a score to settle with the sheriff."

Robyn ran his eyes over the assembled fae folk. Revenge was in his grasp, and he had little care for its cost.

The band traveled to the sign of the White Hart, whereupon Maren vanished within. Robyn lingered with great unease in the shadows, his silent company behind him. He'd deemed it best to coax from Zephrine Humes names of his co-conspirators before dispatching the greedy fool.

When at last she decamped the tavern, she appeared in the company of a knavish lout, his meaty arm around her slender waist. He stumbled drunkenly beside her, then crushed her to him and planted his slavering lips upon her face.

Repulsed by his effrontery, Robyn started from his hiding place, but Alana snatched his arm and pulled him back. "Wait and watch." Her whisper sounded in his head rather than his ears.

The rogue with Maren tried to pull away from her, but he was stuck fast. His arms flailed, as he struggled to push her away, to no avail. It seemed to Robyn that the man was deflating like a wineskin as its contents poured out. The mason rubbed his eyes. Now Maren's companion was limp as a woolen stocking. Then he crumbled to dust, some borne away on the breeze, and some settling to the ground.

Maren licked her lips and strode toward the group, her emerald eyes fairly crackling with energy. Fear and anger battled in Robyn's breast. She was meant to press the innkeeper, not some randy carle. And should she turn her deadly embrace upon him, all would be lost.

"Let us away to the forest, then tell us of your encounter," Robyn whispered at her approach.

The company moved with hasty stealth to the darkling forest, though Robyn feared the footfalls of the ogre would wake the town. When they were safe away, they found a small clearing and sat in council.

"Who was that varlet?" Robyn fought to steady his voice so as not to shout.

Maren shrugged. "A common thief, a cutpurse. None will miss him. The tale he told was that upon pawing through contents of the stolen purses, he kept the coins and sold to Innkeeper Humes the rest, and his wife's sister-daughter sold them at the market for a profit. The place is rife with thieves and the like, and yet the sour old innkeeper retired to his bed and left his wife to serve the riffraff until they should quit the place."

"Ill luck for us. I would press Zephrine Humes as a vintner presses a grape." Robin crossed his arms. "Most taverns are thus, though the White Hart is less rancorous than most. What of the innkeeper's plot? Had he news of that?"

"Mayhap. He and a small band of outlaws were hired to guard a stone mason whilst he worked during the night to chip away at the foundations of a wall in the new tavern, then disguise the damage."

Robyn gritted his teeth. "How much did Humes pay these brigands?"

"Nought. They were paid by his cousin, the miller. He feared if even a groat more grain was subverted to the brewing of ale, there would not be grist enough for the mill."

"Tatton Birde!" Robyn scoffed. "A coin never stuck to his palm. His ten younglings might have some flesh upon their bones if only their father could keep himself from the dice tables." He sighed and shook his head. "I fear your dispatch of the knave was over-hasty. I would fain know if he and his company were one and the same as those who slew my family."

Friar Amok slapped his leg. "We should be off to rattle the miller's brains and pluck their names from his lips."

Legion raised his staff and shook it.

"With his wife and ten bairns about?" Maren asked.

"Nay." Robin rose to his feet. "I'll warrant he'll be headed to the tables on the morrow after he's collected his fees for the milling. We shall wait for him in the gloaming wood and reave him of his secrets."

Robyn supped in the late afternoon, and though he bade his companions to join him, they refused. Afterwards, the mason took up his quiver and bow, then strode into the forest. The band made their way to a trail that the miller was like to tread on his excursion to the gaming tables and concealed themselves amongst the shrubbery. Ere long, Robyn's guess was proved right when whistling reached their ears.

Tatton Birde, still dusted with barley flour from his day's work, stepped lightly down the path, a broken tune upon his lips.

With arrow already nocked, Robyn stepped from the thicket, his bow raised. "Hold, Miller Birde!"

The whistling ceased and the wiry fellow looked at him askance. "How now, Mason? Is not one price upon your head enough? You have turned to robbing travelers?"

"I care not for your purse, though I wot your wife would have it. I am here on a different errand. It has become known to me that you and your treacherous cousin caused the collapse of Cordell Presleye's would-be tavern and hung the blame around my neck."

Birde set his foot behind him as if he would turn and flee. Legion and Willem now blocked his retreat, although the miller seemed not to know of it, their approach having been so stealthy.

The miller sniveled and dropped to his knees. "It was not my idea! Zephrine pledged by his troth that the Guild would protect you and no harm would come to ought."

"And yet the blood of four innocents lies heavy upon your head." Robyn's cheeks flamed hot and his hands trembled with such wroth that if he had loosed his bolt, it would fall well wide of its mark.

"Not ours alone!" Birde sobbed. "The priest from St. Dunstan's Abbey set forth the idea when last he delivered beer to the White Hart. He did avow that Presleye's tavern would brew their own ale, rather than purchase beer from the monastery. And he was right ill-tempered about it."

"Not Father Osbert."

"The very same!"

At this, Robyn was near blind with rage. It was no small wonder that the wicket priest was loathe to meet his eyes whence Cynebald brought him to give funeral rites to Lari and his children. The two hellish hounds of Friar Amok came to sit at Robyn's feet, and Birde bawled like a hungry calf.

"As your cousin has bound you into his business, know you when the next beer wagon comes from St. Dunstan's?"

The miller could not take his eyes from the dogs, and he wept and tore his hair. "The morrow next," he gasped between sobs.

Such a keening arose from the trees that the miller quailed and threw himself prostrate before Robyn. "What fell thing makes such cries?"

"Hand over your purse, Tatton Birde."

"But—"

"That sound, miller, is your fate catching up with you. Your good wife will have need of your coins, as your path shall not cross hers again."

Robyn was aware enough of bean sidhe lore that he knew it must be Alana's wailing, but whether she called Death to her or merely recognized its approach was beyond his ken.

Birde's eyes widened as he sorrowfully reached within his tunic and handed a leather pouch over to Robyn. "Mercy! I beg of you! Take not the father from my children."

"I will give you the same mercy you and your lot gave *my* children." The mason drew back his bow, but ere the arrow took flight, Willem and Legion fell upon the wretched miller.

225

Robyn turned on his heel and strode back into the forest, Birde's shrieks bouncing off the stone that had taken the place of his heart.

Robyn betook himself alone to the mill. The sunrise was closer than the sunset, and he dared not knock upon the widow's door as she would know him. Instead, he let himself into the henhouse and dropped the miller's pouch of coins into one of the nest boxes.

When he returned to his companions, he found Legion picking his teeth with a rib bone and Willem's cap was a brighter shade of red.

Robyn adjusted his cloak. Would the same fate befall him, once his revenge was complete? It mattered little. He had no heart for either masonry or farming without his family and dreamed only of joining them.

He cleared his throat as he approached the assembled band. "We must set a trap for the faithless priest."

Friar Amok grinned, his crumbling teeth glinting in the firelight. "Beer should loosen his tongue, I reckon."

Maren quirked an eyebrow. "Shall we approach him on the highroad, saying, 'How, now, good Father! Shall we all have some of your fine beer?' and expect he will hop down from his wagon and give us a tipple?"

Legion's laugh was like unto boulders rubbing one upon the other. "No. We block his path through the wildwood and drown him in one of his own barrels if need be. Beer is a fine marinade for stringy meat."

Robyn shuddered at the thought of Father Osbert, whom last he'd seen giving funeral rites to his murdered family, becoming food for an ogre. But hadn't he also conspired in their murder? The mason pulled his green scarf tighter around his neck.

Willem capered about, clapping his bony hands, his iron claws clinking and scraping together. "Yes! Yes. Block up the road. Take the beer, bleed the priest. He will talk ere his last breath flees his body."

Only Alana sat silent, combing her long black hair.

In the end, it was decided that Robyn and Friar Amok, who could guise as fair, would go on the morrow to get the lay of the land where Father Osbert must surely pass with his wagonload of beer. Then they would reckon how best to set the trap for the priest.

The jests of Legion and Willem on how best to serve up Osbert had soured Robyn's stomach. He betook himself to his night's rest, his belly empty.

The day of Father Osbert's delivery to the White Hart arrived with a dusting of snow. After Robyn broke his fast, he and his faery band set off to trap the priest. Though Robyn shivered under his cloak, the others cared aught for the chill.

Friar Amok, who had lived in many an abbey and knew well the ways of the clergy, thought the priest would most likely leave after lauds, the dawn prayers. His journey should take four hours, perhaps five, and his arrival at the White Hart most surely would be just in time for the midday meal.

The company set off after their morning meal, the early sun already melting the thin layer of snow. So dense was the forest that most of the white powder remained on the naked branches of the sleeping trees, an offering to Helios, and its melt dripped onto the party like frozen stars.

Robyn chose a spot where trees near kissed the road on one side and an old Roman hillfort rose on the other. The beer wagon was too long to turn round in such a narrow spot. He and Alana concealed themselves so as to block him from going forward. Legion and Willem would stop him moving backward, and Friar Amok and Maren were stationed at either side of the road should the priest leap from the wagon and take to his heels. There they settled in to wait.

At the sound of voices, Robyn peeked from the thicket. Dread doused his skin like a cold stream of water. Some of the company of rogues and bandits that also called the forest home were riding shank's mare down the road. At the head of the troupe was a thing that Robyn could not tell whether it was beast or man.

It was taller than he and covered in black hair. As it plodded closer, he discerned that its face was hidden by a cowl of the same hairy hide that made up its britches and tunic. But whether it was a large man or just went on two legs like one, he could not determine. He ducked his head and held his breath as they passed.

At last, the clop of hooves and squeak of the beer wagon reached their ears. Alana handed Robyn two bits of beeswax, rolled into cylinders and tapered at one end. She pointed to her ears, then stepped into the road. Robyn recalled the Holly King's warning and stuck the wax in his ears forthwith.

A brawny Highlander walked at each side of the wagon while Father Osbert drove. He let out a gasp when his eyes fell on Alana, and he reined the plodding oxen to a stop.

"How, now, miss! Are you in need of aid?" the friar called.

She threw back her hood and her mouth began to move.

Robyn had only ever seen her hooded and was stunned to see what lay beneath. Alana's face would have been the envy of even queens in the highest courts, were it not for her eyes. They were white from edge to edge with no hint of color.

It was then he took note of the priest and his henchmen. They three stood still as oaks rooted to the spot as Alana approached them. Robyn was grateful for the wax, for if this was the effect her voice had on mortal men, he would become trapped in the web of her spell-song and have no part in this adventure. His ears caught the occasional note, but the full force of her power passed over him. He leapt from his hide to follow Alana.

When the treacherous friar shook himself, Robyn surmised the singing had stopped. Quick as a wink, he pulled the wax from his ears. "Hold, Father Osbert!"

The priest leaned forward. "Robyn Mason? What is the meaning of this?"

The morning's frost had chilled his granite heart and he set upon his grim purpose with icy resolve. "When good Cynebald brought you to say the rites for my family, I did not know at the time you had a hand in their slaughter. It was no wonder you could not bear to meet my eyes. But when the tale was told that you, Zephrine Humes, and Tatton Birde schemed against the building of the new tavern, I understood the meaning."

The priest spluttered, then regained his tongue. "So now you keep the company of witches? You will both burn for this. Out of my way!"

The grim Highlanders drew their Claymore swords.

Alana began to wail, a high, keening lament that sounded as if it flowed from a well of deepest sorrow. The Highlanders blanched, re-sheathed their blades, and fled. Of course, the Celts of the north would know the bean sidhe's cry heralded death.

Robyn tsk-tsked as the priest cursed their fleeing forms. The mason made no move when the cleric jumped from the wagon, as if to run into the forest.

Friar Amok appeared from behind a tree and the deceitful priest nearly bowled himself head-over-heels with his sudden halt. When he regained his balance, he crossed himself and raised the wooden cross that dangled from a thong around his neck. "Back, demon! Back I say! The power of God compels you!"

Amok laughed. "I am beholden to a much older God than yours. Your words pour over me like water from the back of a drake!" His red eyes burned brighter, and a cold shiver scuttled down Robyn's spine.

Robyn had come around to the side of the wagon by this time. "I will hear your confession, priest, so you will not die with unshriven soul."

"You would not dare. A murderer cannot pass into Heaven!"

"Then I shall see you in Hell."

Father Osbert's Adam's apple bobbed, and he changed tack. "It was not I! It was the verderer, Oswin Reevese, who handed you and yours over to the sheriff. He signed your death warrant. I am innocent!"

Oswin Reevese. Robyn had seen him from time to time when he was hunting and knew the man well enough to know he was the brother of Zephrine Humes' wife. The sheriff would take the ranger's word in an instant if he claimed a man was poaching.

Robyn fumed. *Was there no one in this wretched village who was not a party to my destruction?* His lips pressed into a thin line. "Even so, you still have the blood of Cordell Presleye's son on your head, though I have no doubt a lie would spring to your tongue as fast as an arrow to save your own skin."

"I confess! I confess I have conspired against you, and may God forgive me. But the death of the taverner's son was an accident. No one was meant to lose their life."

"It is up to St. Peter if the gates of Heaven open to you, and you shall find out by and by."

The oxen began lowing and stamping their hooves. Unable to flee, they dragged the front of the wagon off the road and lodged it in the trees. Maren appeared as if from nowhere and spoke to them in a low, soothing voice. In no time, she calmed the animals enough to unhitch them. Free of their traces, they lumbered as quickly as an ox can go in the direction of St. Dunstan's Abbey.

The ground shook as Legion in three long strides brought himself to within a yard of the quavering priest.

Osbert dropped to his knees, hands clasped as if in prayer. "Robyn Mason, I beg of you. Spare my life."

"Do you not think my wife begged for her children to be spared? There is not enough water in all the oceans to wash their blood from your hands." He turned to the ogre. "Do as you will with him. Free him, roast him. I care not. But when you have finished, please remove this beer wagon blocking the road. There is a leprosaria not far down that track. Perhaps haul it thence, as I reckon the sick get little pleasure in those hospitals."

With that, he slipped the wax back into his ears and turned his feet in the direction of their camp.

Robyn was forced to bide his time in confronting the father of the conspiracy, as Zephrine Humes had been keeping himself inside his tavern, surrounded by people, but the weasel must poke his head from his burrow sooner or later.

The moon had waned and waxed again ere Robyn espied which paths Oswin Reevese trod in the deep forest and learned the pattern of the ranger's comings and goings. The verderer always engaged at least two laborers by the day for each of his particular errands, and Robyn's neighbor Heath was sometime one of that number. It was a hard way to earn two pence, but Robyn himself had considered it since his fortune had turned after the tavern collapse.

So that no harm befell Heath, the mason would take care that his friend was not in the forest when the ranger was taken.

The company had broken their fast and sat planning the capture of the perfidious verderer.

"Shall we away then?" Friar Amok scratched the ears of one of his hellhounds, which closed its fiery eyes and lowered its massive head. "The Twisted Oak is at least an hour's march from here."

"Yes." Robyn rose to his feet. "I have already spotted Heath digging the last of his turnips this morning."

"Turnips!" Willem's lip curled. "Has he no wife to grub in the garden?"

"No. Heath has never married. His youth was wasted in the failed Crusade, and the scars he earned there put off many a maid."

Maren pursed her lips as she dusted dry grass from her skirt. "More's the pity. You speak well of him."

"Yes. I hunt often with him, Cynebald, and Greysen. They are all good fellows of hardy stock, and I would not trade a one of them for all a king's ransom."

Once their feet were set upon the trail to the Twisted Oak, they moved like shadows through the trees. Even Legion, with all his bulk, could move as quiet as a dormouse when he cared to.

After an hour and a quarter had passed, they arrived at the ancient tree. Gnarled limbs curled from a trunk that was wider than an oxcart, and the heaviest of them rested on the ground. All the company, save Legion, could clamber up into the crown of the tree and rest unseen among boughs thicker than the body of a stout man.

They found places to secrete themselves and settled in to wait until Oswin the verderer should come along the path.

Robyn's eyelids had begun to droop before the ranger finally made his appearance. One of the men with him was a laborer from the village who often worked at the mill, and the other he did not know.

With an arrow nocked, he stepped onto the path, blocking the trio. "How, now, ranger! Hold, so I may have a word."

Oswin's lip curled into a sneer. "Well, well, Robyn Mason. Have you come to surrender to me and fatten my purse?"

"I have come to chasten your false tongue."

The ranger's eyes narrowed, drawing his thin lips up. "There are three of us and only one of you. And I will not be called a liar by a wild dog!"

Robyn clenched his jaw. "Oh, my fangs you will yet see. I have never taken aught but what was allowed—small game and smaller birds. And yet you accused me to the sheriff of poaching. I will not swing for your lies." He pulled the arrow back another inch, the taut bowstring creaking.

Oswin's nostrils flared. "I was shown ample proof! A haunch of venison. The feathers of a swan. The wing of a pheasant."

"How came you by this…proof?" Robyn's voice was closer to the growl of an animal than to the speech of man. "I have never done such a thing. Tell me verderer, when did last you see a swan in this forest?"

"But—"

An arrow whistled past Oswin's ear and stuck fast in a tree over Robyn's shoulder. The fletching was dyed red and the shaft was black.

Robyn whipped his gaze toward the road. The tall man clad in hair-covered hide and some of his company had slipped from the forest with nary a sound. *Does this thief come to rob us both?*

The ranger whirled to face the newcomer. "Guy of Gis-bourne!" His tone carried more of surprise than fear.

Robyn's mouth was dry of a sudden. The murderous repu-tation of that outlaw was known far and wide, though few who met him lived to tell the tale. Some said he was a giant in a green elven cloak, others that he was a forest troll clad in red, and yet others that he was merely a man in clothes as black as the devil's heart. It seemed the sturdy verderer had some acquaintance with the villainous fellow, as he knew the rogue the instant he clapped eyes upon him.

In a voice that sounded like boots tramping upon gravel, Gis-bourne spoke. "Well done, ranger. You have saved me some trou-ble. Be off with you. This is none of your affair."

The verderer's face flushed to purple. "You do not have leave to command me! I will collect the boun—"

Somewhere behind Gisbourne, a bow twanged and a black arrow found its mark. Oswin the verderer fell down dead as a hammer.

Gisbourne cast back his hood. Scars criss-crossed his left cheek and there was a wide notch in his ear. Stringy, dark hair clung to his blocky face and his piglike eyes were black as a pot of pitch. A smirk sat upon his thick lips. "How, now, Robin the mason. It is a shame to kill the goose that laid the golden eggs, and yet today you must die."

"What nonsense is that?" Robyn snarled.

Gisbourne threw back his head and laughed. "I am thrice paid because of you. A handsome purse of gold was given to me to slaughter your family, which I gladly did. Your wife was a beautiful woman and her skin was so soft." He licked his greasy lips with an obscene tongue.

It was all Robyn could do not to hurl himself upon the villain. Fury burned so fiercely it heated his very skin and the blood of his veins roared in his ears. "That is but one. Or do you think one is three?" he spat.

Gisbourne's fat lips thinned into a grin. "No. That scabby tavern owner paid me to take your head, and then I will turn it in to the sheriff for the bounty."

Robyn's rage cooled to icy resolve. Either he or Gisbourne would take his last breath on this day. "If you want my head, come and take it."

Motion to his right caused Robyn to turn. A minion of Gisbourne's had been creeping up upon him. One of Friar Amok's hellhounds leapt at the outlaw's throat with a growl. Legion was not far behind, his longstaff raised. Around him, the sounds of combat and the growling of dogs arose.

He turned in time to meet Gisbourne's charge and knock him back. Gisbourne drew his sword, and Robyn had nought but a hunting knife. He spied a fallen oak limb the size of a heavy staff and ran to seize it. Long those two strove against each other, Gisbourne hacking at Robyn's branch until at last it broke.

Gisbourne swung his deadly blade at Robyn and in leaping to avoid it, he caught his foot on the root of a tree and fell on his back. With a rapacious grin, Gisbourne raised his sword, clasping the hilt in both hands to plunge it into Robyn's breast. In the beat of a heart, he moved aside and raised his dagger in both hands. Gisbourne's blade only caught the edge of Robyn's tunic, but the dagger's path was true. It struck below the outlaw's ribs and pierced his shriveled heart.

His mouth gaped in surprise, then he fell like a rotten tree.

Robyn lay on his back, panting, his hands sticky with Gisbourne's cooling blood. He had thought slaying the one who slaughtered his family would give him peace, but his heart was no less empty. Mayhap when Zephrine Humes breathed his last, his task would be complete, and order would be restored to him. A plan to serve a generous helping of revenge to the treacherous taverner was even now being birthed in his restless mind.

Friar Amok grasped the heft of Gisbourne's sword, pulled it free, and tossed it aside. Robyn took his extended hand and allowed himself to be pulled up.

Maren wiped a streak of blood from her chin. "This band of thieves will trouble this wood no more."

Robyn nodded. His arms and shoulders had already begun to stiffen from the pummeling he had taken from Gisbourne. "Legion!"

The ogre strode over, the ground shaking under his heavy tread.

"Legion, how many of that parcel of rogues could you carry?"

"Four of the six with ease."

"Amok, you and Willem assist Legion to deliver these corpses to the sheriff. Wait until nightfall, then leave them at the gallows. Leave Gisbourne to me."

"Alana and Maren, I require your aid."

Robyn was awakened from a dead sleep by hot breath on his cheek. His lids snapped open to see the glowing eyes of one of the Holly King's stags. The footman was already holding open the door of the coach.

With a sigh, Robyn raised his weary bones and climbed into the carriage.

Inside, the Holly King sat alone. "Well met, Robyn Mason. How fares your tour of revenge?"

Robyn doubted that not a bird took wing in the forest but the king knew of it. "The murderer has met with cold steel, yet the one who bred all this coil still hides like a rat in a hole."

The king stroked his beard. "I would ask a small favor of you."

Robyn recalled running with prison guards hot on his heels after the last small favor he had performed for the Holly King, and his heart sank. Yet, he could deny his benefactor nothing. "Another trifling thing, my liege?"

"You have seen, have you not, the proclamations pinned to pillar and post in the village about the Yule festival and games?"

"I have."

The king grinned. "Excellent. You shall enter the competition and win the golden arrow."

"Sir, I am a middling archer at best."

The Holly King gestured to a quiver and a long bow Robyn had not noticed when he entered the coach. "One of these arrows fired from this bow cannot miss its mark. Secure the golden arrow, by fair means or foul, and bring it to me."

"Consider it done." He did not care to be sidetracked on what seemed a frivolous quest, but his five companions aided him at the pleasure of the Holly King, and he could ill afford to lose them.

"You are still battle-weary from this afternoon's adventure. Go to your rest."

The carriage door swung open.

"Thank you, my liege." Robyn picked up the bow and quiver and climbed out of the coach.

Robyn's nose wrinkled as he waited in the shadows. Guy of Gisbourne's hairy clothes reeked aplenty of their own accord, ere his blood had soaked them. The mason pulled the hood down so his face could not be seen. Friar Amok stepped out of the White Hart Tavern and nodded in his direction.

Robyn slipped around to the back entrance and rapped on the oaken door. No one came, so he raised his hand to give it another clout. It creaked open, and Zephrine Humes' wife stood before him. Her hands flew to her mouth.

Keeping his voice as gravelly as he could muster, Robyn said, "I have business with your husband."

She nodded and fled inside, without so much as closing the door behind her.

Presently, Humes strode into the kitchen and espied Robyn waiting for him. He stopped within an arm's length of the visitor. "Is it done?"

Robyn nodded, but said nothing. From a pack on his back, he pulled out his own bow and knife.

Humes studied the weapons, all the while gnawing the inside of his cheek. "Fine. A moment." He handed them back to Robyn, turned on his heel, and disappeared into the tavern.

By and by, Humes returned and handed Robyn a heavy leather pouch. "Now go, before someone sees you!"

Robyn tucked the pouch into his pack, along with the bow. The knife he kept in his hand.

Humes eyed the blade and took a step back. "Do you think to rob me in my own tavern, Gisbourne? Is your payment not enough?"

Robyn threw back the hood.

"You!"

"Indeed. You murdered my family and besmirched my reputation. Then you paid the same villain to reave my head from my shoulders. I am no priest, but I will hear your confession, lest you die unshriven."

Light from the kitchen fire glinted off the steel of the knife. Friar Amok peered through the doorway behind Robyn.

Humes dropped to his knees, his hands clasped in supplication. "Prithee, stay your hand! I had no thought to wrong you so! He said the Guild would protect you!"

"He?"

"Yes. Are you not a freemason? The Guild would find you work and though Presleye's new tavern might collapse, you would carry on much as before." Humes choked back a sob. "That stripling, his son, was never meant to be inside. His blood is upon my hands, and yet I kept my silence. We all did. But then my wife…." He ground the heels of his hands into his eyes.

"What of your wife?" Robyn clenched his teeth.

It took the taverner several moments to collect himself. "She went with her sister to the oven to bake bread." Humes sniveled and wiped his nose on his sleeve. "Your wife was there. My wife's sister was indiscreet. When your wife caught wind of the tale of the tavern… she was furious and had harsh words for the two. She said upon your arrival home from the hunt, she would tell you all that she had heard. If you carried this news to the sheriff, we'd all dance at the end of his rope."

"So Oswin the verderer is the author of my ruination."

"No. No, of course not. Though he may have been stuffed with his own importance, he was bound to the law as pages are bound in a book. It was no great thing to trick him, using the venison and pheasant Father Osbert brought from St. Dunstan's. Duly outraged, he set off forthwith to the sheriff."

"So, Father Osbert—"

"I will hear no hard words against him! He was a good man. You do not understand the peril St. Dunstan's is in. The abbot gave a pair of silver candlesticks to a widow woman to sell so her children would have bread in the winter. The candlesticks had been gifted to the abbey by the bishop, who was sore affronted by the abbot's generosity. He withholds tithes, starving the abbey. If the brothers had no beer to sell, they would be nought but dry bones by now. But they could ill afford to lose even a pence to another brewer. He had no hand in the deaths of your family. His only crime was subterfuge to keep the wolf from the door."

That only leaves the miller. "Your cousin, then. What did he know of Guilds?"

"Tatton? Nothing, I reckon. He was a fool, but his heart was kind. Did you know his youngest son was a cripple? So desperate for his treatment was Tatton that he pinned his hopes on winning at the gambling tables. Had he set the money by, he would have had a goodly store. I tried to reason with him, but my arguments fell on deaf ears. He gave his wife barely enough to feed the family. My cousin, mooncalf that he was, could not be turned from the gambling dens, and if the mill's income was reduced by less grain being ground to flour, his children would have borne the brunt of it."

"Then who set Gisbourne against my family?"

Humes dropped his head and sobs wracked his body. "It was I. When your good wife threatened to go to the sheriff, I was in such fear of my life. Had I known I was cutting my own throat, I would have let the chips fall where they may." He shuddered. "I have never seen such fury, not even yours. He said he would boil me alive in my own pottage." Humes laughed bitterly and raised his eyes to Robyn's. "The sheriff will hang me, and you are here to cut out my heart. I tried to forestall your revenge, yet here you are like a nemesis. For my sins, God has left my fate in the hands of Lady fortune, and her wheel is on the downturn. I am nought but a dead man walking."

"You brought this ruin upon your own head. Could your consortium not parlay with Cordell Presleye? I'll warrant he'd trade any amount of gold for the life of his son. And by God's bones, who is this other man who would avenge my family? Name him!" Robyn's hand shook so that he could scarcely hold the knife.

"Avenge? I suppose. But only because he coveted your wife for himself. Ever he spoke of her in loving terms. It was he who suggested setting you up to take the blame for the failed wall. And the false report of poaching, for which he contrived to lure you from your home."

A sick feeling twisted through Robyn's gut, as if he'd eaten spoiled meat. "Name. Him."

Humes released the breath from his body in a loud gust. "Heath Wilkinse."

Robyn staggered, as if struck a blow to the heart.

Taking advantage of his distraction, Humes grabbed the knife from Robyn's quaking hand and plunged it into his own breast.

Thunderstruck, Robyn hardly noticed the taverner's hot blood pooling around his boots. Friar Amok stepped past him and removed the blade from Humes' chest. He pulled Robyn along like an intransigent child through the pitch-black forest to their camp, his hellhounds leading the way.

This betrayal shattered Robyn's heart anew, and he sat at the camp, witless and refusing all food.

After two days, Maren knelt before him. "Come, Robyn. Put by your grief for now. We must prepare for the Yule Festival. For this adventure, we have need of gold. Amok bids us go to the sheriff's office and collect the bounty on Gisbourne's head."

"I cannot strut like a cock into his lair with a price on my own head. That would be a fool's errand."

"Alana reports that he is alone in his offices for at least the morning. Shall we hie us hence, with the villain's sword and clothes?"

The sheriff brushed hair the color of dust from his face and looked up from his papers as Robyn and Alana entered his office, bearing the relics of the slain outlaw.

"What is the meaning of this!"

From beneath his hood, Robyn said, "We have come to collect the bounty on this outlaw. Ten pounds Sterling for Guy of Gisbourne, alive or dead."

The sheriff scoffed. "There is no bounty on his clothes. Good day."

"Did you not find the corpses of his gang laid stiff upon the gallows not four days ago? Do you think Gisbourne would give up his sword and suit of hide to me if breath were left in his body?"

"I'll wot this rogue was the bane of my existence, and I thank you for dispatching him, but who are you that speaks to me with such cheek?" The sheriff's sharp features were rendered even more rodent-like by the squinting of his eyes.

"We are but concerned citizens, your worship, doing our part to make the forest safer for all to travel."

Robyn pulled the wax cylinders Alana had given him from his tunic and plugged his ears, as the sheriff rose to his feet and grasped the hilt of his sword in consternation.

Alana began to sing and the sheriff's eyes lost their focus. He turned to a cupboard behind him and withdrew a strongbox. From there, he counted out ten pounds, which Robyn collected in a pouch and stashed in his tunic. Alana continued to sing as they backed out of the office. They slipped into the wildwood before the sheriff could recover his senses.

When they returned to the camp, Maren and Friar Amok filled a pouch with a few pounds and took themselves to the village to procure what would be needed for the festival. The hounds stayed behind.

Robyn, the grip of his despair loosened, paced before the campfire like a cow beset by biting flies.

"Heath Wilkines was as a brother to me, and I loved him dear. His treachery has ripped the heart from me and tossed it into the fire. Though I am duty bound, I have little care for festival or Yule. Can not one of you string this enchanted bow and reap the reward?"

Willem grinned. "No. The golden arrow was stolen by a man and a man must return it."

"Stolen?"

"You have no idea what you have been tasked, have you?" Willem shot a glance at Legion.

"Has it meaning, then, other than as a rich prize?"

The ogre and the redcap threw back their heads in laughter to such an extent the hellhounds trotted circles round them, whining.

When he had recovered himself, Willem put his steel-clawed hands upon his hips. "The arrow has a golden shaft, but the tip is iron, leafed in gold. It is the warmth of summer, even as the seed of winter's chill is planted in its heart. The Oak King must shoot it from his bow when he awakes at Ostara, else the winter will not yield to spring. It was stolen, by means yet to be made clear. Ere he fell to the Holly King, he went to his sacred grove to pull it from the ground, but found it not."

Robyn sighed and cast his eyes downward. "It is ill such heavy burden would be set upon my weary shoulders. I fear I have not heart enough to see this adventure through."

Merriment flowed like the sea around Robyn and his co-hort, yet joy touched him not. Dressed as a nun, and cloaked and veiled to boot, he stood with Friar Amok to draw lots for the archery contest.

"Good day to ye, Friar!" The man, bald as a hen's egg, gave Amok a gap-toothed grin and put forth a leather pouch.

"Nay, I could not string a bow to save my life. Our good Sister Ysoria here will take her chances at the targets."

The bald man's brows arched near to the crown of his head. "A woman! Surely not, Father. Saints forfend! Pray do not jest with me."

"Do you fear the local archers would be bested by a nun?"

"Certainly not! Has a woman even the strength to draw a long bow?" He eyed the yew bow that curved along the friar's back.

"Let her choose a lot, and you shall find out."

"I must assess the entry fee, even for clergy."

"Done and done." Amok pulled a purse from his tunic and handed over a silver penny. 'Sister Ysoria' took the proffered chit from the bald man with a slight bow of the head.

As they turned from the table, Robyn made eye contact with Maren. Although she was dressed as one of the villagers, she wore a nun's tunic beneath her dress. There was no disguising Legion, Willem, or Alana, and they waited at the eaves of the forest, if perchance their help was needed. Friar Amok had reluctantly left the hellhounds to guard the camp.

If all went to plan, Robyn would use the enchanted bow and his own arrows at the start of the competition. He did not need to win any round but the last, merely shoot well enough to keep advancing. All the better if Sister Ysoria seemed to struggle at the beginning. It would play upon the others' vanity and let their guard fall through false comfort. Friar Amok had the Holly King's quiver hidden in his cassock and would swap one for the other ere the start of the last match.

While they waited for the archery competition to begin, Robyn and Friar Amok wandered about the festival. As they stood at the table of a local weaver, admiring the colorful cloth, the sheriff approached.

"How, now, Friar! Sister," he greeted the pair as if he knew them.

Friar Amok made the sign of the cross. "May the peace of Christ be upon you, friend. Tis a fine day the Lord has given us for celebration."

The eyes of the sheriff fell upon Sister Ysoria, waiting for a salutation.

Friar Amok cleared his throat. "Please forgive Sister Ysoria. She is of the Cistercian order and speaks only during prayers. She has stopped at St. Dunstan's hostelry on her pilgrimage to Canterbury."

The sheriff's lips pursed ever so slightly, and he nodded slowly. "How comes a nun to enter an archery competition? The village has never seen the like."

Without a pause, Amok said, "As a young child, Sister Ysoria's father was taken from the family by the Great Mortality. As the oldest of ten, she took up his bow and learned to hunt for small game to feed her siblings."

The sheriff's eyebrow arched sharply. "She told you this, did she?"

"The Mother Superior sent letters of introduction for the sister's travels."

"I see." The sheriff stared hard at the nun's veil. "Then I wish you well, Sister. It would be a novel thing indeed should a woman of the cloth win our contest. Good day to you both."

The sheriff strolled away, casting his eye this way and that at the goods on offer, or more likely, any who might be poised to make off with them.

Robyn turned to Amok and whispered, "He suspects."

"Hold to the plan. He can prove nothing."

A horn sounded, calling the archers to their targets. Robyn found the one that was marked with the same colors of his chit. Amok stood near as he strung his bow. He purposefully struggled with the enterprise and had scarcely nocked an arrow when the horn was blown to commence the shooting.

After the targets were inspected, Robyn passed into the next round, and the next. At the end of the third round, the judge trudged back and forth betwixt Robyn's target and another three lanes down. He called upon the mayor and the bald man who sold the chits. The three stood at one target, then the other, debating among themselves, with many a backward glance at Sister Ysoria.'

"This bodes ill," Robyn whispered through clenched teeth. His eyes flew to the golden prize set upon a table in front of the mayor's seat. Then he spied Maren in the crowd. Her gaze cut to the arrow and back to meet Robyn's.

"Hear, hear!" the judge shouted. "There is not a hair's breadth between the good Sister's arrows and those of Hayden Westcott. The two shall each shoot an arrow into a single target. The closest to center advances to the final round. Hayden, move yourself to join Sister Ysoria."

Friar Amok began at once to offer a loud and elaborate blessing, with much waving of arms and entreaties to heaven. In the meantime, Sister Ysoria knelt to pray and made the exchange of quivers.

When the mundane arrows were safely concealed, Amok bid Ysoria to rise. "May Christ himself guide your arrow, Sister." He turned to Hayden. "Blessings upon you! I humbly insist you take the first shot."

With a smirk upon his lips, Hayden Westcott stepped up to the line and drew his bow. He exhaled and let the bolt fly. From where Robyn stood, it looked dead center of the target. He swallowed his rising bile, hoping that the arrows of the Holly King were true to his promise.

As he nocked the enchanted arrow and drew it back against the bow, he felt a surge of energy, as if the twain, once united, became a living thing. It so jangled his nerves that he nearly dropped the bow. But he raised it, focused on the target, and set the arrow free, the twang of the bowstring so loud in his ears it could have been Gabriel's trumpet.

A great *crack* shattered the air as Robyn's arrow split Hayden Westcott's in half. The crowd gasped and the judge, the mayor, and the bald man ran to the target.

"It would seem the good friar has indeed called down a miracle! Hayden's bolt is dead center of the target, and Sister Ysoria's is dead center of that."

With that, the other archers unstrung their bows.

"What chance have I against God's will?" cried one.

"It's a miracle! A miracle!" shouted another.

That cry rippled through the crowd. Robyn and Amok found themselves beset with villagers.

"Please, Father. Call down a miracle for my son! He's broken his leg and it will not heal."

"My crop has failed. Bring a blessing to my family so my children may not starve!"

"My mother is dying. Heal her, I beg of you."

Hands grabbed for Friar Amok's cassock, as it seemed everyone from three villages around pleaded for a miracle. Someone pressed a silver penny into Robyn's hand. He caught the man's wrist and gave the penny back. Then he crossed himself and clasped his hands together in prayer.

"I see you have also taken a vow of poverty," Amok grumbled.

The pain of the villagers cascaded over Robyn until he felt he would drown in their sorrows. No miracle had been called down from on high, for the enchantment lay upon bow and arrows alike. Unless the people longed for archery perfection, he could do nothing to help them, and it tore at his soul. When he thought he could hear no more of their grief without his own heart bursting asunder, the ground began to shake.

With a roar, Legion stormed into the festival, his longstaff raised high. Entreaties for help turned to screams of terror. Sister Ysoria was nearly swept off her legs as the villagers took to their heels in panic.

"Fee, fie, foe, fum!" the ogre growled at the top of his lungs.

Amok snickered under his hood. He raised his arms to the sky, palms up. The wind rose and the pale sun was covered over by grey clouds. "In the name of God and his holy host! Leave this place!"

Legion's hands flew to protect his face and stumbled backward several paces before turning and legging it out of there.

Robyn surveyed the grounds. Moments before, the place had been heaving with people, now there was not a soul, save Sister Ysoria and Friar Amok. "Well, then. All that remains is to claim the golden arrow."

When he turned to the mayor's table, the prize was nowhere to be seen.

"No!" With a groan, Robyn charged to the officials' box. He searched high and low, but no trace of the arrow could be found.

"Come, Robyn!" Friar Amok was hastening toward him. "The sheriff gathers his men. We must away!"

"But the prize!"

"There is no help for it. We must go."

Disheartened, Robyn and Friar Amok arrived at the camp. The mason caught sight of the carriage before his eyes fell upon the Holly King, who stood conversing with Maren and Alana. Robyn's shoulders drooped. He had no wish to apprise the king of his failure.

Amok's hellhounds trotted up to greet him, spiked tails wagging.

Maren gesticulated as the Holly King roared with laughter. Robyn hung his head and stepped meekly to the three.

"Ah! There you are, Sister!" The king's cheeks were flushed with good cheer. "Maren has been regaling us with the tale of the festival."

Robyn tore off the veil and wimple. "And yet it was all for nought. In the furor, someone absconded with the golden arrow. I have failed the cause, my liege."

Silence weighed upon Robyn's shoulders as a boulder.

Maren's bright laugh was like unto a silver bell. "I stood near the tables while the mayor was dithering about your target. A most unsavory pair cast envious eyes upon the golden prize, so I pocketed it for safekeeping."

Joy swelled in Robyn's heart such that he nearly embraced Maren, then thought the better of it. She withdrew a soft leather sack from her tunic and handed it over to him. He reached inside to take out the arrow, but the instant his fingers closed round the shaft, down he fell upon the ground as if in a swoon.

The darkness cleared from Robyn's eyes, and he found himself standing in the autumn wood. He tried to take a step, but found his feet planted fast to the earth.

"Swithin! Mummy said take neither wren nor robin. Let it be!"

Robyn could not draw his breath. Swithin? Eadda? What sorcery was this? He tried to call out to his children, but no sound could he utter. He could do nought but stand and watch as a tiny brown wren fluttered past, with Swithin close behind, his white-blond hair sparkling in the late afternoon sun. Robyn wanted nothing more in the world but to run to his children and embrace them both. But his feet were rooted and his tongue was muted.

The bird perched upon a slender branch in a holly bush. Swithin stood still, casting his eyes upon the earth. At last, he bent and picked up a small stone. Quick as a weasel, he hurled it at the bird.

Eadda screamed. "I'm going to fetch Mummy!"

Robyn could not tell if the bird had fallen or merely flown away. Eadda's running footfalls amongst the leaf litter quickly faded. Swithin crept into the thicket.

"God's bones!" Swithin cried from the bushes.

Robyn cringed, wishing he'd better governed his tongue around the bairns.

The lad emerged, holding in his hands the Oak King's golden arrow.

No! Put it back! Leave it lay! Try as he might, the bridge between his thoughts and his tongue was broken.

Heavy footsteps crushed the dry leaves as they hurried toward Robyn's son. "Swithin?"

Heath Wilkinse!

"Uncle! Uncle! Look what I've found!" Swithin held out his find.

Heath took the arrow and cast his eye from one end to the other, turning the bolt this way and that. "It is a thing of beauty, aye. But tis far too heavy for a proper hunt, eh?"

Swithin frowned. "It must weigh as much as Eadda! I wanted my own arrows, Uncle. Father said I could join the hunt in the spring."

"Yes. That he has said to me as well. I fear even I haven't strength enough to draw the bow that could launch this arrow." He raised the weighty bolt. "But if it's arrows you seek, then let me buy this one from you for a silver penny, and you can fill your quiver with arrows of suitable size."

With this, Swithin's eyes brightened and he held out his hand. Heath pulled his pouch from his tunic and retrieved a shiny coin for Swithin. The arrow he placed in his game bag.

Knave! You knew full well hard times had befallen us, yet you took this prize from a trusting child.

"I suppose Eadda has told her tale to your mother by now. You had best be on your way home."

With a loud sigh, Swithin tucked the penny into his pocket. "Yes, Uncle."

Light footsteps crunched away down the trail. Now Robyn, through no volition of his own, followed Heath. He wondered if he floated behind him like a phantom, and if his erstwhile friend but turned his head, he would recoil in terror.

As Robyn followed Heath through the forest, he noted the shiny golden tip of the arrowhead peeked out the top of the bag if Heath moved in a particular way.

This bodes ill.

Robyn recognized the forest track and was not at all surprised when they came anon to the village. It was market day, and the streets held more people than a wild boar has hairs upon its back, it seemed.

Alackaday! Robyn spied the very same cutpurse from the White Hart Tavern who had revealed the treachery of the taverner and the miller to Maren. Even as he knew it would be to no avail, Robyn tried to shout a warning. Silent as a shadow, the thief moved close to Heath. In less time than it takes to draw breath, the knave had slipped the game bag from Heath's shoulder and fled into the throng.

"Thief! Thief!" Heath shouted as he gave chase.

Robyn's view shifted to the cutpurse, who slipped into an alley and made his way out of the crowded marketplace and into the wildwood. By and by, he came to a lean-to deep in the thicket.

He sat upon a fallen tree and dumped the contents of Heath's game bag upon the forest floor.

"Ha! My supper is provided." He straightened out the limp rabbit and picked up the golden arrow. "Well, well, well. What have we here?" He turned the shaft this way and that, ran his fingers over the yellow fletching, and pricked his thumb upon the point. "Oww!" The thief raised his bloody thumb to his mouth.

Robyn had endured watching the robber cook his meal and take a long nap. At last, he had shaken his lazy bones and hid the arrow in what Robyn guessed was one of the many secret pockets inside his tunic.

The mason knew in an instant that the thief had set his feet upon the path to the White Hart Tavern. When he arrived, he unclipped a leather-covered tankard from his belt and banged it down on the bar. "Fill me jack, Humes."

"Have you coin?"

"Take it out of our next deal."

Zephrine Humes snorted. "You are as like to stretch the hemp as pick another pocket. I'll have my silver now, thank you."

With a sour face, the thief laid a coin upon the bar, whereupon Humes took the battered jack and filled it. The cutpurse took his drink and slunk off to the dice tables to try his luck.

The mayor was there. And the miller. Robyn knew the faces but not the names of the other men gathered in the gambling den.

In short order, the small piles of coins passed from the other players to the hoard in front of the mayor. Beaming like a sated Mammon, he moved to sweep his gains into a leather pouch.

"Hold!" the cutpurse raised a hand.

"Lady Fortune had frowned upon you this night. Pray take your outrage to her."

"One last round. All or nothing."

The mayor gestured to the empty table. "I would oblige you, but you have nothing left to stake."

The thief reached into his tunic and withdrew the golden arrow. "I wager this. Surely it is equal at least to your winnings."

The mayor took it from him and weighed it in his hand. "A bar of iron, leafed in gold." He cocked his head and sucked his teeth. "Still, it will make a fair prize for the Yule archery contest. I'll warrant I can save a few coins from the town's coffers and the rubes won't be any the wiser. Very well, then. I will wager one quarter measure of my winnings."

A scowl breezed across the thief's features, then bravado stained his grin as he rolled the dice. He swore at the results.

The mayor made his play, trouncing the other man's score. "Well then. I shall take my spoils." He lifted the arrow. "You have done a service to your village, although I am sure it was not your intent. Good evening."

Darkness descended over Robyn's vision like a pall. He opened his eyes, and the world appeared as if through a mist. Slowly it cleared, and he sat up. Legion clasped his hand and pulled him to his feet.

Robyn shook his head quickly. "I can scarce believe Heath would cheat a child. I had always thought him a just and honorable man. And yet his soul is as ruined as his face."

The Holly King stroked his beard. "Mayhap. But have you considered that he, like the mayor, perceived the golden arrow to be a cheap forgery, and worth little? Forsooth, who would leave a rich treasure lying about the forest?"

"That may yet be true, but the envy in his heart and the lust for my wife has caused all our downfall. His redemption cannot be bought with a mere silver penny."

Robyn handed over the golden arrow.

The king nodded gravely. "With your heart bent on revenge, have you thought to light candles for the dead?"

"I forsook God when he forsook me."

"But have you forsaken the souls of your wife and children?"

Even as anger flowed as blood through his veins, he knew the folly of raising his voice to the Holly King. With a curt bow, he turned on his heel and strode away into the forest.

The longer he walked, the more his fury cooled, and the words of the Holly King stung him. He had been so overtaken with grief and rage that he had taken no thought to the innocent souls of his family. They would have had no funeral rites had Cynebald not called in the treacherous Father Osbert. There's the rub—he gave them a requiem with their blood on his hands. A hot tear cooled on his cheek. Lari's gentle soul would be crushed by the weight of the vengeance that burned like hellfire within his breast. Swithin and Eadda would be sore afraid of the violent man their father had become. He hung his head and turned his feet toward the chapel.

The winter sun kissed the misty horizon even as Robyn arrived. Pinpricks of light flickered in the twilight church and the resinous scent of burning rosemary and beeswax wafted to Robyn's nose. As he set foot into the sanctuary, he spied a figure kneeling at the altar, three votive candles burning in front of him.

Anger, grief, and shame strove with each other in Robyn's heart. "You!"

Heath rose and faced his erstwhile friend. Tears glistened on his scarred face.

"How dare you?" Robyn cried. "If not for your reckless deeds, my family—*my* family—would not now be food for worms."

Heath squared his shoulders. "How dare *I*? You have been so set on revenge I fear your wroth is more about the blow to your vanity than the death of your wife and children. In death, you cared not a whit to call the priest to bless their souls, nor even burn a candle in remembrance. Yes, to my shame, I sinned against you. And for that I have been sorely punished. Perhaps God will someday forgive me."

"He might, but I will not," Robyn snarled. "Your covetousness is both our ruin."

"Lari deserved better." Heath took three strides toward Robyn. "How many times did I make up the shortfall when you spent your coins at the tavern with the freemasons instead of on flour for your children's bread?"

Robyn blinked and furrowed his brow. "I knew nothing of this."

"Because I bade her not to tell you, lest you felt dishonored. And do you recall the spring two years past, when she lost the fruit of her womb? You told her not to fret as it was the will of God and more babes would come. You and Cynebald left to frolic at the spring fair. Lari spilled her grief to me and I held her in my arms while she soaked my shoulder with her tears."

"So you have been plotting this for some time." Robyn's words crackled with frost.

"Christ's blood, man! You vent anger at me for giving comfort to Lari instead of shame upon yourself for your callousness when her heart was rent asunder. But if your honor so demands it, take my life. I will surrender it to you gladly and consider my debt paid." Heath threw back his arms and raised his chin, baring his throat.

Robyn took three strides, drawing his knife as he went. And while he would have battled to the death, he could not raise his hand to take a freely given sacrifice. As he stood transfixed, the sound of boots on stone echoed in the nave.

Robyn whirled about to see Zephrine Humes' wife, along with the sheriff and several of his men, armed from head to heel.

"That's him!" the widow screeched. "He is the one who slew my husband!"

The group stepped forward.

"Hold!" yelled Heath. "We claim sanctuary. You cannot enter here."

A sly smile curled the sheriff's thin lips. "No need for us to enter."

He gave a glance to one of his men, who took an arrow from his quiver and drew his bow.

Heath shoved Robyn to the side and grunted before falling to the cold stone floor, an arrow buried in his chest.

"No!" Robyn knelt at his friend's side.

Blood frothed around Heath's lips and his eyes met Robyn's. "Fly, fool!" he gurgled.

The spell of horror broken, Robyn lunged for an un-shuttered window.

"By hook or by crook, I will have my revenge, Robyn Mason. And neither kith nor kin can aid you!" the Widow Humes shouted after him as he fled into the thicket.

Robyn ran until his lungs were on fire, and his legs were stone. He sat himself upon a rock and panted like a hunted fox gone to ground. At last, his gulping breaths slowed, and he bowed his head in his hands. *What have I become? Perhaps a better fate would have been the henchman's arrow through my own heart. Long I loved Heath as my own brother, and yet I meant to slay him. In a church, no less. He freely traded his life for mine, and if our fates were reversed, I fear I would not have the grace to grant him the same mercy.*

The clip-clop of hooves and the rattle of a carriage interrupted his despair. Without raising his head, he beheld the cloven hooves of stags as the coach drew to a stop. With a sigh, he rose. The mousy footman held open the door and Robyn climbed inside.

The Holly King sat tall on the cushion, a look of bemusement upon his face.

"How, now, Robyn! Is revenge as sweet a dish as you dreamed?"

"It is bitter as rue, as you knew it would be."

The king kept the smile from his lips, if not from his voice. "It would seem you find yourself at loose ends. I would set before you a small task. A trifling thing, really."

If you enjoyed this book, please consider leaving a review at your favorite book site. Reviews help other readers find and enjoy new books!

To explore more content from Artemis Greenleaf, A.B. Richards, Pandora Martindale, and Holly Dey, please visit BlackMareBooks. com